# cocoa beach
# *Cottage*

## SWEENEY HOUSE
## BOOK 1

# CECELIA
# SCOTT

Cecelia Scott

Sweeney House Book 1

*Cocoa Beach Cottage*

Copyright © 2022 Cecelia Scott

Cover designed by Sarah Brown (http://www.sarahdesigns.co/)

## Introduction To Sweeney House

The Sweeney House is a landmark inn on the shores of Cocoa Beach, built and owned by the same family for decades. After the unexpected passing of their beloved patriarch, Jay, this family must come together like never before. They may have lost their leader, but the Sweeneys are made of strong stuff. Together on the island paradise where they grew up, this family meets every challenge with hope, humor, and heart, bathed in sunshine and the unconditional love they learned from their father.

For release dates, preorder alerts, updates and more, sign up for my newsletter! Or go to www.ceceliascott.com and follow me on Facebook!

# Chapter One

## Sam

Civil. She could be civil, right? How hard could it be to sip coffee and stare at her soon-to-be-ex-husband and pretend to be...*civil*? Not kind. Not warm. Certainly not loving. Not after he'd cheated on her, ended their nearly twenty-five-year marriage, and unraveled her entire life.

But even civil was a challenge for Samantha Sweeney Parker as she sat in the back corner booth at The Piping Cup across from Max, wondering why she was here. What fresh new hell did he have planned, bringing her here with no lawyers? The house was settled, he would pay her half of the profit from a sale. There would be alimony. He'd get Ben every other weekend.

Weren't they done discussing this? It had been six months since her daughter had come home early on her medical school winter break and walked in on him...

She shook off the mental image of what Taylor had seen that day. It was still raw and hurt her brain just to think about it.

Instead, she took a deep drink of coffee and tried to picture the man she fell in love with—the enchanting young Max Parker with dreamy eyes and that charming smile.

A man so captivating that she'd ended up unexpect-edly pregnant at nineteen, and married at lightning speed. Despite the unplanned nature of everything, Sam had been happy. Her husband had been mesmerizing and successful and a decent father to their two children. He, Ben, and Taylor had been all she ever needed.

Even in the early days when he was in med school and up to his eyeballs in crazy hours as a resident, she'd been happy. And then as he rose to be a leading ortho-pedic surgeon at Orlando General Hospital and her focus was motherhood, she'd been extremely happy. Finally, when they were just a few years away from an empty nest and a chance to be a couple again...she discovered her husband was small, selfish, and, sadly, a cliché doctor who had an affair with a nurse.

Only it wasn't an affair. Max was in *love*, and had done everything in his power to make this divorce fast and easy...for him.

Forget civil. He wasn't worth it.

"Why am I here, Max?" she asked on an annoyed sigh, abandoning the strained pleasantries of this interaction.

"Look, Sammi," he said in a lowered tone, using the nickname Sam had always despised. "I just wanted to sit down with you and tell you this in person. Face to face."

*How gentlemanly of you. If only you had decided to "sit down in person" and tell me face to face that you were sleeping with someone else rather than having our*

*daughter catch you in the act and have to break the news
to me herself.*

Sam pushed away the words in her head because
screaming them at him would just open up the floodgates
of pain and anger and betrayal. She'd spent six months
trying to close those gates, and accept that she would
never understand how he could so carelessly throw away
their family and shatter what felt like a picture-perfect
life.

She wrapped her hands around the mug of coffee,
and took a long, hard look at the man she'd loved for more
than two decades.

He was still objectively handsome, even with sprin-
kles of gray in his whiskers and at his temples. In fact, he
looked fit and tanned and…happy.

Which kind of only made her hate him more, if that
was possible.

"Tell me what?" she pressed, leveling her gaze,
leaning into the cushion of the booth. "There's not much
left to discuss, is there? All I want to do now is move on
and focus on making sure the kids are all right. Especially
Ben."

She winced at the thought of her sixteen-year-old
son, who barely spoke a word these days and mostly hid
in his room. Ben had become even more closed off since
she'd moved them into a rented townhouse on the
outskirts of Winter Park. There was no way she'd stay in
that house after…after what Max did *in their very own
bedroom.* All she wanted was…for this to be over.

A few more months, maybe by the end of this

summer. Then she'd be officially divorced and free of him.

Max cleared his throat and attempted a smile. "I just thought I owed you the courtesy of a conversation. Before you heard about this through rumors or your friends or whatever. I know how word gets around quickly here."

Sam rolled her eyes, because he wasn't wrong about that. Winter Park, a small, upscale suburb of Orlando, had a fast-churning rumor mill that chewed up the local gossip and spit it out with shocking speed. The other moms at Ben's high school had been looking at her with a weird mixture of pity and judgment ever since word of Max's affair got out, and she could hear their hushed whispers from a mile away.

"What now, Max? What could you possibly have to tell me that could somehow make my life even worse?"

She waited for his eyes to flash with sympathy or regret, but they didn't. Good heavens, he looked...kind of proud of himself.

"Kayla..." Max said after a long pause, making Sam lift her cup to hide her curled lip at the mention of his girlfriend's name. "Kayla is, um..." Max ran a hand through his black and gray hair, looking down at the table before saying the last word. "Pregnant."

Sam practically spat out the sip of coffee she'd just taken. "Excuse me?"

The whole world felt like it stopped turning and she could hardly move or think or breathe.

*This can't be for real. This has to be some sort of sick joke.*

But Max's expression was stone-cold serious, and all Sam could do was stare at him, wondering if she'd ever really known him at all.

"You're..." She stammered. "You're having a *baby* with her?"

"I know, it's totally unexpected." Max smiled. He actually *smiled*. "And I figured you might have a hard time with this, so I wanted you to hear it first from me."

That didn't make it better. In fact, it made it way worse. Sam would have rather heard this from *anyone* but him.

She threw up her hands and almost laughed, feeling as if the universe was literally playing a game to see how many curveballs it could throw her way. There was nothing left to do but just sit back and get hit.

"Congratulations, Max. That's...wow. That is some news."

"I know it's crazy, but...I'm not that..." He lifted a shoulder, which was definitely beefier than she remembered, like he'd been hitting the gym a whole lot more than he had when they were married. "This sort of feels like a second chance for me, you know? A chance to do it right. I know I messed up badly with you and Tay and Ben, and I just feel like I've been given this opportunity to try again. Have a fresh start."

Sam felt her jaw go slack. "A second chance?" Her voice quivered as she repeated the repulsive phrase. "A *fresh start*? Taylor and Ben are your children. You can't just wipe them away and start over."

Max Parker was just about the last person on Earth who deserved a second chance.

*He* was the one who made a horrible mistake and chose to ruin everything, and yet Sam was the one who felt like her life was completely falling apart. But *he* got the second chance?

"I'm not wiping them away, Sammi. I'll always be there for our kids, whatever they need. And Kayla, too."

She shot him a withering look. "I thought she 'didn't want to try and be their mom.'"

As if that little strumpet could replace Sam.

He ignored the dig, as he always did when she said something nasty about his "girlfriend." Who was now about to be the mother of his third child.

Seriously?

"Anyway, I'm getting another shot at being a dad. Starting from scratch. Don't you think that's a good thing for me?"

"Just fabulous," she dragged out the word and started planning her escape as she reached for her purse. "So, I'm going to—"

"There's one more thing."

Her shoulders slumped with a sigh. "Don't tell me—it's twins."

Chuckling, he shook his head. "No, no. At least, I don't think so. Now that would be—"

"Max. What is it?"

He cleared his throat again. Never a good sign. "We're keeping the house."

For a long moment, at least six slamming beats of her

heart, all she could do was stare at him. "Did you say... 'we're'? As in..."

"Kayla's moving in."

"What?" She had to fight the urge to lunge over the table and wrap her hands around his neck and throttle him.

"It makes so much sense, Sammi—"

"To who? Nothing makes sense, Max! Not you or your girlfriend or your baby or you living in my house that I—"

"Shhh." He glanced around as if her rising voice embarrassed him. Oh, honey, she was just getting started. "Financial sense. I'll refinance and give you half the profits. I already contacted my attorney and he's sending an addendum to yours and—"

"Stop!" She stood up suddenly, grabbing her purse and swinging it over her shoulder so hard it thumped her in the back. "Fine. I don't care. You win. Keep my house where we raised our kids and get your second chance. I don't care. I'll pick up the pieces of your mess while you go on and start a whole new life."

Without waiting for his response, Sam stormed out of The Piping Cup, fighting the sting of tears and vibrating with the familiar pain of betrayal.

The bells on the front door chimed as she rushed through it, wiping a tear from her cheek and heading down the sidewalk of downtown Winter Park. The early June heat made the precious red-brick sidewalks even warmer, with sun bouncing off the glass display windows of the high-end stores that lined this strip.

But all that was lost on Sam as she replayed the conversation and tried to think what upset her the most. The baby? Yeah, horrible. The house? Unspeakable.

*A second chance?* So staggeringly unfair, she wanted to howl and punch and stomp and then roll into a ball and cry.

A second chance? She hadn't even gotten a *first* one. Sam had never been anything except Max's wife, and Taylor and Ben's mom. That's it. She'd married Max at nineteen, had Taylor five months later. No college, no degree, no job. Just this family and this suburban town and their pretty house that Kayla would no doubt redecorate, wiping away Sam's whole existence. What else did she have to show for her forty-three years on this Earth?

Yes, Taylor, her darling daughter who was her best friend. And Ben, her teenaged son who so desperately needed her. But...not as a mother, as a person?

Who was Sam Sweeney Parker? Who had she been before she was the other half of Dr. and Mrs. Max Parker? She'd lived a simple beach life, having grown up on an idyllic barrier island about an hour east of Orlando in the well-known sleepy surf town of Cocoa Beach. There, her parents, Dottie and Jay, had run a ten-room beachfront inn called Sweeney House for forty years. They raised their four kids in an adjacent three-story guest house known simply as "the cottage."

But her father, Jay, had passed away last year due to a stroke, and although Mom put on a good face, Sam and her three siblings knew that she took the loss of her great love really, really hard.

Sam loved her family, and liked knowing her parents —and a few of her siblings—were only an hour away. But even with the short distance, her trips over there had been brief and rare.

She always had excuses—sports and events during the school year, camps and vacations in the summer. But if she was being honest, the truth was that none of her family truly liked or trusted Max, and she always chose him first. And the feelings were mutual. Max had a way of making sure she kept them at arm's length and focused her loyalty solely on him.

Big mistake, considering "loyalty" meant nothing to him and his stupid second chance.

Who didn't want a do-over? Who didn't want a fresh start, new home, and a new life?

On a ragged sigh, Sam looked up to see where she'd gone in her blind rage. Oh, of course: O'Leary's. No surprise she'd head straight to the dive bar where she knew she'd find much-needed comfort.

She pulled open the heavy door, took a breath, and caught the bartender's eye. She felt better already.

# Chapter Two

## *Taylor*

"Mom!" Taylor Parker smiled at the unexpected surprise of her mother coming through the front door of O'Leary's, grateful, for once, that the bar was basically empty. "Thank God you're here. I might die of boredom. It's been so dead all day, and—"

As soon as Taylor laid eyes on her mother's tearstained face and downturned mouth, she stopped talking and rushed to the end of the bar. "Mom? What happened? Are you okay?"

"Oh, Tay." Her mother slumped down onto a stool and leaned her elbows on the bar, blinking red-rimmed eyes.

She looked even sadder than usual lately, which was saying something. Truth was, Taylor hadn't seen her mom truly happy since that horrible, horrible day six months ago.

The quick flashback made Taylor cringe and hurt for a second all over again.

"What's going on?" she asked her mom, feeling worry rise in her chest.

Taylor knew her mother couldn't handle any more

tough times or bad news. Sam Sweeney Parker, angel that she was, did not deserve one single ounce more of pain.

"I just had coffee with your father." Mom looked up through her smeared mascara and curled a lip, but she was still beautiful.

Although, since Christmas, she'd gotten very thin and rarely smiled. Her long, caramel-colored hair was knotted and messy, and her blue eyes, which Taylor was used to being bright and warm and comforting, were gray with pain.

"Why would you do that?" Taylor blinked in surprise, quickly glancing over her shoulder to make sure the bar manager wasn't around to yell at her for doing nothing.

There were no customers, after all.

"He had something he wanted to tell me, and he claimed it could only be said in person."

"Oh, boy. That doesn't sound good." What new misery could her gross and disappointing excuse for a father have in store for them now?

"Hold onto your hat for this one, honey." Her mom gave her a warning look.

Taylor leaned closer. "Do you need a drink?"

Mom snorted. "You know I never drink before five. But for this? I may have to make an exception."

"If I don't pour you a drink soon, Harry's gonna come out here and yell at me for *completely* not working." Taylor glanced over her shoulder again at the back room where her manager worked.

"Screw it." Mom threw her hands up. "I'll take a Blue Moon."

"Good choice." Taylor poured the beer into a glass and finished it with an orange slice, sliding it across the bar. "Okay, now that you're officially a customer..." She rolled her eyes in the general direction of Harry. "What did Dad want?"

Mom grabbed the glass and put a sizeable dent in the beer before letting out a long, deep sigh. "Kayla is pregnant."

Taylor gasped, her hand flying to her mouth as she watched her mother take another long sip, visibly broken by this. "No!"

Mom pushed her hair behind her ear. "I know, Tay. It's unbelievable."

"He's having a kid with her?" Taylor groaned and leaned against the side of the bar, shaking her head with disgust. "I mean, cheating on you and breaking up our family and scarring me for life wasn't enough?"

Taylor shuddered at the memory of finding her dad wearing nothing but boxers as he walked out of her parents' bedroom, the sound of some woman's laughter behind him.

The day Taylor found them together, her entire life changed. Literally, a total pivot that could never be undone. She'd been in her second year of medical school, a determined student who would someday be a surgeon just like her dear Daddy.

Before the semester officially ended, she withdrew from the UCF College of Medicine, kept her apartment not far from here, and started tending bar, a thinly-veiled rebellion against the man who used to call her "Doctor Junior."

*Take that, loser. Your protégé is a bartender.*

She'd rarely spoken to him since then, and had no intention of changing that. But...a baby? Like, she was going to have a half-sister or -brother who would be twenty-four years younger than she was? Gross.

"There's more," Mom said as she took a second sip.

"Oh, God. What?"

"She's moving into our house. And they are keeping it."

Taylor stared. Swallowed. Closed her eyes and tried not to sob in front of Mom. "I...can't." He and that...that... woman would be living in their family home? They would be cooking in Mom's beautiful gourmet kitchen? Barbequing by the pool? Living the good life at 42 Laurel Oak Drive?

*No!*

"You want to know the worst part, Tay?" Mom, who always felt more like a best friend than a mother, slid her a look.

"That *wasn't* the worst part?" Taylor choked.

"He called it a 'second chance.'" Mom held up air quotes, mocking him. "He literally used that phrase. 'Fresh start.' Said he saw it as an opportunity to start over and do better this time. Another shot at being a dad."

That last part stabbed Taylor like a knife to the gut. So, he did care about being a good dad. Just not enough to be one for her.

Taylor's brows shot sky high. She stood in total shock and dismay, wondering how on Earth her own father could possibly be such a terrible, cold person. "Start over? He has a family already! Well, he *had* one." Taylor slung a bar rag over her shoulder and paced back and forth furiously. "Because if I wasn't already completely and totally done with him, whoo baby, I am now."

Mom sat up, reaching for Taylor's hand. "Tay, he's your dad. Try not to hold the world's most enormous grudge."

"Too late for that, Momma. I love my grudges."

"I know you do."

"I tend to them like little pets."

Her mother almost snorted. "I just don't want you to spend your life hating your own father. I feel so...responsible."

"Responsible?" Taylor rushed back over to her mom, leaning down onto the bar to level her gaze with her mother's. "Please don't ever say that, Mom. None of this is your fault. Not one single bit."

Sam pursed her lips like maybe she didn't entirely believe that, but it pained Taylor to think of her mom feeling any bit of the blame for this dumpster fire. "Maybe I wasn't enough."

"Stop it."

"Well, I married him." She gave a wavering smile. "I'm responsible for *that*."

"You did everything right, Mom. Never question that." She reached across the bar and squeezed her mother's hand, aching with love for this woman.

Taylor had spent every day of her life adoring her sweet mother and being her best friend. The two of them were always two peas in a pod, and while Taylor grew up respecting and thinking highly of her dad, he was never the soft, loving, and unconditionally supportive place to fall that Mom was.

They'd never strayed from their closeness, spending thousands of hours walking around the mall or sipping coffee and chatting on the back porch. Even though her dad was the successful, renowned, high-earning surgeon, the older Taylor got, the more she realized her mom was the real superstar.

"I'm at such a loss, Taylor." Mom pushed her long hair behind one shoulder and finished off the rest of the Blue Moon. "I mean, *I* want a fresh start. Desperately. Badly. And frankly, I deserve one more than he does."

"Re-freaking-tweet."

Her mother smiled as if she didn't quite know what that meant, and didn't want a social media language lesson at that moment. "I walk around this town, and all I see are memories and ghosts and images of a life I'll never have again."

Taylor rested her hip against the bar and shook her head. "I get that. You and Dad lived your whole lives here."

"Not my whole life, just once I moved in with him, a pregnant nineteen-year-old. Once I left Cocoa Beach, I was here for the next twenty-four years. This is the only other place I've ever called home besides the cottage. This is home, whether I like it or not."

"Well it sure doesn't feel like it right now." Taylor mindlessly wiped the bar with a rag, even though it hadn't gotten any dirtier since the last twelve times she'd wiped it down.

"But, wow, the idea of just...taking off. Starting over. Being free of the past and..." Her mother shook her head. "I shouldn't even fantasize about it. I can't go anywhere."

Taylor couldn't imagine it; she was truly a homebody with absolutely no urge to pick up and go have an adventure. Sure, she wasn't tethered to a job, a relationship, or a house. She could hop in her 2005 Honda Civic, get on the highway, and start a new life somewhere.

But she could never bring herself to leave her mother, especially when they were such a support for each other. And even though he was insanely moody and quiet and impossible to reach, Taylor knew that, in a weird way, her little brother, Ben, needed her, too.

Still...it was hard not to entertain the idea in the face of Dad's staggering betrayal.

"A fresh start sure does sound nice," Taylor said, not entirely planning for the words to be spoken out loud. "I can't even stand being in the same town as him. Driving on the same streets, breathing the same air."

"Taylor." Mom cracked a smile, her eyes brightening just the tiniest bit as she looked up at her daughter. "You are so dramatic."

"I'm not, actually. I can feel his evil presence. It's like a..." Taylor curled her lip, wiping the same spot on the bar yet again. "A virus."

"You shouldn't talk about your dad that way," Mom said, arching a brow.

"Mom." Taylor crossed her arms. "Seriously?"

"He's still—"

"Dead to me," Taylor interjected, slinging the rag over her shoulder and pacing back and forth behind the bar. "That's what he is."

The two women sat in silence for a while, both of them feeling the heavy presence of grief and sadness and complete and utter confusion about where to go next.

"You know," Taylor said slowly, lifting a shoulder and eyeing her mom. "We could get out of Winter Park. We could leave and have our *own* fresh start. Together. With Ben, too. Better than his and stupid Kayla's."

"I'm not exactly rolling in funds for something like that, Tay." Sam looked up through her dark lashes, eyes flashing. "Until the divorce is final, I can't afford to just move. He's already covering my rent on the townhouse; he isn't going to pay for me to have another place. Plus, we've got Ben to think about. We can't uproot him. He has school. He'll be a junior in the fall, and—"

"The place I have in mind would be totally free, actually." A smile grew on Taylor's face as the idea in her head started to take full form. "And I personally think Ben would love it."

Her mom drew back, confused. "What are you talking about?"

"I'm talking about Cocoa Beach."

"And, what, check into Sweeney House?"

Taylor narrowed her eyes, flipping a lock of dark hair

over her shoulder for added emphasis. "The cottage, Mom. It's empty. Didn't you say Grandma moved into a suite in the inn because the Grandpa memories were getting to her?"

Mom pushed out a sad lip and nodded. "Poor thing."

"Then she'd love to have us!" Taylor said. "That house is huge and right on the beach."

"It's also where I grew up," Mom said. "Talk about backsliding. Just think of the Facebook posts. 'Moving home with my mother at forty-three! Go, me!'"

"Don't think of it that way," Taylor insisted. "It's an opportunity to—"

"Oh, honey, no." Her mom shook her head and frowned a little. "We can't move to the cottage and hide from the world."

"Why the heck not? Grandma would love it. She's so lonely."

"I don't know if she wants us to...descend. Plus, you know she and I can go at it pretty hard."

"Not anymore. That was when you were a young and wayward teenager."

Mom rolled her eyes. "So wayward."

"She would totally adore it if we were there, and you know it. I mean, all your siblings are too busy to spend much time with her. Why should we stay here? Other than, you know, the demise of our family and complete betrayal and heartache. And..." She waved her rag vaguely at the empty bar. "Of course, this fabulous work-place of mine."

Mom laughed softly.

"Which, if you ask me, are all perfect reasons to head to the beach."

Mom puffed out a sigh. "It really feels like admitting defeat or something. Is that stupid?"

"No," Taylor said, matter-of-fact. "Let's admit defeat. Throw up our hands and say, 'You win, Max Parker. Enjoy your stupid new life and your replacement family. You totally defeated us, so we're clearing it straight out of here. See you never.'"

"We're *never* coming back?" Her mother choked out the question.

"Well, I don't know. Isn't Ben done with school this week? He's just going to spend the next two and a half months playing video games, driving around with his sketchy friends, or sulking. He is a master sulker, as you know. What if we just go for the summer?"

"I don't know, Tay—"

Suddenly, the door of O'Leary's swung open with the ring of a bell, and in strolled three mid-forties moms decked out in head-to-toe Lululemon athleisure, looking around like they'd never seen the inside of a bar.

"Oh, God." Mom groaned and ducked her head to face the other way.

"What?" Taylor asked quietly. "You know them?"

She nodded. "From Ben's school," she said in a hushed voice, brushing her hair in front of her face as if she was trying to hide.

Taylor inched away from her mom to greet the posse of Pilates princesses. "Hi, welcome to O'Leary's. Can I get you guys something?"

"I told you this place was a total dive," one woman stage-whispered to another.

Curling her lip, Taylor cleared her throat noisily, annoyed that the women barely noticed her.

"Uh, hi there." The blonde one at the front of the trio stepped forward and slid a pair of enormous designer sunglasses on top of her head. "No, we don't need anything. We're just checking out some local spots. I'm head of the booster club for my son's little league team, and we're looking for a place to throw the end-of-the-season banquet. I, um..." she forced a fake smile. "Think we're gonna have to keep looking."

"Really?" Taylor asked. "Because O'Leary's just screams 'kid paradise.'" She tried to tone down the sarcasm and remember how desperately they needed customers. "You sure you don't want a beer?"

The blonde's gaze slid to the nearly empty glass in front of Taylor's mother. "In the middle of the day? I hardly..." Then her gaze moved up. "Samantha? Oh, my stars, is that you?"

*Oh, crap.*

"Hi, Therese." Taylor's mom managed a wave and pushed her hair away from her face, sitting up straight and quickly attempting to fix herself.

"Oh, Sam. You poor soul." The woman rushed over to her and gave Sam one of the fakest hugs Taylor had ever seen, with the other two right behind her like sharks that smelled chum in the water.

"I'm fine, really," Mom insisted, slipping out of the hug and standing up.

"We all heard," one of the others said with an insane amount of sympathy, putting her arm on Mom's shoulder.

"Heard what?" Taylor interjected, walking over to the end of the bar to try and break up this horrific moment for her mother.

"About..." The woman who seemed to be called Therese lowered her voice to a whisper. "The new baby."

Taylor felt her jaw clench. "That's not really any of your business."

"Well, Kayla is in our hot yoga class, and she's just so overjoyed, she couldn't help but share the news." One of the women shrugged and gave a forced pitying smile.

Taylor's heart sank and her blood boiled. She looked at her mom, who was visibly pained by the whole interaction, but putting on a brave and steady and graceful face, as Sam Sweeney always did.

Taylor...not so graceful. "That's a private family matter, ladies, so if we're not going to work for your event, you can leave my mom and me alone."

"Oh my goodness, honey. We're just trying to help." Therese raised her brows, barely making any lines on her smooth, shiny forehead.

"You're not helping," Taylor said, a little less aggression in her tone. "Can you please just let us be?"

"Bye, Sam." Therese patted Mom's arm again, condescension dripping off every word. "We'll be praying for you."

After the judgment committee left, Taylor groaned loudly and leaned against the bar, throwing her head back and shutting her eyes. "What is *wrong* with people?"

Mom was quiet for a few beats, gathering her wits. Then, she stood very slowly and lifted her chin. "You're right, Tay."

"About what?"

"Let's go stay at Cocoa Beach Cottage for the summer."

Taylor lit up with excitement, a smile beaming on her face. "Really? You want to?"

Mom let out a noisy sigh and shuddered as she glanced toward the door of O'Leary's. "I can't take it here anymore. I need a fresh start. And so do you."

Taylor glanced down at the black jeans and green T-shirt she'd washed and worn a thousand times. She ran her fingers across her stained bar apron and her trusty rag. "Well, it's sure gonna be hard to leave," she whispered, fighting a smile.

Mom laughed. "Don't burn all your bridges. Let's go for the summer and reset ourselves. Ben will...go. He won't like it, but—"

"He doesn't like anything," Taylor said.

"The beach? What kid doesn't want a summer at the beach?"

Ben might be that kid, but Taylor kept it to herself, going for optimistic, because her mother needed that. "It could be really good for him, help him open up more his junior year. And it will be good for you, too. And Grandma."

"What about you?"

She shrugged. "Hey, like I said—what kid doesn't want a summer at the beach?" she teased. "This one wouldn't mind it at all. So, when do you want to head out? Early next week?"

"I was thinking more like..." Mom bit her lip and shot Taylor a look. "Tomorrow morning."

Taylor just laughed. "That's the thing about you, Mom. When you're all in, you're *all* in."

"I am all in!"

# Chapter Three

## *Dottie*

Dottie gripped the metal key tightly, took a slow, deep breath and closed her eyes before unlocking the cottage. She hardly ever stepped foot in it these days. The pain of the emptiness was too much to bear.

She could handle the inn, living and working there every day, as she had since she and Jay opened Sweeney House a year after they got married.

With the constantly changing guests, the inn was bearable for her. Two stories with five uniquely decorated and historic bedrooms on each floor, Sweeney House was work, not home. It didn't have much in the way of amenities but, hey, they built it in the late sixties and the beach was the only amenity anyone needed, according to Jay.

With its stunningly gorgeous location and every special, unique detail, it still did great business for the droves of tourists and surfers who flocked to Cocoa Beach. It wasn't too terribly updated, but Dottie's wonderful staff kept it clean and tidy and the outdated finishings didn't seem to hurt business.

But the cottage? Oh, that was a different story for her.

The quaint, three-story yellow beach house with white shutters and colorful flower boxes under the windows was where Dottie's heart resided.

And consequently, where it broke every time she walked in and didn't hear Jay's booming voice or wry chuckle.

To anyone else, the cottage was one heck of a piece of prime Florida waterfront property. The whole back of the house directly faced the ocean, with giant glass sliding doors and huge windows. It had a balcony and two wooden decks that had been thoroughly enjoyed by their kids for many, many years.

Every square inch, every weathered floorboard from top to bottom, was rich with memories of raising four boisterous, hilarious, and brilliant Sweeney kids. Just walking up to the front door she could feel the laughter and play of her young children and the screech of Jay's old tires as his bright yellow Chevy pickup pulled in from work.

They had brought the twins, John and Julie, home to this house, forty-nine years ago. Oh, had they been in over their heads with that set of Double Trouble, as Jay called them. But they had each other, and they laughed their way through every single day.

Then Sam came along, and then Erica a couple years later, and those two ended up sharing one of the upstairs bedrooms for a few years, staying up late in the night giggling and chatting and covering the walls in boy-band posters.

Julie used to play her music in the loft when the twins were teenagers, practicing the electric guitar for hours on end, while John would hush her over and over because he was studying in his room.

The cottage was only ever the home to the Sweeney family, who had all grown and left and built lives and families and homes of their own.

Once the kids had grown, it had become an empty nest, which Dottie and Jay enjoyed together immensely. The cottage had taken on a new kind of joy, a quiet peace that surrounded the couple as they lived out their golden years, still overseeing their inn and inviting their children to visit every chance they got.

But now that Jay was gone, it wasn't an empty nest. It was just...empty.

Not for long, though, because in about half an hour or so, Sam was coming home. And as much as it pained Dottie to step through this front door and back into every familiar smell and sight and corner of what was once her little bit of paradise, she knew she had to get it ready for Sam, Taylor, and Ben's arrival.

Before Dottie had a chance to replace the sheets or add some fresh towels to the bathroom, her gaze fell straight onto the worn-out recliner that sat by the window in the corner of the living room.

Her eyes instantly filled up as the sharp knife of grief once again twisted her chest. She could practically still see the deep dent in the chair from where Jay would sit every day, reading articles from the newspaper out loud to Dottie as she cooked them breakfast and poured coffee.

Next to the recliner was her favorite spot, a completely mismatched, formal-looking blue velvet chair, which Dottie found at an antique store and loved. It didn't fit the vibe of the inn, so they put it in the cottage and it became her go-to place, right next to Jay.

With tears in her eyes and an ache in her heart, she slowly walked through the living room and sat down in her familiar blue chair, looking at the empty recliner next to her.

"I miss you so much, honey." She smiled tearfully, setting her hand on the armrest right in the groove created by his hand.

She could practically see him there, his gray hair, his giant, beaming smile, flipping through the newspaper and shaking his head as he announced daily that, "This world is going to hell in a handbasket, darlin'."

"Well, you were right." Dottie laughed, knowing full well she was talking to an empty chair, but so desperately needing Jay's advice with her current predicament. "You used to always say Sam would be back. You'd tell me, 'It might be months or years or decades, but she'll be back.'"

And, of course, he was right. And it was complicated in a way Jay might not ever understand, because Sam's spontaneous decision threw a very unexpected monkey-wrench in the plans Dottie had been quietly crafting over the last few months.

"It's wonderful, it truly is," she continued as if he were sitting right there, listening. "I couldn't be happier to have another one of our beautiful kids back on the island."

Dottie swallowed, looking out the big living room window at the bright blue ocean and powdery white sand of the beach.

"But...I...I did have a plan of my own." She made a face, knowing that if he really was here, he wouldn't like this plan.

But then, if he really *was* sitting here, she wouldn't have to make this plan.

"I'm selling," she said simply. "I have a realtor lining up a deal right now, because I just...I can't stand it here without you, Jay."

A tear snaked down her cheek, but she couldn't let go of the armrest to wipe it away. When did she become so weak? Dottie had always been a strong, vibrant woman who hardly felt her age one bit. But the death of her great love seemed to have left her frail and lost, a distant version of her old self who'd run this inn with energy and life.

Could she ever get her strength back? Without him, it seemed impossible. He *was* her strength.

"It's too lonely with you gone. It's too sad. I know you never wanted me to sell the inn or the cottage. I know you wanted to keep it in the family forever. But..." She sucked in a shuddering breath, the pain practically choking her. "You were never supposed to leave me! I was never supposed to do this without you. I *can't* do this without you."

She paused for a long time, as if she was waiting for a response, even though there was never going to be one.

"My mind is made up," she said, hearing the determination in her voice as if she knew he was up there in heaven trying to talk her out of this. "I'm selling the inn and the cottage and I'll be set for life and free of my memories. I just..." She grunted. "I wasn't counting on Sam and Taylor and Ben announcing they'd like to live here for the summer."

She flopped down against the blue velvet back of her chair, shaking her head. "And I can't say no! I'm so lost without you, honey. So unbelievably lost. Selling is the practical thing to do, but I can't tell Sam about my plans. I can't tell any of the kids. They'll be devastated. But I need to set myself up, you know. I don't want to depend on anyone and...and now I'm rambling to an empty recliner."

With a groan of pity and defeat, Dottie slowly stood up, running her fingers along the cracked leather of Jay's armrest one last time. Rooting for some much-needed self-discipline, she walked away and busied herself by checking around the cottage to make sure everything had been readied and spruced up by the inn staff as she'd asked.

As she did, the echo of her own confession was as loud as her shoes on the hardwood floor.

*Lost.* Dottie Sweeney was totally and completely lost, and she thought she'd find her way by selling the cottage and the inn.

But now, she had to switch from grieving widow to loving mom. That shouldn't be hard. It was probably the easiest and most joyful transition she could make. She'd worry about the sale of the inn and the cottage later, because right now, one of her babies needed her. And there was nothing more important to Dottie in the entire world.

And it was Samantha, who had gone away, ran off with a guy and kept her distance for far too many years. Sam, who always weighed the most on Dottie's heart, although all of her children owned a piece of that heart.

Erica Sweeney-Armstrong, her youngest, was fiercely independent and freakishly ambitious. At thirty-nine, she was a happily married rocket scientist, living in a big, beachside house with her husband and working every day as an aerospace engineer for NASA at the Kennedy Space Center.

Dottie was grateful for Erica's career choice, not just because it was mind-blowing and impressive, but because it kept her youngest daughter permanently local.

John, one of the twins, was the steady and stable man of the family, and had effortlessly assumed the patriarchal role of caring for everyone after Jay passed. He owned and ran a successful local ad agency, and also chose to stay in Cocoa Beach, living not far away in a new gated neighborhood with his wife, Imani, and three adorable kids.

Julie, his twin sister, was not nearly as settled. She and her boyfriend, Roman, were wildly passionate musicians who traveled the world in a van, home-schooling their teenage daughter, Bliss. They had a band and played every gig they could get their hands on, chasing their big break and always searching for something new.

Dottie didn't see much of Julie these days, but she didn't worry about her nearly as much as she worried about Sam. Because Julie—even though she was wild and tattooed and definitely did not act like the forty-nine-year-old mother of a teenager—knew who she was. She wasn't lost.

Sam, on the other hand, never truly discovered herself. She had spent her life in the shadow of a man who Dottie never truly trusted.

She'd have to be careful not to say, "I told you so." Not that she wanted to. No, all she could think about was holding her poor, broken daughter and her sweet grandkids and getting them settled in at the cottage.

And, God knew, Dottie could use the company around the cottage and Sweeney House.

She stood on the edge of the driveway and watched as a light blue SUV rolled down the long path to the beach house.

"Oh, my girl." Dottie walked over to the car as it crunched to a stop on the shell-covered driveway.

A familiar, salty breeze blew Dottie's soft gray curls all around her face, and she could taste the ocean in the air. The palm trees that lined the driveway of the inn swayed in the gentle wind, their rich, green leaves like a painting on the clear blue sky behind them.

"Mommy." Sam stepped out of the driver's seat of the SUV and instantly slumped down into her mother's arms, making Dottie's heart soar.

It had been so long since she'd felt truly needed. But Sam needed her now. And Dottie needed the distraction.

Now, she could at least focus her attention on being a mom and grandmother, and maybe that would ease some of the emptiness and pain of missing Jay.

"I've got the whole cottage completely ready, and you'll all have your own rooms to stay in, totally private."

Sam sniffled and pulled away from the hug, smiling at her mother. "You're the best. I really don't want to put you out, but we just, I just—" Her voice cracked.

"Oh, baby." Dottie held Sam's beautiful face in her hands, seeing that same blue-gray she'd admired in Jay's eyes for fifty years. Sam looked tired and a bit ragged, but her skin was still soft and smooth and her features were aging with such beauty and grace. "You are not putting anyone out. You're *home*. You can always come home."

Dottie felt a quick pang of guilt as she thought about her real estate agent, who was likely working on selling the place at that very moment, but quickly pushed it away. One battle at a time. And that would be a battle with Sam, so, for now at least, she'd keep that plan to herself.

Sam took a deep breath and got a suitcase and duffle bag out of the back. "Come on, Benny." She whipped open the back door of the SUV.

Dottie craned her neck to look inside, where Ben sat with headphones over his ears and his face glued to his cell phone.

He was such a cute young boy, in desperate need of a haircut. He had his mother's eyes and a quiet mystery about him, and Dottie longed for him to laugh and smile once again.

"Hello, Grandson." Dottie grinned at him as she leaned into the car. "You're going to have to put away the video games. You're at the beach now. Uncle John has already agreed to take you out fishing this weekend. Won't that be fun?"

"Hey, Grandma." Ben barely lifted his head from the screen.

"I'm sorry, Mom. He's..." Sam glanced at her, more pain welling in her eyes. "He's just going through a lot. We all are."

"Well, you're here now. And nobody can be sad at the Cocoa Beach cottage." Dottie wrapped an arm around Sam and squeezed her close. "I simply will not allow it. Where's Taylor?"

"She'll be here any second," Sam answered. "She's coming in her own car so she'd have it here. Plus, she packed a bunch of stuff and brought her cat, Mr. Minx." Sam crinkled her nose. "You sure you're okay with this? It's only for the summer."

"More than okay," Dottie assured her with another hug. "You're a godsend, dear."

As they started to gather the bags and finally got Ben to take off his headphones and carry a suitcase, Taylor's little red Honda came crunching up the driveway with the windows rolled down.

Dottie smiled through a pang of sadness, so wishing Jay could be here to see Taylor one more time, all grown and beautiful. A carbon copy of Sam in so many ways.

"The fun has arrived," Taylor announced, lifting her sunglasses onto her head as she pulled the car up and smiled at her grandmother.

"You look as beautiful as ever." Dottie wrapped Taylor in a hug as soon as she stepped out of the car. "More like your mom every day."

She had long, chocolate-brown hair that glistened in the sunlight and big, blue-gray eyes like Sam.

"I sure hope so. I don't want a single feature of mine to resemble He Who Shall Not Be Named," Taylor whispered playfully.

Dottie laughed with her granddaughter, feeling yet another rise of anger at Max Parker.

She'd known. She'd known all along. She'd told Sam a thousand times not to marry him, that she could stay there, raise the baby in Cocoa Beach, have all the help in the world. She didn't have to sign her life away to be with a man who oozed selfishness, only for him to ruin it twenty-something years later.

When Sam married Max, she and her parents grew distant for a few years. They didn't like Max and Max didn't like them, and Sam had to choose. She chose Max.

That was understandable, since she was young, pregnant, and in love. She wouldn't listen to anyone saying anything about Max. Would Dottie have listened at nineteen years old if someone had told her not to be with Jay?

Not that anyone would, but still. She'd have moved mountains for their love.

So Dottie had been right all along. Big deal. Dottie

didn't want to be *right*; she wanted to heal her daughter's broken heart as best she could.

"Oh, Grandma." Taylor leaned her head back and shut her eyes, taking a deep breath as the sun bathed her young, beautiful face in warmth and light. "I always forget how wonderful the air is here. It's so clean and clear and ocean fresh."

"It's my slice of paradise." Dottie offered to take a tote bag from Taylor's car and swung it over her shoulder, trying to swallow yet another pang of guilt that came with the weight of the secret she was keeping. She'd tell them eventually, when the time was right. And they'd understand.

But not now. Not when they just got here.

"There's my baby brother." Taylor locked her car up and pulled a rolling suitcase behind her as she ran up the driveway to ruffle Ben's hair lovingly. "I haven't seen you in, like, a week, kid. What have you been up to?"

"Hey," Ben grunted, barely audible. "Not much, really."

Dottie gave a mock gasp. "So you do speak English after all?"

Ben just managed a mopey nod and looked at his mom, who was getting the rest of their things out of her SUV. "Mom, where can I set up my PS5? Is there a TV in my room?"

"Oh, yes!" Dottie interjected, happy to announce something that was sure to bring a smile to Ben's face. "You will have your own room in the cottage, young man, and there is a nice fifty-inch flatscreen just waiting for you up there! It's got everything you could need, all kinds of—"

"Thanks, Grandma." With that, he headed straight into the cottage, not another word spoken.

"Now you see why we call him Mr. Sunshine," Taylor quipped, wrapping her arm around Dottie's shoulders as they went along the sandy path out back that ran right to the front door of the cottage. It was all covered in sand, as always, with the ocean air practically spraying them as they walked.

Dottie adored this life, this beachside existence bathed in sunshine and happiness. But she adored it with Jay. Now, without him, even the bluest of skies looked gray.

She hoped that the presence of Sam and her grandkids would maybe start to fill in some of that color, at least for the time being, until she left this place forever.

"Ah, the cottage," Sam said on a sigh as they walked into the cozy, memory-filled home on the water. "It never changes, does it, Mom?"

"Not in a million years," Dottie replied.

Sam was right, the cottage never changed. Frankly, nothing in the entire inn ever changed. Why would it? Dottie and Jay had picked out every last detail of it together.

When he came back from Vietnam after serving in the Air Force, Jay had been stationed at Patrick Air Force Base, just a few miles down the road. They had fallen in love with Cocoa Beach, which had been a tiny, undiscovered beach town back then. It didn't even merit a mark on the map until NASA put launch pads about fifteen miles north at Cape Canaveral.

After that, it became a playground for astronauts and famous as the setting for a classic TV show, *I Dream of Jeannie,* that she and Jay used to watch and love.

Way back then, land was cheap, so they'd gobbled some of it with money they'd saved. Then they'd pored over every detail—every doorhandle, every piece of fabric, every bit of different and fun-colored wallpaper in each of the bathrooms.

As the years went by, the inn had become like their fifth baby, and Dottie didn't dare change a thing about it, because it had all been loved, influenced, and impacted by Jay.

Not to mention, her kids had grown up in the cottage next door, and Dottie knew that she'd have to be mindful of their feelings about selling it.

But it was hers to sell, not theirs. And she needed to get away from the haunted memories.

"I'll let you all get settled in." Dottie set down a duffle bag in the entryway of the cottage, giving Sam one last hug. "But don't get too comfy. We have a family dinner at six."

Sam drew back, her eyes flashing a little. "Tonight? Already?"

"Of course!" Dottie clasped her hands together, floating over to the living room to fluff a throw pillow on the couch. "John and Erica are dying to see you and give you a warm welcome back to the island! Isn't it wonderful? Three of my four babies, all in the same zip code again." She shut her eyes and smiled. "Oh, if only I could get your vagabond of a sister back around here."

Taylor scoffed as she wheeled in a suitcase, stopping it with her foot. "Good luck with that. Trying to get Aunt Julie to stay in one place is practically mission impossible."

"No kidding," Sam agreed, pulling her long hair back into a ponytail. "They have a one-of-kind life, that's for sure."

"Julie has always followed her heart," Dottie said wistfully. "It's taken her to many, many wonderful places."

"Wow." Sam flopped down on the big, turquoise sectional that filled the living room. It was against a tall, sliding glass door that looked out onto a wooden deck on the beach, letting in beams of warmth and sunlight. "It's so crazy being back here. I mean, we've come for holidays and things, but...never a whole summer."

"Yeah. The good kind of crazy," Taylor added, yanking open the slider to let in the salty ocean air. "We need this so badly."

"Where's Ben?" Dottie asked, peering down the hallway and up the stairs, where the brooding sixteen-year-old had undoubtedly already disappeared.

"Being a miserable teenager." Taylor glanced over her shoulder with an eye roll as she stepped out onto the beach deck. "Where else?"

"I hope he knows he's more than welcome at dinner." Dottie frowned. "His cousins are going to be there, and I think some family love and good roasted chicken would brighten that boy right up. Plus, it wouldn't hurt for him to get close to his Uncle John. He could use a father figure right now."

"He has a father, Mom," Sam said quickly.

"Hardly," Taylor whispered, making Dottie feel relieved that she wasn't the only one in the room who thought Max Parker was no longer qualified to be a role model to anyone.

Sam stood up and walked over to Dottie, then gestured for Taylor to come back in and join their little circle.

"Listen, you guys," she said in a hushed voice, peering over her shoulder to make sure Ben was definitely out of earshot. "Max is still Ben's dad. And I know the three of us are all more than ready to hate him forever, and it's within our rights to do that. But I need to make sure Ben knows he can still love his father and have a good relationship with him. I think it's important." Sam shut her eyes tightly, her lashes fluttering. "When I think about my relationship with my dad growing up, how influential he was for me, how much I needed him, I just..."

Dottie held a hand to her chest, knowing that Jay was the greatest father anyone could have ever asked for, and all of her kids had grown up to realize and appreciate how special he was. "I know, honey. He was the best there is."

"It kills me that my kids won't have that," Sam admitted, her voice cracking. She turned to Taylor with misty eyes. "And you...you're all grown up and you can choose what kind of relationship you have with Max, that's your decision. But Ben...he needs his dad. I can't let his heart fill with hate."

"Well..." Dottie wrapped one arm around her daughter and the other around her granddaughter, holding them close for a group hug. "I think that is wildly mature of you, Sam."

"You're a better woman than I am," Taylor said with a soft laugh. "But you're looking out for Ben, and I think that's good."

"He's my son." She smiled, pulling away from Dottie and Taylor. "And, Mom..."

"Yes?" Dottie, tilted her head, admiring her beautiful, selfless, heartbroken daughter, feeling proud of the wonderful mother Sam had become.

"Thank you. For...everything. I think this summer is going to be just what we need."

Dottie kissed Sam's cheek and brushed back a strand of her hair. "You stay as long as you need. Remember, you can always come home."

"Home." Taylor echoed the word, bouncing back over to the open glass door and dancing around on the sunny deck. "Not a bad place to call home, is it?"

"It's paradise." Sam stepped out and joined her daughter. "It'll always be home to me."

Dottie felt another sudden stab of guilt for her looming secret, and the realtor who she practically had on speed dial at this point.

But how could she have known that Sam would choose to finally come home at the very moment she was about to sell the inn and cottage? She couldn't tell her now.

As Dottie walked back to the main building of the inn along the sandy, shell-covered path, she smiled to herself, feeling Jay's strong and comforting presence with every crash of the waves.

*"She'll be back."*

And back she was.

# Chapter Four

## Sam

The last thing Sam wanted was a literal pity party, complete with wine and roasted chicken. But there would be a decent bit of sympathy from her older brother and younger sister at dinner tonight, whether she wanted it or not. She tried not to feel sorry for herself, and she tried even harder not to be embarrassed at the complete and utter dumpster fire her life had turned into.

It was Max's choice, she kept reminding herself. He was the one who screwed everything up, not her.

And yet, here she was, forty-three and living in her childhood home with her mom taking care of her and her two kids. A pity party might be inevitable. At least there'd be snacks and wine.

As Dottie got everything set up for dinner in the big dining room of the cottage, Sam took one last look in the mirror and wondered if her brother and sister would think she looked like she'd been going through it pretty badly. Well, she had been.

She slowly walked around the living room, running her hand along the worn white wooden banister of the staircase. She remembered twelve-year-old Julie trying to slide down that banister, and her twin brother John threatening to tell Mom and Dad.

Sam so clearly recalled standing in the living room at six years old, watching her wild and reckless and free-spirited older sister fly down the railing, shrieking with laughter as Julie's long, curly hair flowed all around her.

She remembered envying Julie's self-assurance and confidence and bold fearlessness. She remembered wishing she was more like Julie, like someone who would slide down the banister without a care in the world.

Then she meandered over to the kitchen table, remembering how Erica would sit there for hours and hours, studying for the SATs and doing ungodly amounts of homework. Sam had also envied Erica's ambition and focus, wishing she could find something to dedicate herself to the way Erica pursued academics.

She had always felt a little overshadowed by her incredibly strong and unforgettable siblings, but tonight, as Sam walked through the cottage, thinking about the memories that lived in every corner of that house seemed to bring her a certain level of comfort.

She may not know who she was, but at least she had this family, where she'd always fit in and have a place.

The smell of that house, the beachy wallpaper and giant windows and mismatched old school furniture washed over Sam like a bath of nostalgia, and she was relieved to feel the peace and warmth of being back in the cottage.

And that sense only intensified a few minutes later when John Sweeney entered the house.

Sam's only brother had always been the most dependable, reliable "fixer" the Sweeney women so often needed, especially after Jay passed.

Tall, in shape, and well-dressed, John gave Sam a familiar, brotherly smile and wrapped his arms around her for a hug.

"Hey, sis." John patted her back. "It's great to see you. I can't believe you're back. How are you holding up?"

Sam pulled away, plastering on a smile and lifting her chin. "I'm doing okay. I really am. It's good to be here."

"I'll bet. We're happy to have you, and if you need anything at all, please don't hesitate. We're here for you."

"Thanks, John." Sam leaned her head against her brother's shoulder, already feeling more at ease.

"Sam, hey!" Imani Sweeney walked in, her long, dark braids bouncing flawlessly around her shoulders. "It's been way too long."

Sam smiled and hugged John's picture-perfect wife, the stunning, magnetic, beautiful Black woman who entered every room with an air of calm, grace and elegance. Imani sometimes seemed to be everything Sam wished she was but...wasn't.

The stay-at-home mom and doting wife who *didn't* get cheated on. Who had a man who adored her, was loyal to her, and a marriage that was so painfully well-functioning it didn't even seem real at times.

John and Imani were...it. The textbook gorgeous family with the white picket fence life that Sam always felt like she was just a hair shy of.

Well, not anymore. Now she wasn't even in the same universe as that life.

It wasn't even possible to be jealous of Imani, because she was the sweetest person alive, the best imaginable sister-in-law. and the whole family loved her. She was part of it, and had been for years, since she and John met in their mid-twenties and had been inseparable ever since.

"Imani, hi." Sam greeted her sister-in-law, whose eyes were even more sparkling and deep brown than she remembered. "I've missed you."

"It's good to see you, it really is. Damien is so excited to hang with his cousin, Ben, this summer. Hopefully, they can have some quality teenage boy time." She laughed, referring to her oldest kid, who was *nothing* like Ben.

Fifteen and their oldest, Damien played about nine sports, was president of every imaginable club and committee, had a thousand friends, and was just about the happiest kid alive.

"Aunt Sam!" One by one, John and Imani's three children, aged nine, twelve, and fifteen, all came into the house.

"Hey, you guys!" Sam hugged Damien first. "My gosh, bud, you're growing like a weed! I think you might have a full inch on me."

Damien, who was a stunning blend of Imani and John, with mocha-colored skin, bright hazel eyes, and a head of thick dark curls, grinned and straightened his back dramatically. "The doctor says I'm gonna be taller than my dad by the end of high school."

"Well, that's quite a worthy goal." Sam chuckled, sliding a look over to John.

"Is Ben here?" Damien asked eagerly.

"He's upstairs. If you want to attempt to dig him out of that hole, please be my guest. Word on the street is he has a PS5." She wiggled her brows jokingly.

Damien gasped and looked over at his dad for approval. "Can I go play?"

John raised his brows and smiled, jutting his chin toward the stairs. "Go have fun with your cousin. You know the video game rules, though."

Damien nodded. "Thirty minutes at a time and no shooting games. I know!" He darted up the stairs.

Sam cringed visibly and leaned over to John. "The, uh, shooting game thing might not be as strictly followed in the Parker household..."

Her brother laughed and waved a hand in the direction Damien had gone. "It's fine. Damien won't play anything he's not supposed to."

"Is he always that...chipper?" Sam laughed, shaking her head.

John shrugged humbly. "Yeah, he's a good kid." Clearly sensing Sam's concern for her own son, he placed a hand on her shoulder. "Don't worry about Ben. I'm sure he'll cheer up after a summer in Cocoa Beach. It's a tough time."

Damien was so bright and happy and engaged. Sam had just kept telling herself that all teenage boys were angsty and troubled like Ben, but somehow John's kid seemed to have missed that aspect of growing up.

"Are those my cousins I hear?" Taylor's joyful voice echoed through the hallway as the kitchen started filling up with family, wine glasses got poured, and charcuterie boards got munched on.

"Tay Tay!" John's youngest child, nine-year-old Ellen, skipped excitedly over to Taylor and gave her a big hug.

"Hi, Taylor." Liam, the twelve-year-old who was as sweet and perfect as the rest of the family, came over to greet Taylor.

"You guys want to go pet Mr. Minx? He's out on the back deck."

The two young kids nodded enthusiastically, and Taylor led them out to the back deck where the ocean air was starting to cool down as the sun set, and the waves crashed gently across the sand.

Taylor's cat, white and fluffy Mr. Minx, was perched like the King of Cocoa Beach on a chaise lounge.

"Here you go, my children." Mom floated in with two glasses of wine and handed one to John and one to Sam. "Imani, red or white?"

"White for me, please." Imani smiled.

"You got it. Erica and Will are on their way. She ended up having to work late. Again." Dottie groaned and shook her head as she poured Imani a glass of wine. "Poor girl."

"No pity for her." Imani sipped the wine. "The

woman is a literal rocket scientist. Talk about a role model for young women."

Sam cringed. "Well, I'm absolutely nothing, so it probably cancels out somehow and brings down the family role model average."

John glared at her, narrowing his eyes. "Come on, Sam. You're not nothing. Life kicked you on your butt, and you're going to get back up again. Just...give it time."

"I know. I'm sorry." Sam glanced at Imani apologetically. "I want to get all the sympathy out and over with, done on the first night, okay?"

Imani placed a hand with perfectly manicured nails on Sam's arm. "I can't imagine what you're going through."

"That's what I'm talking about," Sam teased with a wink. "But seriously? I'm taking it one day at a time, am currently residing in paradise, and ready to...rebound."

"And you will," John said with all that Sweeney confidence that had somehow skipped her.

"Hello, family!"

Erica. Right on time—the crown jewel of the Sweeney family and her darling of a husband. Even from here, she could see her sister's beautiful face, framed with her shiny brown hair, somehow looking not a day over thirty instead of the thirty-nine she was. Erica's brown eyes were big and bright and somehow always seemed to reflect just how brilliant she was.

Good thing Sam loved the heck out of her baby sister.

"Hi, Erica." Sam headed right over to give her a hug. "Flawless as always."

Erica choked. "You're not looking hard enough," she teased as she gave Sam a loving squeeze.

Almost immediately, Sam felt more relaxed and at home in her sister's familiar embrace. Why was she so worried about pity and sympathy and how she looked to these people?

They were family, and they loved her.

Erica couldn't help that she was a freakishly impressive workaholic who had an aerospace engineering degree from MIT and launched rockets for NASA.

She was humble about it, for the most part, and at the end of the day, she was still Sam's little sister. Still the girl who'd always wanted to tag along with Sam and her friends at the mall and tried to copy all of Sam's outfits and makeup.

Now, Sam wished she could copy Erica's entire life. And that was something to be celebrated, not embarrassed about.

"Sam, how the heck are ya?" William Armstrong, Erica's great-looking and always-attentive husband, came over to greet her, a warm smile easily reaching his green eyes.

"Better now that I'm with this crew," she said, and wondered if they knew how much she meant it.

"Well, we're happy you're here." Will placed a hand on her shoulder, looking out toward the beach. "It's hard to be sad in paradise, right?"

"It certainly helps to be home."

"I'm gonna go see if Dottie needs any help in the kitchen." Will headed over to greet Mom.

"Of course he is. Because being Mr. Perfect is a twenty-four-seven gig," Sam cracked with a playful elbow to Erica.

"He's so good at it, though," Erica volleyed, then eyed Sam. "You're gonna be okay. You know that, don't you?"

"Trying so hard to hold that thought."

"Coming here was smart," Erica said matter-of-fact. "And the kids, too? For the whole summer? Max is okay with that?"

"It'll give him more time to go to Lamaze classes."

Erica rolled her eyes. "I heard. Where are Ben and Taylor?"

"Taylor's outside on the deck with Liam and Ellen, and Ben is upstairs probably scaring the life out of poor Damien."

Her sister snorted. "Damien doesn't scare easily."

"Yeah? You haven't been around Ben lately."

"Oh, you're finally here!" Mom walked over to them, giving Erica a hug and taking a minute to soak in the fact that two of her three daughters were together in her home. "White or red for you, Erica?"

"I'll just take a water, actually. Thanks, Mom."

Sam narrowed her eyes at her sister. "No wine anymore? Things really are changing around here."

She laughed softly and waved a dismissive hand as they walked together to the deck. "I've got so much going on with work, and with this new top-secret clearance and all, I've really got to keep a clear head."

"You're so cool it hurts."

It was dusk now, and the sky was almost indigo, with

the early light of the moon starting to reflect on the ocean waves. A warm, salty breeze swirled through the air, smelling and tasting like home to Sam.

Liam and Ellen giggled wildly as they chased around Taylor's cat with a toy, and the calm hum of the ocean set a soft white noise in the background of everything.

"I mean it," Erica said softly, leaning into her. "You made the right choice coming back."

Sam took a long, deep breath, watching as the palm trees that surrounded the cottage swayed in the soft wind. "I think I did."

"Kids! Dinner!" Mom called out to the deck.

"Coming!" Sam said over her shoulder, turning back to the ocean as the younger children jetted into the house for dinner.

"Mom seems happy. Well, as happy as she's been since Dad died," Erica said softly, leaning close to Sam. "She's been so weak and fragile ever since he passed, it's been tough to see. You coming here was good for her. Maybe we'll get some of the old Dottie magic back."

"I'm glad, and I really hope so." Sam smiled. "Also, it doesn't have to constantly be about me and my train-wreck life. I do want to hear about your stuff. Well, the stuff I *can* hear about, Mrs. Top-Secret Clearance."

Her sister laughed sharply, tilting her head back as they walked inside to sit down at the table. "Nothing too interesting, I promise."

The flash in Erica's eyes made Sam think that may not be entirely true, but she decided she'd get to that later.

John called up the stairs for Damien and Ben to come down and eat, and Will helped Mom set the table and get everything ready for dinner.

"Mom, this looks beautiful. Thank you." Sam took a deep inhale, smelling the savory, earthy rosemary that covered that roasted chicken on the table.

The table was piled with platters of buttery smashed potatoes, green beans with bacon bits, and warm garlic rolls in a basket.

"It's your welcome home dinner, honey." Dottie assumed her seat at the head of the table and flipped a napkin into her lap. "And I know how you guys love my special rosemary chicken."

"Rosemary chicken? Grandma, that's my favorite!" Damien's comically cheery voice entered the room as he grinned and sat down at the seat next to his mom.

Sam looked for Ben, who was slowly skulking his way into the dining room. She had hoped that some of Damien's brightness would rub off on her son, but there seemed to be no such connection.

But his hood wasn't up anymore. Score one for Damien's influence on Mr. Sunshine.

"Hi, sweetie." Sam smiled at Ben, waving him into the empty seat between her and John. "Come sit."

Ben forced a generic wave for the family and a smile that looked like it caused him physical pain before sitting down and piling some food on his plate.

At least he was eating.

There was a short pause as everyone got their dinners and settled in for the meal, and for a split-second Sam held her breath, silently praying that the conversation would be about anything but her and Max and the divorce and the *new baby*. And the house. Oh, God, the house.

John glanced at her and caught her eye, seemingly reading her mind yet again in his protective, older brother way. "So, Erica. Tell us about the new launch you've been working on. An updated Mars rover, right?"

*Thank you, John.*

Sam breathed a quiet sigh of relief, sliding a smile over to Taylor beside her, who reached down and gave her hand a quick squeeze.

They were in this together, and they had this family for support.

And at this point, that was invaluable.

Sam ate her dinner, enjoying every bite more than she'd enjoyed a meal in years, as she watched her siblings fall back into their familiar, consistent roles.

John, the dependable, stable, rock-solid older brother who gave great advice and fixed every imaginable problem.

Erica, the baby who'd made it her life's mission to prove herself to be the most successful, intelligent, and impressive member of the family. She'd come a long way from standing up in her dinner chair to make a point, but the memory made Sam smile.

Julie, of course, was off somewhere out West in her touring van with her boyfriend and daughter. But she was with them in spirit.

And then there was Sam. Floating somewhere in the

middle of strong personalities, a close-knit dynamic, and millions of memories.

She'd have to find a new way to fit back into this family after years of distance. But for the first time since that dreadful day when Taylor called her in tears to share the trauma of seeing her father in the act of cheating, Sam felt optimistic.

# Chapter Five

## *Erica*

"It really is nice to have Sam back." Erica looked out the window of their SUV as Will drove down the smooth road of the well-lit, high-end neighborhood of Riverside Palms. "We haven't been as close these past several years, but I have a good feeling about her being home. Now that Max is out of the picture, I feel like I can finally have my sister back."

Will smiled at her, looking over from the driver's seat with the shadows of his sharp cheekbones and jawline visible in the car light. She never tired of looking at him, feeling a swell of affection and gratitude that she had him at her side.

"I'm really happy for you," he said. "I know you guys used to be so close."

"Yeah." Erica exhaled, trying to keep up the small talk and ignore the jittery, relentless thoughts about the other pressing issue on her mind. "It's good. It's really good."

That issue would be the elephant in the room—or car, rather—that Erica and Will were sort of dancing around since they left the cottage. It sat right between them.

For a few beats of silence, Erica could feel her heart

slam against her ribs as she made the announcement. "I'm going to do it tonight."

"What? Really?" He shook his head. "Babe, no. Don't you think you should wait until the morning? I mean, isn't it supposed to be more accurate—"

"Will, come on. I'm two and a *half* days late." She grinned brightly at him, excitement swirling through her.

"Half days?" He cracked a smile. "How can you be a half-day late?"

She puffed out a breath. "When you track your cycle as closely as I do, you can be a half-day late."

This had to be it. This had to be the month. It was her time to get a positive pregnancy test and finally have her dream come true.

"You sure about this? I don't want..." Will stopped himself and swallowed as he pulled the car into their garage. "I don't want you to be disappointed again, Erica. We've had a great night, and—"

"I won't be." She shook her head, buzzing with optimism. "This is it. I can feel it. I know this is it."

As they got out of the car, Erica practically jogged into the house to run upstairs and take the test.

Excitement and anticipation and a good bit of anxiety coursed through her as she headed up the sleek open stairs of their ultra-contemporary home, the one they'd built with extra bedrooms that were so painfully empty right now.

She slipped into the hall bathroom where she kept the tests she'd purchased at CVS a few months ago, hoping she'd only need one, even though she bought five.

"Hey, Erica. Wait." Will jogged up the stairs to keep up with her.

She whipped around. "What?"

"Don't..." He bit his lip. "I just don't want you to get your hopes too high. It's not even a year yet, and you know this can take—"

"Too late!" she exclaimed with a playful shrug. "My hopes are high. But I'm right. I know I'm right. Have I ever been wrong?"

"Not..." Will paused to think. "Not really."

"Okay. I'm gonna take it."

He put his arms around her and pulled her close, giving her a kiss on the forehead. "I love you, no matter what it says. And we are going to be okay..." He pulled away to meet her gaze, those green eyes drawing her in and making her melt. "No matter what it says."

Erica let out a breath and nodded. "I know. Wish me luck."

Her baby was coming, she was certain of it. She could feel it in her heart and soul.

"I'll be right here, okay?" Will stepped to the side, leaning against the wall of the hallway.

He'd learned by now that Erica had to be alone when she took a pregnancy test, which was why she did it in the hall bathroom instead of their master. She couldn't stand sharing the gut-wrenching rollercoaster of watching the test develop with anyone, even Will.

More than that, she couldn't stand watching the hope drain from his eyes when it showed up negative.

With one quick, silent prayer, Erica pulled the stick out of the box, sucked in a deep breath, and took the test.

As per the ritual she had developed all these months —because, yes, she had taken the test a few times even before she was officially late—she placed the stick face down on a tissue while she washed her hands, fixed her hair, and stared in the mirror trying to decide if she *looked* pregnant or the same as always.

Until last year, she had never really prioritized having kids. She'd hardly ever even thought about it. Work was her life, and those rockets were her babies. Erica had lived and breathed engineering since college, and she'd always thought that was enough for her.

And it was, for a long time. But one random day, a week after her thirty-ninth birthday, she ran into Target on her way home from work when Will had asked her to grab some eggs.

As she was walking to the back of the store where the groceries were, something stopped her with a powerful and magnetic force.

A tiny, green and pink onesie hanging on a rack. She'd known she must have blown past the baby clothes in her neighborhood Target a thousand times before, and never even noticed.

But something happened that day. She touched the onesie with her fingers, stunned at how tiny it was. And suddenly she could see Will's eyes on a baby, beaming with green light and joy.

She realized she was thirty-nine, and time had flown, and she had worked. And worked. And worked. That day in Target, she felt a need so strong that she ran home and they started trying that very night.

That was almost a year ago, and every day Erica's baby fever had gone up a degree or two. Now, she was completely burning, and it was starting to get painful.

And so was this wait.

Certain it had been five minutes, Erica squeezed her eyes shut, held her breath, and picked up the test, turning it around.

One line. One. One dark, defined, unmistakable red line, and not even a hint of anything else.

The thud of disappointment was so physical, she felt like her heart literally dropped down to that currently empty uterus and gave it a little punch. She pressed her palm onto the countertop for stability and tried not to cry.

No. This couldn't be. Negative...again?

"What is it? What does it say?" Will tapped the other side of the bathroom door impatiently.

Bless his heart. Erica knew he was just as invested in this journey as she was, but she needed to be alone right now. She could barely talk. She could barely think.

She stared at the single red line on that stupid stick. Why did it have to only be one line? Why couldn't there just be two?

She was sure this would be the month. They'd done everything right, timed it to perfection based on the tracking app. Okay, *both* tracking apps, because what if one had been wrong?

But *something* had been wrong. Stress, sleep deprivation, timing, maybe some lackluster eggs? Whatever,

Erica Armstrong was not pregnant and that was just...wrong.

She cursed under her breath, feeling a sting of frustrated tears in the back of her eyes.

"Erica?" Will said softly, the hope in his voice draining as fast as hers had. "Are you gonna tell me anything?"

She dropped the stick into the little metal wastebasket with an angry thud and walked out of the bathroom.

"Take a guess," she said through a breaking voice, falling into her husband's loving arms.

"Oh, babe." He pulled her in, tight and close, and Erica took a deep breath. He smelled like home...earthy and woodsy and a little bit sweet.

He felt like love and safety and security. And Erica knew, without a doubt in her mind, that he was put in the world to be a dad.

And her body, for one reason or another, was not doing the one thing it was supposed to be able to do.

Her body had never failed her. Not once in nearly forty years. Her body had taken her to the state championships on the high school swim team. Her body had withstood every coffee-fueled all-nighter studying aerospace engineering at MIT. Her body had a mind so sharp she could figure out the mass ratio of a shuttle engine just by looking at it.

Her body and brain were so capable that many people found her amazing and many more found her intimidating.

But that very body was now falling short, incapable of completing the most basic and natural task that a woman was designed to complete.

It should have been a whole lot easier than rocket science, right?

"Hey." Will took her chin between his fingers, tipping her head up to meet his gaze. "Our time is gonna come. I promise."

"But what if it doesn't?" she asked on a hushed sob, holding onto Will's familiar green eyes for some shred of comfort and reassurance. "What if something's...wrong?"

"Nothing's wrong, babe," he said quickly, wrapping an arm around her as they sat down on the floor of the hallway outside the bathroom like walking to their own room would just take too much effort right then. "It just takes a little longer at our age. We aren't exactly spring chickens anymore." He gave a wink that almost made Erica laugh.

"But it's been so many months. And we're doing everything you're supposed to do. You got tested and everything is great. I'm tracking and planning and obsessing. I have a freaking spreadsheet to document when I'm ovulating."

"Well, don't take this the wrong way, but..." He wrapped an arm around her and they leaned against the wall. "That doesn't exactly come as a shock. You have a spreadsheet for everything."

"Yeah, and they work," she said quickly, shaking her head. "They always work. The numbers are there. The cycles are recorded. The projections make perfect sense. It's just not...*happening*."

"It will."

Erica looked up at her husband, holding his gaze, moving to her next phase after planning and spreadsheet: a strategy change. "I think it's time to see a specialist. Run some tests. Get answers."

"You think? I thought at the year point, and that's two more months, so..." Will offered, raising his shoulder.

"Why wait? My clock is ticking, honey. Fast. I'm staring forty smack in the face."

"And you are the hottest almost-forty-year-old in the entire state of Florida, you know that?" He squeezed her side, making her smile as she leaned into him.

"That is so not true."

"Definitely the smartest."

"That..." Erica cocked her head and smiled a little. "That might be true."

Will took a long, deep breath and ran a hand through his blond hair. "You think it'll give you peace of mind to see a fertility specialist and get told that everything is completely normal and perfect?"

She nodded eagerly, inching closer to him. "I really do. And if something is wrong, I want to know sooner rather than later. Don't you?"

"Okay." Will kissed her forehead, keeping his lips on her for an extra beat. "I'll do some research tomorrow and book us an appointment." He pulled away and tapped her temple. "This mind needs peace."

"Desperately." Erica felt more at ease with the

undying support of her husband. "Thank you. I love you."

"I love you more." He stood up, offering Erica his hand to help her off the ground. "Come on. Let's get to bed and enjoy our last bit of time when it's just the two of us. Because I know for a fact we've got a little one in our near future. I'm sure of it."

Erica just smiled and followed him to the bedroom, so hoping that he was right.

Peace of mind. A fertility specialist would bring peace of mind. Because everything was going to be fine and normal, just like Will said.

And if it wasn't, she'd deal with that. They'd deal with it together.

But the thought of that very possibility made her nauseous, and not in the good, pregnant kind of way.

# Chapter Six

## *Taylor*

It must have been somewhere between five-thirty and six in the morning when Taylor woke up, ready to start the day, which was beyond weird and out of character for her.

She was normally a big fan of sleeping in, especially after late-night shifts at the bar. But Taylor wasn't a bartender anymore, at least for the time being. Right now, she was just a girl at the beach.

The earliest slivers of morning light came though the white sheer curtains of her room at the cottage, and Taylor slid out of the silky sheets and walked over to the slider.

Like the living room, the downstairs bedroom where Taylor was staying had big glass doors leading out to a deck directly on the sand of the beach. Grandma and Grandpa had built the cottage with a lot of indoor-outdoor living—or IOL, as her mom called it—in mind. And Taylor was here for it.

Her little apartment in downtown Winter Park couldn't compare to this, that was for sure.

Taylor slid open one glass door, slowly and quietly in an attempt to not wake anyone.

The morning air was warm and a bit sticky, but the salty breeze instantly cooled it down, lifting Taylor's hair around her face.

Mr. Minx, clearly annoyed by Taylor's strangely early activity, stretched and yawned and gave her a slightly dirty look before resuming his perch on the chair in the corner of the room.

"I'll be right back, Minxy," she whispered to her beloved kitty, who just snored and dreamed away.

She stepped out onto the deck, watching the waves calmly splash and spray up against the sand. Glancing down, she gauged the chances of getting caught out here in nothing but the oversized T-shirt that hung halfway down her thighs. Not great, since there wasn't a soul in sight except for a lone surfer a good quarter of a mile away.

Basking in the overwhelming calm of these early hours by the ocean, she walked out onto the sand, feeling it squish between her toes as she got closer to the surf.

Gosh, it was peaceful here. Peaceful in a way that Taylor had forgotten existed. Ever since that day, which she infamously referred to as The Worst Day Of All Time, she hadn't known true, deep, real peace.

Well, she guessed that's what happened when an innocent, hard-working senior in college finished finals and came home early for winter break to surprise her parents and found her dad in bed with some random blonde.

Yeah, that would steal some peace.

Taylor hated that memory. Not because it was gross

and repulsive and upsetting. Of course, it was all of those things. And more. But what she hated the most was the sinking feeling she had gotten in the pit of her stomach after she'd let out a strangled cry and bolted out of the house that day.

She had known in that moment, without a shadow of a doubt, that her family was gone. In a flash. In a second. On a Tuesday afternoon. She also knew she had to be the one to tell her mother, and watch the woman she loved more than anyone in the world crumble to the ground in heartbreak.

That. That was the worst part.

What if she hadn't decided to come home early when she found out she didn't have to take that anatomy final? What if she had just texted Mom and Dad to say she'd arrive that day instead of trying to surprise them? Would Mom have been home getting her favorite dinner ready instead of spending the day Christmas shopping at the Millenia Mall with a friend, leaving Dad to...do that? Would they still be a family? Would he have kept up the lie and the double life for all this time?

It didn't matter. He was history.

Taylor kicked some shells with her feet as she stepped through the sand and out to where the small waves broke against the beach. The water splashed around her ankles, chilling her toes.

She looked out at the ocean, which was a deep shade of blue at this early hour, and wished she could wash those ugly memories away with the tide.

"Such a freaking jerk," she mumbled to herself,

walking a bit deeper into the ocean, the water spraying up at her knees now.

An unfamiliar male voice startled Taylor in the darkness of the early morning. "Excuse me?"

"Huh?" She jumped with fear, turning around to try to find the source of the random voice.

Who the heck was on this silent beach before six a.m. besides Taylor?

"Sorry, didn't mean to scare you." A tall, broad man walked closer to Taylor, his long, soaking wet shoulder-length hair falling around his face.

He looked around Taylor's age, maybe a little older, and was wearing a full-body wetsuit, which hugged a muscular frame. He had a surfboard tucked under his arm.

"Oh, no, I'm..." Taylor tugged at the hem of her shirt with an embarrassed laugh. "I'm sorry, I was totally just talking to myself. I didn't think anyone was out here. I was kind of having a...moment."

"A moment, huh?" The wetsuit surfboard guy shot her a crooked, knowing smile and shook out some of his wet hair.

"Yeah, a moment." She tried to smooth down her bedhead and kept her other hand tightly gripping the bottom of the T-shirt. "Like I said, I thought I was alone. It's so early."

"Prime time for catching waves." He notched his head toward the surfboard in his arm, the move highlighting beautifully sculpted features and hair, which was dark with a few golden flecks.

"That makes sense." Taylor nodded, glancing out at the ocean, which had a steady flow of calm, glassy waves.

She knew next to nothing about surfing, but it sure did look like a nice time to be out on the water.

"I'm Kai." He held out a hand.

"Nice to meet you, Kai. I'm Taylor." She reluctantly took her hand off the hem of her T-shirt and slid it into his. "And I do normally have pants on."

"Hey, I wasn't complaining."

Taylor felt her face flush again, and took a second to study Kai. With those chocolatey eyes and sharp cheekbones, he looked as if his ancestors could have been Hawaiian royalty.

Or *he* could have.

"Anyway, I'll, um..." She flicked her thumb over her shoulder back toward her bedroom at the cottage. "I'll let you enjoy your surfing."

"You ever been on a board?" Kai asked, keeping his gaze fixed on Taylor.

"Oh, me?" She laughed sharply. "Uh, no. I don't really do water activities. Unless you count sitting somewhat close to the ocean sipping a Mai Tai under an umbrella."

He chuckled softly, eyeing her. "Hey, that's not a bad way to spend a day. But I'm out here every morning if you ever get a sudden desire to, uh, hang ten."

"Every morning? Do you live locally?" she asked.

He lifted a shoulder nonchalantly. "For now, sort of. I live in Hawaii, that's where I'm from. But I train and compete in Cocoa Beach a lot. I'm here for a couple months working with a coach to get ready for the Ron Jon Invitational."

"You're a professional surfer?" Taylor drew back, impressed.

He smiled again. "Yeah. I dabble."

"That's amazing."

"What do you do? Besides have pants-less moments on the beach before dawn."

Taylor laughed easily. "I'm a bartender. Well, I was. I just got here to spend the summer at my grandma's cottage. She owns Sweeney House, the inn back there, and the little cottage next to it. I'm a little between jobs right now, so I guess I don't really know what I do."

Kai waved the board at her. "Maybe you surf."

"I doubt it."

He angled his head, looking back out at the ocean. "Never know until you try, yeah?" With that, he jogged back out into the water, running through the shallow shore before laying flat on the board and paddling out deeper.

"It was nice meeting you, Kai!" Taylor called as he paddled out to where the waves were forming.

"Aloha, Taylor!" He yelled back, his smooth, deep voice echoing across the water. "Have a beautiful day!"

Taylor smiled to herself as she walked back up the sand and slipped through the slider into her bedroom.

She didn't have much direction or certainty or, well, much of anything. But for some reason, it felt like she was indeed going to have a beautiful day.

# Chapter Seven

## *Dottie*

J ay would have taken one look at Karen Bickford and pronounced her a shark.

*You mess with sharks, darlin', you're going to get bit.*

But didn't she want a shark for a real estate agent? Wasn't that how she could get the best offer imaginable for Sweeney House and the cottage? Yes and yes. But that still didn't make Dottie unafraid of this woman's bite.

"Dottie, this buyer is serious," she ground out the words, pacing her office in heels that had to hurt. "Very serious. An offer like this isn't going to linger while you think about it."

"Well..." Dottie shifted in her chair at the agent's office, smoothing out the fabric of her floral maxi skirt. "What kind of buyer is it? Is it a nice family? With kids, perhaps, to fill the bedrooms of the cottage? To grow up playing out on the beach deck and filling the home with laughter?"

Karen snapped her neck to turn and face Dottie with a fiery glare. "I thought you said you didn't care who buys. You said you didn't want to know."

Dottie drew back and shrugged. "Well, I guess I do care."

"Fine, but the answer is no." She slipped into the chair behind her desk and tapped some papers, a challenging gaze on Dottie. "It's not a family. It's a company. A nationwide hotel chain. Bartram Properties. You've heard of them, I'm sure."

"Oh." Dottie flinched at the name, praying that Jay didn't hear that from heaven.

"They're willing to put up top dollar." The agent held up her hands, clearly frustrated with her wishy-washy, seventy-two-year-old client. "And in this market, top dollar is...top."

"I don't doubt that I'll make a small fortune on the place. I know the value of the location and the land, and I know there's a finite amount of beachfront property in the state of Florida."

*"They're not building new beaches, Dot."*

She tamped down Jay's voice and brushed a curl back and let out a sigh, the knot of her conflicted feelings forming a lump in her throat. Selling was the right thing to do, she knew that. Financially, emotionally, in every way it made sense.

Except when it didn't.

Of course, it was natural that Dottie would question a decision of this magnitude, especially now that Sam and her family were staying through the summer. Dottie couldn't have known that they'd be coming!

But she was really starting to struggle with the choice. The other night, having dinner at the cottage with several of her children around the table along with their spouses and kids, it was the closest thing she'd felt to joy since saying goodbye to Jay.

Was she seriously ready to give up the inn?

Of course she was. She couldn't bear to live the rest of her years there, without the love of her life, having to carry the burden of upkeep and management alone. She saw him everywhere, in every corner and on every wall, and needed his guidance and wisdom on a daily basis.

His fingerprints were all over the inn and the cottage. They'd raised their babies there. That was their spot. Always had been.

It simply didn't feel like a spot that Dottie wanted to have alone.

She needed to set herself up for independence and security for the rest of her life, which selling the inn and cottage would definitely do.

But then again...it was *home*.

"Dottie? Did you hear me?" Karen's impatient voice startled her, making Dottie blink back and refocus her attention away from her endless stream of thoughts about Jay and their years together.

"Oh, sorry, Karen. What did you say?"

Karen took in a slow breath, visibly on her last nerve. "I asked you if you are completely and totally certain you want to sell. Because this is no small amount of money we're dealing with, and I've been working on this for a while. When you initially came to me a couple of months ago, you were a thousand percent sure, and you wanted it sold as fast as possible with no hesitation. Now, I'm sensing some second thoughts. Am I wrong?"

Well, no. She wasn't wrong.

She was having second, third, and fifteenth thoughts, based on the last few sleepless nights. But was that enough to postpone the sale and potentially lose out on a massive chunk of change from some hotel company?

She could get the fresh start she'd been wanting, sock away some money for the grandkids, and finally be free of the suffocating grief she felt every day at that inn. Not to mention the cottage, which she could hardly step foot in without breaking down.

The thing was, ever since Sam had arrived, the grief didn't seem so suffocating. She didn't cry at the family dinner the other night, she'd laughed. Quite a bit, actually.

John and Erica were in town, sure, but they were busy with their own jobs and families and lives, and what difference would it make to them if Dottie didn't own the inn anymore?

Oh, yes, they'd romanticize their childhood home and whine about giving it up, but

Sweeney House belonged to Dottie and Jay, and the decision was hers and hers alone.

But then...Sam showed up. Her girl came home, and needed her mother. Finally. After all those long years of being kept at a distance and pushed away...Sam needed her. How could Dottie rip out the rug from underneath Sam's feet when her life had already so drastically fallen apart? What kind of mother would that make her?

"Can I just..." Dottie spoke slowly, trying to gauge Karen's current level of frustration. "Can I just get a little more time? The summer? I do want to sell, I do, it's just that now isn't as good a time as I thought."

"The market could turn on a dime, Dottie. This offer could be significantly lower, if it exists at all. There aren't a lot of buyers for a ten-room inn that needs a lot of work."

"I'll take that chance," Dottie said, shutting her eyes for a second. "I *do* want to sell Sweeney House. And the cottage. Package deal, like we talked about. I just need a little more time. You see, my daughter came home very suddenly with her two kids after her husband cheated on her with a nurse, and her life is a mess and her kids are, well, also kind of a mess and she needs to be home." She was rambling but didn't care. "I can't take this home away from my family right now. These are unexpected circumstances."

Karen sighed softly. "I'm sorry. About your daughter. Men can seriously be the worst. Sounds like that guy might be giving my ex-husband a run for his money on awfulness."

Dottie laughed quietly, relieved to find a whisper of warmth in this woman. Maybe there was a heart in there after all. "Some are rotten. Some are gold." She locked eyes with the other woman, feeling a sudden emotion squeeze at her heart. "Mine was gold."

"I'm...I'm sorry, Dottie." Karen leaned back and gave a sympathetic smile. "I sometimes tend to get so wrapped up in the business of real estate, I forget how deeply emotions can be attached to a place. Especially some-where as beautiful and special as Sweeney House. And, of course, the darling cottage. I know what it means to you and your family."

Dottie smiled, quick to forgive Karen's previous icy demeanor and pleased to see the good she knew was inside everyone. "That's quite all right, Karen. I under-stand that it's a job to you. And I don't mean to be so inconsistent, I just..." She lifted a shoulder. "Have had some recent unexpected life changes."

"I hear you." Karen stood back up, brushing her stick-straight blond hair behind her ears and adjusting the black-framed glasses perched on her nose. "But just to be clear..."

"I still want to sell," Dottie insisted, sounding a bit more certain than she actually was, but she knew she had to commit. "Just not now."

Karen nodded and made a note. "I'll put a hold on the property for now, and tell the buyer there's going to be a small personal delay. But I can't hold them off for too long, or they'll lose interest. And you'll lose all this money."

Dottie pursed her lips and nodded, thinking. "You said it was Bartram Properties, right?"

"Yes, that's the one."

"That's a big chain. What are they going to do to the place? Will they keep it as-is? Oh, please don't tell me they plan on putting in a bunch of barn doors and shiplap trying to make it look like a farmhouse on the beach. Jay would have—" She caught herself. "I would not like that.

I think it would ruin the integrity of Sweeney House." She added a laugh. "Not that they'd ask me for decorating advice, but there are some very valuable antiques in there."

"Oh, um..." Karen scooted forward to the edge of her desk. "Dottie, they're not..." She paused, as if she was struggling to finish this sentence. "They're not going to keep the inn. Or the cottage, for that matter."

Dottie jolted back in her seat, totally confused. "What do you mean? They're *buying* it, aren't they?"

"Well, they're buying the...property. The piece of land on the beach. I think the business proposal was to just level it to the ground and put a brand-new hotel on the spot. It's a prime location."

Dottie could hardly speak. "L-level it? You mean they want to get rid of Sweeney House? And the cottage?"

Karen inhaled sharply. "Dottie, when you said you wanted to sell, you said you wanted to sell as soon as possible. For the maximum profit. A big corporation like this is probably the only way you're going to be able to do that. And what they decide to do with the property once they own it is..." She gave an apologetic smile. "Up to them."

"I know, I know." Dottie could feel her heart sinking at the thought of it. Sweeney House was a staple of the community. Every Cocoa Beach local knew it. It was a landmark. It was...home. "But...getting rid of it entirely?"

The thought made Dottie want to cry, literally.

"Think on it," Karen said, tapping the screen of her iPhone. "I'm sorry, I've got a meeting in two minutes."

Dottie knew she needed to stand up and leave, but she was frozen in place.

"Okay." Dottie finally stood up, pulling her little pink handbag over her shoulder and fixing her hair, still reeling with shock and conflict. "Thanks for your time. I'll get back to you."

"Please do," Karen said, lifting up her phone to take a call as she waved goodbye to Dottie.

As she walked out, she tried to process what she'd just learned. A company that was going to level Sweeney House to the ground? And put some generic ten-story glass box in its place?

But Karen was right. Dottie wanted to move on with her life. And selling meant that she would no longer have a say in anything that happened to the place. That was the whole point, wasn't it? To get her hands off of it and her heart somewhere it could start to heal?

As Dottie drove home down the familiar stretch of A1A, she watched the palm trees sway in the breeze and looked up at every beachside hotel and condo she passed. They were all interchangeable.

There was nothing else like Sweeney House.

It was just like Jay always used to say.

*"My darling, times...they are a-changin'."*

Dottie's eyes filled up at how clearly she could still hear his voice. Times *were* a-changin', even if Dottie didn't want them to.

# Chapter Eight

## Sam

"I'm so glad we got to do this!" Imani grinned at the women around the table, her bright eyes beaming. "It has been way too long since I've had a proper girls' night."

"I probably have you beat in that department," Erica chimed in, raising a brow. "My only late nights these days consist of sitting in a room with nine nerdy male engineers talking about whether or not the laminar boundary layer is streamlined enough."

Imani groaned. "Okay, you're right. I'd rather be gluing sparkly letters on poster boards for Ellen's school projects. Which is how most of my nights went until school finally got out."

Sam laughed, thanking the waiter as he came around with four tropical, fully decorated pina coladas and handed one each to her, Imani, Erica, and Taylor.

"This is *amaaaazing*," Taylor sang, closing her eyes with pleasure as she took the first sweet sip of the fruity drink. "Ever since I started working at O'Leary's, the only thing I ever drink is beer. I need some sweetness in my life."

"We are so glad you came to girls' night." Sam

wrapped an arm around her daughter.

"Of course!" Erica raised her glass. "The next generation of Sweeney women is in good hands with you, young one."

The four women sat around an outdoor high-top at Sharky's Sea Shack, a local tiki-style bar and restaurant with quirky live music and a fabulous beach view. It was all situated outside on a big deck, overlooking the ocean and the sand, where people would go sometimes to dance after they'd had a few drinks.

Cocoa Beach was a small town, and after looking around for a few minutes, Sam seemed to see a few faces she recognized.

The sun was setting as they sipped their drinks, chatted, and laughed, painting the sky a warm shade of orange and cooling down the weather to the absolute perfect degree.

The bar hummed with conversation and music, and the ocean waves crashed not too far in the distance, making Sam feel familiar and comfortable.

Tracy Ellis, the woman who owned and managed Sharky's for as long as Sam could remember, bounced around to different tables and greeted the locals she knew so well.

"Well, if it isn't the Sweeney women!" Tracy, with a long braid and some bedazzled jean shorts, walked over and smiled, waving her hands.

"Tracy, how are you?" Sam gave her a hug.

"I'm good, I'm good. Same old, you know." She waved a hand in the direction of the bar, flashing her insanely long nails. She leaned down close to Sam and lowered her voice. "Got me a doctor boyfriend, so I'm sitting kind of pretty right now."

Imani laughed. "That's great, Tracy."

"He's a cutie, too." She smacked her chewing gum. "Might just have to keep this one."

"Mmm." Sam arched a brow. "Be careful with doctors."

"Oh..." Tracy leaned forward and held a hand to her chest. "I heard about what happened with your husband. Dottie filled me in. I am just so darn sorry. Some men can be real scumbags. 'Specially the rich ones."

She snorted. "Thank you, and it's been tough but I'm doing better." Sam looked around the table. "I've got my family, which has been wonderfully helpful."

"That's the most important thing. And this must be your daughter."

"This is Taylor, my pride and joy," Sam announced. "She's here for the summer."

"You are just a gorgeous drink of water and look exactly like your mother." Tracy gave another wave. "All right, I'll leave you gals to it. And, Sam, if you need anything at all, don't hesitate. We take care of each other on this island."

"I appreciate that. Thank you, Tracy."

"Y'all have a fun night now!" She blew a kiss and floated away.

Sam smiled to herself and shook her head, remembering just how close-knit the community of Cocoa Beach actually was.

"So, how have you been settling in?" Imani asked Sam, not wanting to get too deep into the nitty gritty of Sam's tragic life, but still bringing it up, which Sam appreciated.

"You know, I'm doing okay." She stirred her frozen drink. "Obviously, I'm still really hurt, and maybe a little lost?"

"Mom," Taylor whispered, gently placing her hand on her mother's arm.

"No, no, it's fine, honey. I'm getting there. I guess right now I just wish I had some sort of...purpose."

Erica, Imani, and Taylor all kept their attention on Sam as she talked, and she felt comfortable enough to really share with them what was going on in her heart. After all, they were her family.

"The weirdest thing is that the cheating itself wasn't even the worst part," she confessed, leaning in. "It was awful, don't get me wrong. But, I don't know, Max and I had been disconnected. I didn't realize it, but I guess I took him for granted and, well, obviously that went both ways."

"Don't blame yourself." Erica put a hand on Sam's. "Just because you two grew apart and the marriage wasn't ideal is no excuse for infidelity."

"And you left as soon as he cheated," Imani added, stirring her drink. "You're strong for that. Not everyone does."

"Everyone *should*," Erica said with a dry laugh.

"But like I said, the cheating wasn't the worst of it." Sam brushed some hair behind her ears as a warm breeze blew through the outdoor deck and swirled salty ocean air all around them. "The worst part has been trying to figure out who the hell I am without him. I mean, you guys know." She gestured at Erica and Imani. "All I've ever been is Max's wife."

They did know. Erica was her sister, and had grown up adoring Sam and wanting to be just like her. And Imani had been around forever, as she and John had been together since college. They knew Sam inside and out, and despite Sam living in her own world and Max forcing her family to keep a good distance, they still knew her better than anyone. And that would never change.

"I mean..." Imani lifted a shoulder. "I'm a wife and a mom, and that's about all I am these days, and it's fine. Don't beat yourself up."

"But you had an amazing career before Damien was born," Sam said, referring to Imani's impressive journalism career she worked tirelessly at for over six years before she and John had their first child.

She was successful and independent, and had made a name for herself and lived in a world outside of just her marriage. Of course, she stopped working to be a mom to three wonderful kids, but she'd had the career. She'd been the successful woman. She had something to show for her life.

And she'd always have that. Something Sam would never have.

"I did, but..." Imani flipped some of her long braids. "Being a mom is wonderful. Don't diminish that. Not to say I don't miss my work sometimes, but..." She gestured at Taylor. "Look at the amazing person you raised. She turned out totally awesome, and I seriously give you all the credit for that."

Taylor lifted a shoulder and winked at her mom. "It's true. I owe all of my fabulousness to you."

"See?" Erica added with a laugh. "Don't sell yourself so short, Sam. You have a daughter who's your best friend and has your back no matter what. There's a lot to be said for that."

"Well, that is true." Sam smiled, wrapping an arm around Taylor, knowing full well that despite all the mess and chaos and heartbreak that came from her relationship with Max, nothing could affect her relationship with Taylor.

"And, you know, Sam, on the career front..." Erica tilted her drink across the table. "You're forty-three, not ninety-three. You can do whatever you want. You have so much time, and it's never too late to start something new."

Sam laughed at her sister's never-ending well of ambition, swirling her pina colada and looking down at it. "I don't have a degree, Erica. I literally have a high school diploma and exactly zero years of work experience."

Erica shrugged, leaning back into the wooden barstool. "So, start now."

"I don't even know where to begin. I don't have passions or talents or interests. I'm not like you guys. I know I sound like a broken record, but I'm lost."

"Of course you are," Taylor said softly, looking at her mother. "Look at what you've been through. Who wouldn't be lost right now?"

"She's right," Imani added, lifting a brow. "If you ask me, you're handling the entire thing like a total champ."

"Well, thank you. I appreciate that. I'm trying to put on a brave face. For Ben, mostly."

Erica gave a sympathetic smile. "How's he doing?"

"How should I know? He won't say more than three words to me in a twenty-four-hour period." Sam sighed.

"He should spend more time with Damien," Imani suggested eagerly. "They're cousins and only a year apart! I know they're very different, but I bet they could be wonderful friends. Damien is such a little extrovert, maybe he'd bring Shy Ben right out of his shell."

"Ben's not shy, he's miserable," Sam shot back, the words sounding a little snippier than she intended.

"I'm sorry," Imani said quickly.

"No, I'm...I'm sorry." Sam waved a hand and gave her a smile. "It's just been really, really tough for him. Seeing his family fall apart and basically losing his father. Or all respect for him, at least."

"He and I used to be so close," Taylor mused, lifting her straw from the cup to lick off some of the whipped cream. "Then, when all the crap happened with Dad, he just...shut me out. Shut everyone out. I thought maybe it would bring us closer, like we could lean on each other, but he put up some serious brick walls. So I leaned on Mom instead."

"He idolized his father," Sam said. "He had him on such a pedestal."

Taylor scoffed. "Um, hello? So did I, the girl who was literally in her second year of medical school because I wanted to be his little surgeon protégé, despite how much I hated it. I was *Doctor Junior,*" she finished the sentence in a mocking tone, licking the whipped cream again. "Now about all I can do is make a mean Old Fashioned and fend off drunk guys."

Imani snorted, giving Taylor an adoring smile.

"You're older, though, Tay," Erica said. "You know who you are."

"Not exactly yet, but I do know I'm not a doctor. But Ben?"

"Is at such a tender age," Imani said with the wisdom that comes with motherhood, giving a slow nod of understanding.

"I know, it's bad." Sam sighed, shaking her head. "My current strategy is to just let it run its course. He'll open up when he opens up. Maybe. Someday."

"And don't forget about you, Sam," Erica insisted. "You deserve a whole new life, too. There are times when you should prioritize yourself as much as your family."

Sam sat back in the chair, wondering what this magical "new life" could actually look like for her. She wasn't like Erica or Imani, who were so sure of who they were. If they lost their husbands, they'd still have...something. An identity.

Sam felt like that's what she lacked the most. An identity.

"I'll help you," Taylor promised with a smile. "We all will. That's the beauty of being here in Cocoa Beach, Mom. We're not on our own anymore. Look around!"

"You certainly are not." Erica took Sam's hand and

gave it a tight squeeze. "And I know I work like a million hours a week, but I'm here for you. I mean, hey, I made it out tonight, didn't I?"

Sam laughed. "You did. And thank you."

"We love you," Imani added. "I know you're technically my sister-in-law, but at this point you feel like a real sister to me. And, feel free to totally hate this idea, but you could maybe consider talking to John to see if there's anything you could do at Coastal Marketing. It wouldn't be, like, the job of your dreams, but to get you by for now, it might be worth asking."

"That's not a bad idea, actually. It would feel good just to have a purpose. And an income."

"See?" Taylor shook her mom's arm around excitedly. "We're already coming up with brilliant ideas of how to help you. And speaking of jobs, I'm gonna start peeking around for something, too."

"Bartending?" Sam asked.

"I don't know. Any other ideas what I can do with a degree in biology?" She rolled her eyes. "Mixology is all I know."

"You'll find something, Taylor. There's so much tourism and fun places around here," Imani said, gesturing around vaguely. "Just keep your eyes and ears open and talk to people."

"You may want to start by wiping that whipped cream off your nose, though, Tay." Sam laughed, reaching for her daughter's nose where there was, in fact, a smudge of whipped cream on the tip.

"Huh? Where?" Taylor giggled, reaching for a

napkin.

"Hang on, I almost got it." Sam wiped her nose, but Taylor kept moving. "Hold still."

"Don't lick your finger, Mom. Ew!"

"Well, it's sticky. I've got to get it—"

"Taylor?" An unexpected male voice startled them all, making Taylor and Sam freeze right in the middle of their whipped cream nose battle.

Who was this? Sam looked up to see a tall, well-built young man in his mid-twenties, with striking features and long, dark hair. He was wearing colorful board shorts and a Hawaiian shirt that was open down the middle. Would it have killed him to close a couple of buttons?

And, wait a second—how did this guy know Taylor?

"Oh, oh my gosh." Taylor went bright red in the cheeks and stood up, her hand flying to her face to cover the remnants of whipped cream. "Kai, hey! What are you...what are you doing here?"

He ran a hand through that movie-star hair, looking at Taylor like he might want to lick that whipped cream off himself, instantly raising Sam's guard. "I hang out here a lot. I chill with some of the other surfers who are training, and this spot doesn't get too overrun with tourists, so we like it."

A surfer, huh?

"It's definitely a great spot," Taylor said nervously.

Erica, Imani, and Sam all exchanged looks as they watched the youthful, flirty interaction, all mutually wondering who this cute, young mystery surfer was and how the heck he knew Taylor.

"Oh, sorry, I'm so rude!" Taylor whipped around, her eyes dancing. "Kai, this is my mom, Sam, and two of my aunts, Erica and Imani."

"Hey, great to meet you guys." He leaned down and shook each of their hands. "I'm Kai."

"Holy crap, you're Kai Leilani!" Imani blurted out, her whole expression lighting up.

"You know him, too?" Sam laughed with confusion.

"Everyone knows him, he's a famous surfer!" Imani exclaimed. "My son, Damien, is a huge fan. He's headed to surf camp this summer for the fifth year in a row, and you're basically his idol."

Kai's brown eyes glimmered as he chuckled. "No way. I love that! I'll have to take him out on the waves sometime."

Imani drew back and grinned at the possibility of bringing her son that much joy. "That'd be incredible."

"Wait, what?" Taylor drew back. "I know you said you surfed, but...Damien knows you?"

Erica nodded slowly. "Oh, yeah, I know who you are, too. My husband and I go to the invitational every year! It's wonderful to meet you!"

Taylor shook her head. "Oh my gosh, when I ran into you the other day, I had no idea you were, like, famous."

Kai shrugs casually. "It's not a big deal."

"When did you meet him the other day?" Sam asked, growing more and more intrigued by the fact that Taylor knew this guy and somehow forgot to mention him to her.

"On the beach," Kai answered, leaning his palms

against the back of Taylor's chair. "During one of her early morning moments."

"Early morning *what*?" Sam snorted. "Taylor is *not* a morning person."

"It was just a weird day," Taylor explained. "I was up and couldn't go back to sleep. Mr. Minx was being fussy, so I went out to the beach to just walk and chill, and I ran into Kai. Briefly. I didn't realize who he was." She turned to him, her cheeks flushed. "Sorry."

"Please don't apologize." He laughed. "I'm just a guy from Hawaii."

"Oh my gosh, it's Kai Leilani!" Suddenly, three teenage girls swarmed out of nowhere.

"Can you sign my surfboard?" one of them asked with so much excitement she looked like she might spontaneously combust. "It's just outside in the parking lot in my dad's truck. Please, omigod, it would be the coolest thing *ever*!"

"Um, sure, of course." Kai shot an apologetic look to the women. "It was really great to meet you all." He waved, then turned directly to Taylor, looking at her with a fiery gaze. "Taylor, I'll...see you around?"

Erica shot Sam a knowing look, and Sam held back a laugh, entertained by every second of this allegedly famous and insanely cute surfer being completely captivated by her daughter.

"Sure!" Taylor answered with a wave as Kai headed off to go sign surfboards and live in the fantasies of fourteen-year-old girls.

Taylor sat back down slowly, sipping her nearly

empty pina colada and staring straight down as the silence at the table was hilariously overwhelming.

"Um, Tay?" Sam raised her brows slowly, staring at her daughter. "You want to, uh, fill us in on...*that*?"

"Oh, it's nothing really, Mom. I just met him out on the beach that morning. We chatted for, like, five minutes. I had no clue he was such a big deal. That was it. I'm surprised he even remembered me."

"Remembered you?" Imani laughed sharply. "Honey, he was completely crazy about you. It was all over his face."

"What?" Taylor waved her hands dismissively. "No way. I was a total wreck when I met him. I didn't even have pants on, which was mortifying, and plus, he's famous, apparently. I think you guys might be blowing it out of proportion."

"You didn't have *pants* on?" Sam asked, widening her gaze. "Since when are there things you don't tell me? How did I not hear about the pants-less encounter with the gorgeous surfer? That is top-tier mother-daughter news, hello."

"Because it was nothing!" Taylor insisted, laughing and shaking her head.

"Nonsense." Erica flicked her wrist. "We all saw how he was looking at you. You'd have to be blind to miss those eyes."

"Taylor, I'll..." Imani lowered her voice to imitate a man, talking slowly. "I'll see you around?" She wiggled her brows with the deep voice.

The other women cracked up, teasing Taylor and

deciding that this topic was much more fun than Sam's currently tragic existence.

And Sam agreed. Taylor had never dated anyone seriously. She had a couple of little high school relationships, but at UCF, all she'd done was study for med school. And then, well, then the worst day ever happened, and she saw her own father being unfaithful.

Sam guessed that her trust in men was pretty wrecked from that, and rightly so. It pained Sam that Taylor might struggle in relationships because of Max's crappy and disgusting choices, but it was just reality.

Taylor was scarred for life.

But not too scarred to flirt with the cute famous surfer, and that made Sam's heart feel light. Maybe there was hope for her to heal, too. She was far too young to be so jaded.

Couple that with the comfort of her sisters, the unconditional love of her mother, and the warm, familiar hominess of the cottage and Sweeney House, and Sam was starting to heal.

Why, she wondered, had she kept her distance from her amazing family for so long? These women were right here, all those years, only an hour away. Her mom was here, the cottage was here.

Why had she been so isolated?

There was only one clear answer. Max.

Just barely scratching the surface of figuring out her life and where to go from here, but she was starting. And that was something.

Maybe she'd ask John about that job after all.

# Chapter Nine

## Erica

The fertility clinic was freezing cold, making Erica shiver with a chill as she and Will sat in the waiting room, riddled with anxiety.

Seated side by side in cushioned chairs, they watched a variety of patients come and go as they waited. Erica wondered about each of their stories.

She took another peek at her watch and stifled a moan. They'd been waiting for over an hour, and she was missing some seriously important meetings. But she couldn't think about that right now. Dressed in typical NASA engineer clothes—skirt, blouse, and blazer, with all of her work materials in her laptop bag by her side—she was a professional on the outside.

On the inside, she was one distraught, terrified, hopeful wanna-be mother.

All she could think about were the test results they were about to review, and what they would mean. Erica and Will had decided to both go through the fertility testing at the same time, so they could get to an answer as quickly as possible.

They'd doublecheck his count, and rule Will out as a

problem. And for her? Well, she had no idea what they'd find, but whatever it was, she wanted to know.

Answers would help. There was no such thing as a bad answer, Erica believed. Because an answer was a fact, and once you had a fact, you could always figure out what to do with it.

Will threaded his fingers through hers and gave them a comforting squeeze. "How you holding up?"

"Well...I need to get this show on the road because I promised Roger I'd be back in time for the three o'clock blueprint meeting, which I'm supposed to lead."

"Are you ready for it?" Will gave her his signature crooked smile, already clearly knowing the answer to the question.

"Of course I am. The blueprints for the new Eagle engine are flawless. I've spent hours poring over them. I know that Roger will—"

"Armstrong?"

Erica and Will both straightened at the sound of the nurse calling their last name, taking one last look at each other before they stood and walked to the door leading to the back offices and exam rooms.

"Come on back, guys." The nurse smiled kindly, holding the door open for them. "Dr. Beckett has your test results ready."

"Both of us?" Erica asked nervously.

"I believe so, yes." The nurse gestured down the hall to a room on the right. "She's right in there."

Erica laced her fingers through her husband's, holding onto him for dear life, knowing that the results they were about to hear could change everything. They could open doors, answer questions, or wreck her dreams.

Erica sucked in a breath and shut her eyes as they stepped into the office, where Dr. Carol Beckett was sitting on the other side of a desk, her blue eyes kind, her smile warm.

"Mr. and Mrs. Armstrong? Welcome back." She stood up and shook each of their hands. "Have a seat."

Erica's knees felt weak as she lowered herself into the black plush chair across from the doctor, keeping her hand clinging to Will's.

Dr. Beckett leaned her elbows on the desk and looked from one to the other. "How are you two doing?"

As much as Erica respected a kind woman professional, she needed Dr. Beckett to cut to the chase, like, yesterday.

"Nervous," Erica answered quickly, giving a soft laugh.

"We're doing fine," Will added, his voice steady and strong. "Just trying to cover all our bases and get peace of mind. We're very eager to start our family."

"I know you are, and it's wonderful. At Beachside Fertility Clinic, we are going to do absolutely everything we can to make that dream come true."

"What does that mean?" Erica asked quickly, her heart rate spiking. "There's something wrong? We're going to need help?"

"No, no, Erica, please." The doctor held up her hands and laughed slowly. "Please don't panic. I have your test results and I'm going to go over them with you thoroughly, okay? I will answer any and every question you have."

Erica drew in a shuddering breath. "Okay. Can you just tell me...will we be able to have a baby?"

She could practically hear her heartbeat pounding in her ears while she waited for Dr. Beckett's answer.

"It's not quite that simple. Please, let me talk through these results with you. There are options and possibilities. Nothing in the fertility world is black and white."

Erica's heart sank. Options and possibilities didn't sound like...*yes*.

"Let me start with your test results, Will." She gestured at him, pulling up a document on the large computer screen in front of her. "Your tests came back completely normal. Sperm counts are right in the healthy range, and there were no red flags in the bloodwork or analysis."

Will let out a breath and smiled at his wife. "Good. Great! That's awesome, right?"

"What about me?" Erica asked, the lump in her throat getting bigger as she clung to Will's hand. "What about my test?"

"Well, for the most part, everything looks healthy. But we've discovered some signs of endometriosis." She leveled her gaze with Erica's. "Have you ever experienced any kind of pain or abnormalities? Symptoms?"

"None," she answered quickly, shaking her head. "I've never had any symptoms of endometriosis. But it's very common right?"

"Yes." The doctor nodded. "It's one of the most

common diseases we see with the female reproductive system. And asymptomatic cases—like yours—are slightly less common, but they do happen."

Oh. She had endometriosis. Okay, that wasn't...infertility. Was it?

Erica shut her eyes, gathering herself with this new information. "But endometriosis is treatable, right? I mean, it can be fixed?"

"It can be treated, but there is no cure."

Erica gnawed on her lip, desperately needing a whole heck of a lot more clarity and answers than she was getting. "Well, then, let's treat it. And that's that. Once it's better, I should be able to get pregnant, right? I mean, endo—"

"Erica, your case has gone untreated for a long time. Decades, I'd say, which is understandable, since you haven't had the typical pain that would cause a woman to seek help. It's nothing you've done."

Erica cocked her head. "Okay, but..."

"However, the disease has led to a significant amount of scar tissue that has formed in your uterus, and it has caused some serious blockage in both fallopian tubes," Dr. Beckett said slowly, letting the words fall over Erica like shards of glass. "One worse than the other."

"Okay, well, let's unblock it," Erica said, feeling like the world had started swimming a bit. "We'll just fix it. We'll find the solution, and fix it. That's what we do. We can always—"

"Erica." Dr. Beckett locked eyes with her, her brows

knitting together with apologetic sympathy. "It's not quite that simple."

Will squeezed her hand, which was sweaty.

"Let me explain." Dr. Beckett cleared her throat. "One of your tubes is, unfortunately, blocked beyond repair. Treatment and surgery for that condition would likely lend no good results and get you nowhere."

"But..." Erica inhaled sharply. "There's another fallopian tube."

"Yes, there is. And the other one is not as badly blocked. It does show some significant scarring, however, and would make getting pregnant very, very difficult."

She shut her eyes tightly, shaking her head. "Can we fix it? The tube that's not as bad?"

"We can operate on the tube, yes." Dr. Beckett clasped her hands together and placed them on the desk, keeping her gaze steady and calm on Erica's. "But the possibility of clearing it to the level of normalcy, at this point and at your age, is slim."

"It can't be fixed?" Erica shuddered.

"Babe." Will wrapped his arm around her, holding her close. "It's going to be okay."

"We have to be able to fix it. The surgery could work, right? I just—" Erica looked at the doctor again. "Are you saying I can't get pregnant?"

The doctor pressed her lips together. "I am not saying that, actually. I am telling you that, realistically, with your current medical status, age, and the condition of your endometriosis, it is very, very unlikely. We could harvest eggs and try IV but, again, age is a limiting factor here."

Erica just stared at her, hearing nothing but the thrum of blood in her head.

"I realize this is not the news you wanted, Erica. And I am by no means telling you to stop trying. Like I said, it's not impossible. But with the fact that you are thirty-nine, and you only have one fallopian tube that is semi-functional, it is going to be difficult. It could be years."

"It's too late." Erica shut her eyes and felt tears stinging behind them.

"It's not too late," Will chimed in, holding his wife reassuringly. "She just said it isn't impossible, you heard her."

"I'm almost forty." Erica looked at her husband and then back at the doctor. "It's basically impossible."

Dr. Beckett shook her head. "It's very unlikely, not impossible. There is still IVF, although I want to set your expectations realistically. There are other ways to become a mom—"

"Thank you." Erica held up a hand, shutting her eyes as a tear rolled down her cheek. "I know there are other ways, but...I want to just deal with this. Thank you, Dr. Beckett."

"Hang in there." She said, walking them out the door and back to the hallway. "Please call if you have any questions."

"Thanks, Doc." Will nodded at her as they passed through the doorway, holding Erica up as she leaned on him for support in more ways than one.

"Come on. Let's just get to the car." He walked her

through the waiting room, which was a blur, and out into the blinding, blistering sunlight in the parking lot.

"Will, I..." Erica stopped in her tracks before they could reach their black SUV. She quivered with a sob, dropping to the ground, sitting right down on the pavement in her three-hundred-dollar St. John skirt.

"Oh, Erica." He crouched next to her, wrapping his arms around his wife's shaking shoulders.

"We're never going to have a family, Will." She looked up at him, feeling mascara smear all over her face and not caring. "I'm never going to be a mom. I have to get my head around that and I can't."

"Honey. She didn't say never." He gently touched her chin and lifted it up to meet his gaze. "But I know you're hurting." He shut his eyes and clenched his jaw. "So am I."

Erica was so caught up in her own grief, she'd not even taken a second to think about how crushed Will also must be. Especially because their infertility was her problem. He would never be a dad because of her.

"We can look into other options, okay?" He sat fully down on the ground of the parking lot with her as she cried into his chest. "Maybe we can consider the surgery, or IV, or ..."

"The surgery sounded like a waste. She said there's a slim chance it would even help. And do you know how long egg harvesting takes? Years? And it doesn't work most of the time. I can't...I just can't."

"I know. I know."

"I'll be okay." Erica nodded, wishing the whole world

would go away and she could just live in this spot in Will's chest forever, never having to face life again.

"For now..." He ran a hand through her hair. "I think you need to tell Roger that something came up. You're sick, or a family emergency or something, and the blueprint meeting will have to wait."

"No." Erica untangled herself from him, stood up, and brushed the dust and dirt off of her skirt. "No, I'm going to lead the meeting. And I'm going to crush it. And then I'm going to engineer the Eagle and it's going to put three men and a rover on Mars. That's what I'm going to do. That's all I'm meant to do in this life, so I might as well do it right."

Will nodded, standing up. "I'll take you back to the Space Center, then."

Erica wiped off her mascara, took a deep breath and held her chin high.

She had wanted answers. So, so badly. And now she had one. And as much as it sucked and hurt and broke her heart, she had to power on.

# Chapter Ten

## *Taylor*

Taylor Parker was not one to chase boys. Ever. She wouldn't be caught dead having some dumb crush on a guy, and she knew without a doubt that relying on a man was about as good of an idea as relying on a pile of rocks.

She'd seen firsthand just how *reliable* a man can be. She hated her dad for what he'd done, but at least it opened her eyes. At least she knew for sure that men were not, under any circumstances, to be trusted, and needed to be kept at arm's length at all times.

And Taylor had done that spectacularly well. She had never really dated much prior to everything going down in med school, mostly because undergrad was the busiest and most stressful time of her life. She was laser focused on becoming a doctor, and didn't give anyone or anything else the time of day.

After she found out about her dad and dropped out, she was so broken and bruised by what he'd done that she'd sworn off men for, well, forever.

So why on Earth was she awake at 5:22 in the morning—the *morning!*—sliding open the door to the deck and getting ready to wander the beach in hopes of seeing Kai again?

That was so not like her.

But whatever the reason was, she wasn't going to be caught in some ugly old T-shirt and no pants this time.

Taylor slid on a soft pair of gray joggers and opted for a white crop top, tying her hair up in a big, loose bun with some strands hanging out around her face. Casual, cute, but not trying too hard.

Mr. Minx walked up to her and rubbed his head on her leg over and over, making figure eights between her feet and purring loudly.

"Hi, Minxy." Taylor crouched down and scratched his fluffy white fur, giving him a kiss on his soft little head. He chittered in response and nuzzled her some more, and she walked over to his food and water to make sure they were filled up.

She hadn't set an alarm. She wasn't *that* crazy. She just...woke up. Before the sun started beaming through the sheer curtains and it was still silvery and dark.

Maybe Cocoa Beach Taylor was a different person who liked early mornings. Or liked...Kai.

She stepped out onto the deck, blowing a kiss to Mr. Minx and quietly closing the door yet again so she wouldn't wake her mom or brother.

The sand was cool in between her toes, and the air was warm and still. It was almost completely dark, but the earliest rays of sun on the horizon gave her just enough light for her to see.

Taylor walked down to the edge of the water,

glancing left and right so as not to be caught off guard this time. She didn't see a sign of life, and a tiny ribbon of disappointment wormed its way through her chest.

Was she really that desperate? Was she really only awake and out here at five-thirty in hopes of seeing the hot Hawaiian surfer who she couldn't stop thinking about?

No. She was out here on this beach for herself. To think and to ponder and to reflect on—

Wait a second, what was that?

Taylor looked out at the waves of the ocean, narrowing her eyes to make out a figure far out in the water.

Then, a large, swooping wave rose up way out there, deep blue and glassy. And...there he was.

Gliding on a surfboard through the barrel of the wave, looking like some kind of surfing movie poster.

Taylor laughed and shook her head in amazement as she walked toward the shore, watching Kai glide across the surface of the wave, defying all laws of physics as Taylor understood them.

She jogged closer, squinting her eyes to make him out better.

He reached his arm out and skimmed it across the inside of the wave, making a thin line of white bubbles in the scooping circle of water.

"Holy crap," Taylor whispered to herself, completely mesmerized by the graceful beauty of Kai on his surfboard in the early morning light.

As he reached the end of the wave and it crashed

down in the ocean, he flipped the board out from underneath him and dove into the water.

As he popped back up to the surface, he lifted himself up onto the surfboard and looked toward the sand, his gaze finding Taylor.

"That was amazing!" she shouted, the water splashing her ankles as she got close. "No wonder you're famous!"

He laughed, the deep, throaty sound carrying across the water as he waded back toward the shore, picking up the board and jogging toward her.

He shook out his hair, which sprayed little droplets of ocean water all around him. "Hey, you," Kai said, his dark, defined eyes giving her a good look up and down. "You remembered your pants today."

Taylor rolled her eyes and stifled a laugh. "I know it's a stupid question, but how did you learn to surf like that? I mean, I tried boogie boarding once and completely wiped out. Whole thing just flew out from under me and I flipped backwards. My ears got clogged, I cried, it was a rough time."

Kai threw his head back and laughed heartily, squatting down to sit in the sand away from the water.

Taylor sat next to him, holding her knees to her chest and turning to look at him as the early sunlight cast an orange glow on his face.

"My uncle taught me, back in Hawaii. There, everyone surfs. Well, not everyone." He lifted a shoulder and chuckled softly. "But most people. My Uncle Akau was an amazing surfer. Never went pro or anything, but he was incredible. When I was about four, he took me out on the water for the first time."

"And you just got up and surfed?" Taylor asked. "Just like that?"

"Uh, no." Kai raised a brow as a smile hinted at his lips. "It took me two weeks to even stand up. I just kept falling and falling and falling."

Taylor laughed, shaking her head. "Why did you keep going out there then? That's terrible."

"Because I wanted to be like my uncle! I knew I could get it if I kept trying."

"Well, you certainly did." Taylor turned back toward the ocean, thinking about Kai's effortless ride across the waves.

"The first time I found myself inside the barrel of a wave, I thought I was in heaven," he said, his voice low and reverent. "I was instantly addicted to that feeling, and I've been chasing it every day since. The competition and fans and all of that? It's just a perk. But all I really care about is riding waves. It's seriously blissful."

"What's it feel like?"

Kai looked at her, his hair dripping down his forehead. "Everything goes silent. The wave moves you entirely on its own. It's like being a literal part of the ocean. You don't have to balance, you don't have to propel yourself, it just...takes you. It's crazy, it's so cool. Kind of like flying. You would love it."

Their eyes locked, and Taylor could feel herself being pulled to him like a magnet, drawn to his warmth and light and, oh, that smile.

"That's incredible. I wish..." She laughed softly and shrugged. "I wish I had something I felt that much passion for."

Kai put his hand on her arm, giving it a friendly shake. "You do! You just have to find it. What did you do before you came to Cocoa Beach?"

"Poured drinks," Taylor said with a curled lip. "But before that, um, I used to be in school. I was going to be a doctor. A surgeon, actually. Like my dad. But I...changed my mind. So, I started bartending."

"Was that your passion?" Kai asked with no sarcasm.

Taylor snorted. "I mean, the tips are nice. But no. I don't think so."

"If you don't mind me asking..." He picked up some sand and let it fall through his fingers. "Why did you leave school? You didn't want to be a doctor?"

"I didn't want to be anything like my dad. Actually, I really wanted to infuriate him. As much as possible. So, I quit on the one thing he wanted most from me."

Kai drew back, his dark eyes wide. "Just to stick it to your old man?"

"Well, that and the fact that I realized I was doing it more for him, and not at all for myself. I don't think being a surgeon was my passion, either. I kinda hated it."

"What did your dad do to make you so mad at him?" Kai ran a hand through his hair, looking intently at Taylor.

"He cheated on my mom with a nurse," she answered, looking back out at the water as she cringed with the memory. "I caught them."

"You did?" He gasped. "Good God, that's awful."

"Yeah. I came home early for winter break my senior year of college. I wanted to surprise them." She rolled her eyes. "*Surprise!*" Taylor scoffed. "And now he's living with her in my childhood home and expecting a child and my parents are divorced. Or about to be."

"Holy crap, Taylor." Kai blew out a sigh, shaking his head sympathetically. "That is so rough. No wonder you hate him. I can't even blame you."

"It was brutal. And I had to be the one to tell my mother." She shut her eyes.

"And you guys are really close, huh?"

"Best friends." She held up two fingers and crossed them together. "Like this."

"I'm so sorry. I can't imagine how hard that must have been on your family."

Taylor nodded. "It changed everything, that's for sure. My mom was super depressed for a while. She's still trying to find herself and figure out where to go from here. But I think coming to Cocoa Beach was a really good move for us."

"A fresh start," he added.

"Exactly. And my brother, Ben?" Taylor sucked her teeth. "He's not doing so hot. He and my dad were close. And I don't think he likes how much my mom and I hate him now. But also, he hates him, too, I think. He just doesn't want to. He's struggling."

"How old is your brother?"

"Sixteen."

"Ouch."

Taylor laughed. "Yeah. But we're hanging in there." She pulled her knees closer and rested her chin on them, turning to face Kai. "What about you? What's your family like? Aside from your cool uncle, the surfer?"

Kai paused for a second, thinking before he answered. "They're, um, very traditional."

"They're all still in Hawaii, right?"

"Oh, yes," he answered quickly. "They'd sooner die than leave the Islands. When I say traditional, I mean it. My family has lived in Hawaii running a sugarcane farm for a hundred and fifty years. The time-honored Hawaiian culture is the most important thing in the world to them. So, as you can imagine, they aren't huge fans of me traveling the world as a professional surfer."

"Really? I'd think they'd be over the moon with your success." She wrinkled her nose. "Not that I Googled you or anything."

He laughed and lifted up his knuckles to meet hers. "Thank you."

"But seriously, what about your uncle? He was a surfer. Isn't being a surfer, like, the most Hawaiian thing ever?"

Kai chuckled, then shook his head. "To them, it's a waste of time, or at least just something you do for fun, not as a profession. My uncle was a black sheep of sorts. My dad always wrote him off as some sort of pariah because he didn't want to work on the farm. He told me I shouldn't idolize Uncle Akau, and that surfing went against our family values and traditions."

Taylor cocked her head, totally surprised by this

deeper knowledge about Kai. "So they want you to stop? They don't support it?"

"Well, yeah, basically," Kai said softly. "But obviously, I've proven to be a decent surfer. My father told me to"—he held up air quotes—"'get it out of my system,' so that I can come back home and take over the farm and family business."

"Wow. And you're so good." Taylor swallowed, watching the sun start to peek out over the horizon, with bright orange and yellow rays streaking across the grayish blue sky.

He shrugged. "Not important to them. They're waiting for me to finish my silly little surfing phase and come home."

"And work on a sugarcane farm."

Kai sighed deeply. "Family business. Hundred and fifty years in the making. And I have no brothers or sisters to take it over, so...looks like I don't have too much of a choice."

"It must be hard not to have their support." She touched his arm.

"Not as hard as catching your dad in the act of cheating," he replied, the little bit of humor making her giggle lightly.

"True that. I think I've got you beat."

"So, now that we've properly aired out our family trauma..." He stood, reaching out his hand to help Taylor to her feet. "Are you gonna get on this board or what?"

"What? Absolutely not!" She laughed, shaking her head wildly. "I'll drown."

"You will not drown." He angled his head low, his eyes drinking her in. "I won't let anything happen to you."

"I think I'd rather just watch you for now."

Kai rolled his eyes, picking the surfboard up and walking back out to the water. "I'm going to get you on a wave, Taylor. If it's the last thing I do!"

She sat back down in the sand, cheering jokingly as Kai paddled out in the water to surf.

She definitely had a crush. And she couldn't remember the last time she'd had a crush on someone like this. But...it didn't matter. Because nothing about him could ever be permanent. She'd just found out he eventually had to get back to Hawaii, which might as well be a million miles away.

So, nothing could happen between them. Nothing real, anyway.

Still, it was kind of fun to think about.

# Chapter Eleven

## Sam

S am had never interviewed for a job. She'd never made a resume, or created a LinkedIn profile, or met with a recruiter.

What would her resume even say? Expert Range Rover driver and fabulous at choosing throw pillows? Could pack a kid's lunch in record time, fold a load of laundry in under two minutes, and sew on a Boy Scout patch while driving?

Those were some serious skills, but unfortunately, none that belonged on a resume.

Times had changed, and Sam certainly wasn't driving a Range Rover these days. It was time to turn over a new leaf, and, at the age of forty-three, look for her first job.

And what better place to start than with some good old-fashioned nepotism?

As she walked up the driveway to John and Imani's sweet, suburban Florida house, she thought about what might come with asking her brother to get her a job. It wouldn't be her dream job—not that she had one—but it could be a start. A purpose and a paycheck, at the very least.

Sam held her head high and knocked on the front

door, fixing her hair, which the humidity had no doubt destroyed.

"Hey, sis." John smiled and held out his arms as he opened the door. "Come on in. What brings you my way?"

"Well..." Sam stepped inside, admiring the perfectly tasteful coastal décor of John's house.

She'd always noticed decoration and design, and always loved seeing the way other people chose to set up their houses. Sam had her own ideas and imagination about it, but she really liked Imani's taste.

She'd spent so many hours perfecting every detail of the big, beautiful home in Winter Park she'd shared with Max and raised her kids in, that she found she had sort of an eye for that type of thing.

But barring her dream job as an interior designer, she'd like to start with something at an ad agency.

"Your home looks as beautiful as ever." She walked down the little hallway to the living room area, which backed up to a big, sliding glass door that led to a nice backyard. "Is Imani around?"

"She's at soccer with Ellen and Liam. Damien's at debate club practice. So, it's just me." John walked over to the kitchen.

"Debate club?" Sam snorted. "Is there anything that kid doesn't do?"

John smiled with fatherly pride. "Evidently not. Coffee?"

Sam nodded. "Sure, yeah."

John poured two mugs of coffee and handed one to

Sam, who sat on one of the barstools at the kitchen island. "How are you settling in at Mom's? Cottage treating you well?" He took a sip. "Bringing back some memories, I'll bet."

"Oh my gosh, yeah." Sam blew the steam from the top of the coffee cup and wrapped her hands around it. "Tons of them. It's been good, though. Taylor just loves it here. I think she's happy to get out of that grimy bar. Plus, she's made *friends* with a very cute Hawaiian surfer boy, so she's not exactly miserable."

"Wow." John chuckled, crossing his arms over the button-down that he wore to work, laughing as he shook his head. "Settling right in, then. Good for her."

"Yeah. And Ben is..." Sam huffed out a sigh. "Ben."

"He'll come around."

"Hopefully."

"And how about you?" her brother asked. "How are you doing? I mean, it's a big change, and you've been through a lot."

"I'm...better, actually." Sam looked up and smiled. "There's something I wanted to talk to you about. The reason I came here."

John drew back and raised his brows. "It wasn't for the subpar coffee and the inevitable condescending brotherly advice?"

She laughed. "I mean, I'll take some of that to go, but...no." Sam took in a deep breath, setting her mug on the counter and meeting John's gaze. "I was wondering if you might be able to find me a job. At least something temporary."

John paused, his eyes wide with surprise. "Really?"

"Yes. And I know I don't have much in the way of qualifications, or a degree, and I'm not expecting anything amazing, I just need something. Something that will give me a bit of money and, well, purpose, I guess." She swallowed. "I've only ever been a wife and mom. I think I'm ready to be something else, too."

Her brother thought for a minute, running a hand through his hair. He leaned against the countertop and looked at Sam. "Okay. I can't make any promises, but..."

Sam raised her brows, intrigued.

"My agency is looking to hire a new administrative assistant."

"That would be perfect." Hope rose in her chest. She could be an administrative assistant, right? If she knew what to do and how to do it.

"Fran has been there forever, and she's desperate to retire. It would not be glamorous. Lots of filing, scheduling, answering the phone. And the pay would be... mediocre. Coastal Marketing isn't exactly a billion-dollar company. But it's something, and..."

"It's more than something." Sam slid out of the barstool and came around the other side of the island to give her brother a big hug. "That would mean the world to me, John."

He frowned. "You thinking about making Cocoa Beach a permanent home, Sam?"

"No, Ben has school. But I could commute from Winter Park. It's only an hour on the Bee Line, and, honestly? I live there but do not want to work there, too."

"That's true. You might be able to carpool with a few of our staff who live in Orlando. But like I said..." He pulled away and held up a cautionary finger. "No promises. You'll have to interview. I'll put in a good word, and maybe we can work something out."

"You are the best, thank you. Seriously." She smiled at him, letting out a sigh of relief. "I need this."

"I know you do." He patted her shoulder. "I'll talk to the team tomorrow and keep you posted."

Sam grinned. "Your girl's about to be employed."

"Maybe." John raised his brows and visibly fought a smile.

"Maybe," Sam repeated. "It's still more than I've ever been able to say. Anyway, I gotta run. I promised Taylor we'd go shopping in Cocoa Village. And now we have something to celebrate."

"Maybe!" he called after her as she walked out of the living room and toward the front door.

"Right, right. Maybe."

"Hey, Sam," John said, stopping her as she swung open the door to walk outside.

"Yeah?" She turned to look over her shoulder.

"You seem...a lot better. You seem happy."

She smiled and looked up, realizing he was right. She was probably the happiest she'd been since the day she found out about Max's cheating and her whole world fell apart.

"I am, actually," she replied. "Coming here was the best thing I ever did."

"I'm really glad you're here. Family is everything."

Sam inhaled slowly, the salty breeze even reaching John's neighborhood, which was a tiny bit inland. "It sure is."

She headed back to her car with a new bounce in her step. Administrative assistant. She liked the sound of that. Sam reveled at the prospect of finally being *something*, even if it was a small start.

On the drive home, she thought about how she'd gotten so wrapped up in her doctor's wife-Winter Park bubble. She didn't visit Cocoa Beach nearly enough, and even when she did, she had her preconceived thoughts on her siblings. Preconceived by Max, of course.

She'd thought John was Mr. Perfect and was always trying to give unsolicited advice because he'd never made a mistake *ever*. She'd thought Julie was a trainwreck, but now she wondered what her nomadic rock-star sister was really like. She'd thought Erica was a diehard workaholic with no time for fun and *no* respect for stay-at-home moms. But she was actually just a selfless hard worker with a heart of gold.

And Dottie, her sweet mother? Well, she'd thought Dottie would judge her for her failed marriage. She'd thought her mother would arch a brow and say, "I told you so, didn't I?" But Sam couldn't have been more far off. Dottie was a living angel, and Sam deeply regretted every fight they'd ever had and every mean thing she'd ever said to her loving mother. And sadly, there had been a lot of them.

Screaming fights, flying insults, tears and loud arguments and regrets stained the past of Sam's relationship with her mother, and now she struggled to even understand why.

Those were *Max's* wrong and unfair assumptions about her family, and he'd spent years pulling her away from them.

He'd spent their entire marriage cutting her off from the people who loved her. And she'd let him.

She loathed Max even more with that realization. Just despised him. So much so that thinking about it almost put a damper on her lightened mood.

He'd taken twenty-five years of her life. He'd completely wasted them. Yes, she got Taylor and Ben, and she wouldn't change a thing. But the anger she felt toward Max for how he'd completely ruined her life at every imaginable turn made this sunny, cheery day feel a bit dark.

He'd poisoned her. Like a snake with a venomous bite. And now, little by little, day by day, she had to detox. She had to suck all of his poison out of her life, and her kids' lives. And nothing would stop her from doing just that.

# Chapter Twelve

## *Dottie*

Dottie had been up all night, tossing and turning and imagining a big old bulldozer smashing Sweeney House to smithereens.

The image nearly cracked her heart in two, but not as much as the constant reminders of Jay did.

She missed her old self. Her strong, energetic, bubbly self who would float around this inn with vibrance and joy and never met a problem she couldn't tackle.

But it seemed that was all Jay. He brought that out in her. How could she ever get it back without him?

As the early morning light started to brighten the windows of her upstairs suite at the inn, Dottie sat up and looked around the room.

The Executive Suite, they'd called it.

She ran her fingers over the old white headboard behind her. She remembered the day she and Jay found that headboard. They had loved visiting all kinds of antique shops and beachside furniture consignment stores to fill the inn with unique pieces.

The headboard was distressed, whitewashed wood, with long, elegant panels and little knobs on the top of each side that were shaped like seashells. Jay had deemed it "too girly," but Dottie adored it.

Of course, he'd given in, as he always did, and they'd loaded it in the back of that familiar old yellow Chevy pickup truck and brought it straight to the inn.

Just the thought of that truck could bring her to tears.

Dottie smiled to herself as she looked at the seashell-shaped carvings, remembering Jay leaning back, crossing his arms, and saying, *"You were right, darlin'. It looks just wonderful in here."*

The bittersweet memory hit her with a pang, forcing her out of bed so she could move and get busy living, rather than wallowing in her relentless and never-ending sadness.

She found that the grief was worst in the early hours of the morning, when she missed him the most. The world was quiet at those hours, no inn guests to distract her or keep her busy, no employees and staff to chat with or suites to ready for new guests.

Just...emptiness. A space in the bed where he should be.

She needed coffee. Except the coffeemaker in the lobby of Sweeney House was broken. *Okay, okay,* she mumbled mentally as she slid into a robe and slippers. The inn could use some updating. It hardly had a kitchen, and there was certainly no dining area or much of anything besides a small lobby and the bedrooms.

But did it matter? Sweeney House would cease to exist in a matter of months, and until then, guests seemed fine to use that Starbucks down the road.

Anyway, she could get her coffee in the cottage. Sam wouldn't mind her popping in, and they were most likely all still asleep anyway.

She tip-toed through the lobby of the inn, past the sitting area that looked out over the back deck. The sun was barely starting to rise over the horizon, and the wall-to-wall glass sliders let in just enough light to illuminate the familiar route Dottie knew like the back of her hand.

Outside, the path was just as familiar, with that sweet morning smell of salt and honeysuckle, and the pleasant coo of mourning doves just a little louder than the waves.

She tightened the belt of her robe and slipped into the back door of the cottage, which was always unlocked, walking in quietly.

"Oh! Mom!" Sam gasped, turning around from the kitchen counter and holding her hand to her chest. "You scared me. What are you doing here so early?"

"I'm so sorry." Dottie gave an apologetic smile and shut the door behind her. "I was just sneaking in for some coffee. The one-cup thing over at the inn is broken, so I thought I'd get some from my trusty pot over here. Those K-things are for the birds, in my opinion, always breaking."

Sam chuckled. "You sound like Dad. Here." She lifted the glass pot, filled with rick, dark brown coffee. "For you, not the birds."

The deep, earthy smell of the hot coffee perked Dottie up.

"Wonderful." Dottie grabbed a mug and poured

herself a cup, studying her daughter. "What are you doing up so early, anyway?"

"I don't know, honestly." Sam took a sip from her mug and looked out through the glass door at the sunrise over the water. "Just...a lot on my mind."

"Care to share the load?" Dottie nodded toward the back deck, where two chairs facing the ocean sunrise had their mother and daughter names on them.

"I'd love that." Sam smiled, holding Dottie's gaze for a second, and it was almost like getting a glimpse of Jay's eyes.

The two women walked out to the deck, sipping their coffee as they settled into the blue and white cushioned patio furniture, watching a gull swoop over the waves and chase a family of sandpipers down the beach.

"Now, what's on your mind, my girl?" Dottie put her feet up on the shared ottoman and looked at Sam. "Hopefully, focusing on your problems will get my crazy old brain off of my own."

Sam chuckled, shaking her head as she let out a noisy groan. "I don't know, Mom. Yesterday, I went over to John's house, and I asked if there was any way he could find me a job around here, or at least point me in the right direction."

"Oh, Sam." Dottie pressed her hand to her chest. "Don't take that personally if he didn't have anything for you. His ad agency is so small and there's hardly any turnover. I'm sure if he could help you out, he absolutely would."

"No, no," Sam said quickly, waving her hand. "It's

not that at all. He actually might have an opening for an administrative position at the agency."

"Really?" Dottie asked, this news lightening her heart tremendously. There was no greater joy for a parent than to see her kids help and love and support each other. "That sounds wonderful, and what a nice opportunity for you!"

"It would be, yeah." Sam nodded, smiling.

"Well, if that's the case, what the heck has got you down? Other than the obvious heartbreak, which I don't mean to diminish." She placed a hand on her daughter's arm. "I just mean, that sounds like a step in a positive direction."

"You're not diminishing anything at all. And a job is more than a step—it's that purpose I am so desperately seeking." Sam looked out at the ocean, the breeze blowing her hair back to reveal her profile, a mix of strong and beautiful that Dottie always admired, but now she looked troubled.

"What is it?" Dottie urged.

"I guess John's generosity, Imani's sweetness, Erica's ambition, Will's loyalty...my family is filled with such wonderful people." Her eyes got misty, making Dottie feel insanely confused about why this was a sad thing. "And you," Sam added quietly. "I don't appreciate you enough."

"Oh, honey. You being here and trusting me to guide you through this tough time is a greater gift than you realize. And we do have a wonderful family, don't we? I'm beyond blessed."

Dottie reminded herself of that fact frequently, because there had been so many days spent in sadness since Jay had been gone. She had to remember that there were still so many good things.

"But loving your family is a *positive* thing." Dottie gave Sam a gentle smile. "Why is it making you sad?"

"I've missed out on all these years." Sam pressed her lips together. "All this time, I've been less than an hour away. I've kept myself distant from my siblings and their spouses and their families and...you."

She shifted in her seat, visibly uncomfortable, making Dottie's heart tug a little and send her searching for excuses.

"You were busy," Dottie said. "You visited occasionally. And you were wrapped up in Max and the kids and—"

"I chose him." Sam turned to Dottie, her eyes darkening. "I pushed all of my family away for him. I gave him all of my loyalty and attention and put every single one of my eggs in the Max Parker basket. And now what do I have? Scrambled eggs."

Dottie sighed, relieved to be having this conversation. She didn't want Sam to hurt or wallow in regret, but opening up could only help her heal.

"Nothing is scrambled when you have family," Dottie said softly.

"I know you and Dad were never fans of Max." Sam looked at her, giving a tight smile. "Don't you want just one good, 'I told you so,' Mom?"

Dottie chuckled and shook her head. "And be such a cliché?" she teased.

"But like all good clichés, you were right."

"Well, Jay never *got* Max. Never fully trusted him. And I have to say I felt the same way."

"I know. It was no secret." She let out a soft grunt. "I should have trusted Dad's character judgment. He never missed. That's why I couldn't stay close with you and the family throughout my marriage to him. I chose Max. And I chose...wrong."

"You were young, and in love, and pregnant." Dottie took a sip of her coffee and let that sink in. "Don't beat yourself up. Life happens the way it happens."

Sam shut her eyes and turned back toward the beach as another soft gust fluttered her hair. "I know. I just hate that I hurt you. I hate the way we used to fight over it. Such ugly fights."

Dottie's mind flashed back to what felt like hundreds of tearful nights spent arguing back and forth with her strong-willed daughter. It had been so hard for Dottie to get Sam to realize that she and Jay only ever wanted what was best for her.

And Sam...oh, young Sam had known how to push her mother's buttons, that was for sure.

"Oh, we had some doozies, didn't we?" Dottie raised her brows. "I can recall you standing at the top of the staircase screaming, 'It's my life, Mom! Not yours!'"

Sam's eyes fell. "I'm so sorry I was so mean to you."

"Oh, Sam. You were a bit of a tough one. But you want to know something?"

"What?"

"You're kind of my favorite."

Sam burst out with laughter. "You totally can't say that!"

"I don't mean 'favorite,'" Dottie said through a hearty laugh. "I mean, you're the one I sympathize with the most. You're the one I *get* the most."

"Really? How do you mean? We're so different."

"Not that different." Dottie leaned closer to her daughter. "I was the one who was young and defiant and in love and would have gone to the ends of the Earth to be with the man I loved. Jay was all I wanted."

Sam leaned back against the chair, surprised as she pondered Dottie's words.

"I would have screamed my heart out at anyone who tried to stop me from being with Jay. Which is why, eventually, I just let you go. I knew how you were feeling, and it didn't matter what my opinion of Max was. Or your father's. Or anyone else. You were going to be with him. And I was either going to shut up or lose you completely."

"I pushed you so far away."

"You did." Dottie lifted her coffee mug and smiled at Sam. "But you came back."

"*She'll be back.*" Jay's voice echoed through her mind. If only he could be here to see it.

Quiet, Sam rocked back and forth, sipping her coffee as the waves sprayed up on the sand and the morning birds chirped away.

"I'm truly sorry, Mom," she finally said. "For everything. For all of those fights and for pushing you away all those years. You didn't deserve it."

Dottie reached out and took Sam's hand, giving it a squeeze as she held her daughter's gaze. "Honey, you are more than forgiven. And you really ought to learn to forgive, too, or else you're going to be walking around with the weight of hating Max Parker for the rest of your life. And believe me, it'll drag you down."

Sam shut her eyes. "I'm not ready to go there yet. I need to heal."

"Well, consider this cottage and your family a big old Band-Aid, then. And you just heal up. We're all here for you. We never stopped being here for you. And you know, maybe you can change your last name back. Stick with Sweeney, so you don't feel so attached to him anymore."

Sam smiled, turning to her mom. "I love that idea. Sam Sweeney again. I'm so grateful," Sam said. "For you and..." She gestured toward the house and the inn beyond it. "This oasis."

Dottie just took a deep breath, silent as the weight of her secret tugged at her chest. Not now. Not yet. She couldn't break her daughter's heart when she was so close to healing and forgiving and starting over. This moment with her daughter was too beautiful to ruin or stain with something that, for all she knew, could cause another one of those fights.

And, selfishly, she felt her own grief lessen out here with Sam. That loneliness and sorrow that pressed on her when she woke up had evaporated like the morning mist over the ocean, leaving the world vibrant and bright and full of possibilities.

That was the morning mood she wanted, not new confessions and hurt feelings. So she rocked and sipped and soaked up the goodness and didn't think about the inevitable disappointment she'd cause when she sold the inn and the cottage.

# Chapter Thirteen

## *Erica*

Erica shifted her gaze from one monitor to the next, forcing herself to focus on the formulas, the design, and the blueprints.

She could be sad later. She could whine and cry and drink half a bottle of wine tonight at home. That's where she could feel sorry for herself. Not here, at the Kennedy Space Center in her top-floor office, where she had to present herself as the head aerospace engineer on the Eagle rocket.

Here, in her sleek and streamlined office that looked out over the NASA Vehicle Assembly Building and, in the distance, Launchpad 39B, she had to be head engineer, not wanna-be mom. She'd worked tirelessly to attain this position, and managed critical projects with millions of dollars and thousands of people's jobs at stake.

Right now, they mattered more than her poor little disappointment.

On a sigh of pure determination, she sipped her coffee and clicked through the pages of blueprints, comparing them to the equations her team had provided. There had to be something off with the orbital mechanics to cause that estimated trajectory to veer off course.

She'd find it. She always did.

Because solving problems and finding answers was Erica Sweeney-Armstrong's specialty. Except when it came to her own body—the first problem she faced that she truly couldn't solve with math, science, and her oh-so-impressive brain.

Another sip of coffee. More scrolling. No thinking about personal issues involving blocked fallopian tubes. This was Erica's life. This was her destiny. No matter how much she felt it in her bones that she wanted to be a mother, maybe it wasn't in the cards for her, and that was that. She'd be better off accepting that than fighting it, right?

She had a wonderful life. A beautiful house, an amazing husband, and the job of her dreams. She should be happy with that.

Suddenly, the phone on her desk rang, and Erica pressed the button to answer.

"This is Erica Armstrong."

"Hi, Erica," Nate, her assistant who worked down-stairs, greeted her through the phone. "There's someone here to see you, but wants it to be a surprise. Pretty sure it's personal and safe. Should I send her up?"

*Her?* Who would be surprising Erica at work besides Will, who most definitely wasn't a "her"?

"Um, sure." She shrugged and swiveled around in her desk chair. "Thanks, Nate."

By the time a knock on her office door pulled her from an equation she was working on, Erica darn near forgot about the surprise guest. She looked over the screens, craning her neck to see who it was.

"Come in," she called.

"It's a long way from the lobby, so the latte might be cold by now." Sam's voice floated in ahead of her. "But it was a grand gesture anyway."

"Oh my gosh, hi!" Erica popped up, so surprised to see her sister. "This is awesome and so is a latte. Thank you!"

"Here, baby sister." Sam gave her a big hug and handed her the coffee, which was still steaming. "How goes the engineering wars?"

"Beating me. But you look good." She eyed her sister, taking in a change that was noticeable since the day she first arrived at the beach. Her eyes were brighter, her smile was bigger.

"Got time for a five-minute break?" Sam asked. "Or am I slowing down the next rocket launch?"

"For you? Always." Erica gestured toward the gray sofa on the other side of her office and walked over to sit down with Sam.

"Seriously, how's work? The Eagle stuff is going well?" Sam lifted her coffee cup to her mouth and leaned forward.

"It's fine." Erica shook her head. "I'm struggling a bit with the orbital mechanics, because the point of atmospheric entry keeps going all wonky."

"That darn atmospheric entry." Sam tsked and stifled a laugh. "Gets me every time."

Erica laughed, too. "You seem better. You look

better."

"I feel like a human again." Sam took in a breath and nodded slowly. "I still have a long way to go, and some demons to work through, I guess, but I'm hopeful."

Something stabbed Erica's gut, something selfish and personal. She was the furthest thing from hopeful. She didn't want to tell Sam or anyone else about her infertility and bring everything down.

Sam had worked so hard to be happy again, or close to happy. Would unburdening herself just burden her sister? Because it sure was hard to bear the secret alone.

"I do have some news, though," Sam said, making Erica grateful for the segue and change of subject.

She smiled. "What is it?"

"I might have a job. I mean, I have to interview, but it's in the works."

Erica drew back and beamed at her sister with pride. "Sam, that's amazing! What is it?"

"It's...not quite on par with this." She gestured to the spacious surroundings. "But John may have a position as an administrative assistant at his ad agency. The woman who's been working the front desk forever is retiring, and I could step in. In fact, he just texted that the interview is set for later this week."

"Fran? She's so sweet and you'd be perfect for that job. Congratulations!" Erica leaned over and hugged her sister for a long time, feeling genuinely happy for her despite her own personal sorrow. "You're gonna kill it."

"It feels a little small potatoes around here, just answering phones and filing things, but, Erica?" She lifted her brows. "I have honestly never had a job before. And I've never interviewed for one, either."

"You've been a mother," Erica said softly. "That's a big job."

"Pay stinks," she quipped. "Seriously, I'm a little nervous."

"That's normal." Erica took Sam's hand and gave it a loving squeeze. "Just be yourself, Sam. You're vibrant and funny and a quick study. They'd be lucky to have you in any position."

"I don't know the first thing about advertising and marketing."

"You'll learn on the job." Erica shrugged. "When I started here, I didn't know the first thing about rocket science."

"Yeah, because six years in college and an advanced engineering degree didn't teach you a thing."

"True, but you'd be surprised how much you learn by doing," Erica said. "This is big for you, and I think it's going to be a huge step forward. You're gonna start to feel like yourself again. Better, even. A new you."

Sam shook her head, leaning back into the soft leather sofa and sipping her coffee. "I don't even know who the old me was, so it ought to be interesting. I mean, I was a doctor's wife and stay-at-home mom who was great at decorating and never missed a Little League game."

"You're so much more than that." Erica swallowed, a voice in her head crying out to her about how much she wanted the chance to never miss a Little League game.

"Although, don't discount that. The way you've spent your life is beautiful, and it's valuable."

Sam eyed her over her cup, maybe hearing something in Erica's voice that gave away what she was going through.

"You know, I've always felt inferior to you," Sam admitted softly.

"I'm sorry, Sam—"

"Not because of anything you did or said," Sam assured her. "These were my own insecurities. There was always this part of me that thought I would never compare to my insanely smart, ridiculously successful little sister who came along and outshined us all."

Erica laughed, shaking her head. "I never wanted to outshine anyone."

"I know that." Sam nodded, taking her sister's hand. "It was all in my head. And I felt that way because I dedicated my whole life and my entire existence to someone who never truly loved me. And, as silly as it sounds, I may get this tiny little insignificant job, and I just feel like it's the first step to being something...more. Having an identity outside of Max Parker."

"It is. And you *do* have an identity, Sam." Erica inched closer to her, leveling her gaze with Sam's. "You're a mother. That's the greatest thing you can be."

Sam scoffed, flicking a dismissive hand. "Anyone can be a mother."

Erica's heart slammed into her gut. She knew Sam didn't mean anything by the comment, but it stung.

Not *anyone* could be a mother.

The irony of Sam being jealous of Erica, while *Sam* was the one who got pregnant by accident *twice*. If anyone should have been jealous, it was Erica.

And she knew Sam meant to say that Erica's job was more impressive and required hard work and dedication and intelligence and that was all true, but not anyone can be a mother, and Erica was...

Crying. Now. Here. At work, sitting on the couch with Sam, she felt tears fall down her cheeks and her shoulders quiver with a sob.

"Erica! No! What's wrong?" Sam scooted closer to her sister, reaching for her. "What did I say?"

"Nothing, it's...nothing."

"Doesn't look like nothing. Talk to me."

Erica nodded, wanting to spill it all out, but...

"It's just..." Erica wiped her eyes, squeezing them shut as she waved a hand. "It's nothing, really. I'm fine."

"You're obviously not fine." Sam angled her head and searched her sister's tear-stained face. "What on Earth is going on? Are you okay? Is it work? Will?"

"No, no. It's..." Erica huffed out a defeated sigh, taking the time to find the right words. Although, why worry about that? This was her sister, and they'd always be there for each other, no matter what. "I promise I'm okay. Will's perfect."

"Not news to anyone."

Erica gave a soft laugh, so grateful for Sam's humor. "Okay," she said, wiping a tear and praying she didn't have a mascara smear. "We just met with a fertility specialist and..." She made a face. "My chances of ever getting pregnant are really, really infinitesimal."

"Oh, honey!" Sam's jaw fell slack as she pressed her hands to her lips. "No wonder you're upset. And, gah! Did I really say that anyone can be a mother? I'm so sorry. I had no idea."

"It's okay. You couldn't have known."

"I honestly didn't think you wanted kids, that they weren't..." She shook her head and stopped talking. "How long have you been trying?"

"Almost a year and we kept it really private. I tracked every last measurement and hormone and cycle down to the hour."

"And did equations to make sure it was accurate."

Erica managed a smile. "So many."

Sam's eyes shuttered. "Oh, Erica. Are you positive?"

"Yeah. We went to a fertility clinic and we both got tested and had some imaging done. Apparently, I've had asymptomatic endometriosis for many years and that did some damage. Scar tissue that completely blocks one fallopian tube and more on the other one." She waved a hand. "I'll spare you the medical jargon. The point is, according to the doctor, it's highly unlikely for me to ever conceive, especially at my age when the eggs are fewer and less robust. I picked this career, to be honest, years ago. So now, I'm paying the price."

"Well, if you had no symptoms, how could you know? Doctors don't look for endometriosis unless you have really painful periods, as far as I know. And it's common. Don't be hard on yourself." She hugged Erica again, holding her tight, both of them quiet for a moment.

"If there's anything I can do or if you need anything at all, please. I'm here," Sam added. "And I know I haven't been around and there for you for a long time, ever since I got wrapped up in Max and grew apart from the family, but I'm here now. And I'm not going anywhere."

Erica smiled slowly through her tears, admiring this softer, sweeter version of her sister she'd so badly missed. "I'm so glad you are. And thank you. I'll get through it."

"It must feel devastating when you want a child. Is surgery an option? Egg freezing?"

"Surgery wouldn't change much, and the eggs? It could take forever, and I don't want to get pregnant— maybe—at forty-five." She shrugged. "I'm coming to terms with it, and realizing it was the hand I was dealt. And I'm glad I shared it with you. I already feel less weighed down now that I'm not hanging onto this miserable secret."

Sam inched closer and held her sister's gaze. "No more secrets."

"No more distance," Erica replied.

"Deal." Sam smiled, but her eyes narrowed as if she were thinking of something. "Not to step out of bounds or anything, but have you guys considered adoption? I know you just recently got the news, so, of course you need time to process. But I'm sure you and Will would be perfect candidates. And..." She put her hand on Erica's leg, holding her gaze with loving certainty. "You can still be a mom."

Erica leaned back, nodding slowly as she took a sip of coffee that was well and truly cold now. "Of course, the thought had crossed my mind briefly when we first found out. But I never entertained it seriously because I was so wrapped up in not being able to have my own child. My genetics. Will's genetics. Our baby."

"Yeah, beauty and brains abound in that gene pool."

"And when you look at Taylor," Erica said, leaning closer, "don't you see so much of yourself?"

"So much so, it scares me," Sam admitted on a laugh.

"She's beautiful and bright and funny, just like you. And the older she gets, the more I adore her." Erica smiled wistfully.

"She's all that," Sam admitted. "But even if she wasn't, you know, my DNA? I can't imagine loving her less. She's my best friend and my softest place to fall. Every laugh line on my face is due to her, and Ben. Okay, he's responsible for some frown lines."

Erica laughed. "He'll be fine."

"The point is, honey, once you hold a baby and he or she looks at you like you hung the moon and have their next bottle in your hand? Once you rock a sick child to sleep in the middle of the night, or hold their hand on the first day of school, or wipe a tear and know you could and would kill the person who caused it?" Sam smiled. "You really don't care if they have your genes or not. They have your heart."

Erica just stared at her, chills rising on her arms. For a

moment, she couldn't speak. Finally, she swallowed and leaned into Sam.

"And they say I'm the smart one," she joked, her voice thick with emotion.

"Hold that thought, I may need you for a reference."

She laughed and squeezed a little harder. "Have I told you I'm happy you're here?" Erica whispered.

"So, you'll think about adoption?"

"I will," she answered. "You really helped open my eyes." She added a kiss on her sister's cheek. "Auntie Sam. Thank you."

Sam gave her a gentle smile. "Don't give up this dream."

Erica took a deep breath, thinking about how deeply and desperately she wanted to be a mother. It was more than a valid option, maybe it was the way it was always meant to be for her.

"I'm going to look into it." Erica nodded. "The dream is very much alive."

# Chapter Fourteen

## *Taylor*

There had been a time in Taylor's life, not so long ago, when she was convinced that morning people were inherently evil and not to be trusted. And yet, here she was, up before the sun—*again*—opening the curtains to greet the gorgeous day, and feeling downright whimsical and lighthearted.

Had she become the very thing she hated? A...*morning* person?

Or maybe she was a Kai person, because all of this early morning beach time was spent with him. Who wouldn't wake up for flirtatious interactions and casual touches and shared personal stories in the shrouded privacy of pre-dawn light?

Even Mr. Minx was adjusting to Taylor's new sleep schedule, burying himself into the throw blanket on the chair so her bathroom light didn't disturb his precious beauty sleep.

She still walked over to give the cat a scratch and a snuggle, which he lovingly accepted before stretching and going back to sleep.

With an extra kiss on his soft fur, she took one last

look in the mirror before heading into the kitchen to grab a cup of coffee and walk out to the beach.

As Taylor slipped out of her bedroom and shut the door quietly behind her, she noticed some faint, electronic musical sounds coming from down the hallway. What was that? Noise from Ben's room at this hour?

Across the hall, she pressed her ear to his door, wondering if he'd left the TV on all night. But that sounded like distant gunfire and fake explosions and a musical jingle.

"Dang it!" Ben muttered, the sound of his voice making her jerk back from the door. "Died again."

Really? He was playing video games before six a.m.? Even for Ben, that was hardcore.

Fueled by both concern for her younger brother and sheer curiosity, Taylor tapped the door lightly. "Ben? Are you awake?"

"Taylor?"

She cracked the door open, flinching when it squeaked on the old hinges. "Hey, bro," she whispered. "Little early for *Halo*, isn't it?"

"*Call of Duty*." Ben was sitting on the edge of the bed, the room lit up by nothing but the blinding light of the flatscreen. He was holding a controller, wearing plaid sleep pants, and staring at the TV.

"What are you doing up at this hour?" Taylor asked, letting herself in and sitting on the edge of the bed next to him.

"Couldn't sleep."

"All night?"

He shrugged. "Basically. Did my game wake you up? I can use headphones—"

"No, no," Taylor said quickly, her heart warmed by the fact that Ben may have just shown a shred of concern for her. "You're completely fine. I didn't hear it until I came out to the hallway, actually."

"So, then, why are you up?" He turned to her, his face lit up by the blue and white glow of the TV.

Ben had managed to escape teenage acne, with soft, smooth skin that made Taylor jealous. He had light brown eyes, just like their father, and dark blond hair all shaggy in a classic Justin Bieber cut.

He somehow simultaneously looked like her baby brother and some grown-up young man she could hardly recognize.

"I..." Taylor bit her lower lip. "I've kinda been waking up early a lot since we've moved here."

Ben scoffed. "You?"

She was relieved to see a twinkle of humor from the brother who'd been so shut down for months.

"It's totally weird, I know," Taylor said. "But the beach is super nice at this time of day and, well..."

"Is there a guy?" Ben asked, matter-of-fact, his lips almost forming a smile.

Taylor shoved her brother. "Shut up."

Ben fell back on the bed, toying with the video game controller in his hand. "I knew it."

"How? How did you know?" Taylor lay flat on her back next to him, the two of them watching the blades of the old, pale wooden ceiling fan spin around and around.

"Because you're my sister. And I can tell."

"Ah." Taylor tapped his shoulder. "So there still is a soul somewhere in there?"

Ben's eyes flashed as he turned to her, then faced the ceiling again. "Somewhere in there," he said, his voice lowering. "Who's the dude?"

"A cool dude, actually," Taylor said. "And nothing is going to happen. He's more of a friend, I guess. He surfs, and he's from Hawaii."

"How do you know nothing is going to happen? He sounds dope."

"Because his family owns a sugarcane farm in Hawaii that they've lived and worked on for, like, two hundred years. He's the sole heir of that lovely business, so the surfing is temporary and, therefore, so is he." Taylor swallowed the hint of sadness that accented her words.

"That's pretty wild." Ben stared up at the ceiling and tossed the controller around in his hands.

"But he's cool and I like him and..." Taylor sat up, shrugging her shoulders. "It's all part of our fresh start, right? We're here for a new life?"

"We're only here for the summer," Ben answered quickly. "I have school in the fall and I'm not transferring right before my junior year."

Taylor nodded, understanding that completely. She'd have howled if someone had even considered dragging her out of high school that far into the game. "Right. Anyway, I'll leave you to your fun little..." She gestured at the TV, where a violent-looking video game was paused. "Massacres."

Ben gave a quick wave and kept his eyes fixed on the ceiling.

Taylor walked over to the door and pushed it open, about to leave.

"Wait. Taylor?"

She turned around quickly to see her brother sitting up on the edge of the bed. "Yeah?"

"Can I come with you? Down to the beach?"

Taylor felt a big smile pull across her cheeks, and tried not to get too excited about this potential progress from her moody and broody brother. "Absolutely you can."

Ben got up, slipped on a T-shirt, and joined her as they tiptoed barefoot down the hallway.

The two of them headed out the sliding glass door in the living room and onto the beach, which was silver and dark blue before the sunrise.

"Dang, it's not even hot right now," Ben said, kicking some sand up from underneath his feet as they walked toward the shore.

"I know, right?" Taylor felt the breeze lift up her hair as she took a deep breath, the birds chirping in the distance as soft waves crashed on the sand. "It's humid but still kind of cool."

"I haven't been down here yet."

Taylor looked at her brother, her mouth open with shock. "We've been staying here at the beachside cottage on one of the nicest islands on the east coast, and you haven't been *on the beach* yet?"

Ben shrugged and shook his head, his messy hair

bouncing around. "I've just been playing my game, texting friends, whatever."

"I feel like I've hardly talked to you," Taylor nudged, not wanting to push him away, knowing he was in kind of a fragile state.

But maybe she could get somewhere with him, since this was the closest thing they'd had to quality time and actual fun together since they got here. Heck, since their parents split up.

"I've hardly talked to anyone here, honestly."

"Are you doing okay, Ben?" Taylor stopped walking as they reached the water, which splashed up around her ankles. She looked at her brother, who had a good couple of inches on her now, with worry and concern.

"Yeah, I'm fine."

"You don't seem fine. And, look, I know a lot of awful stuff has happened recently, and it's not what either of us wanted, but you know I'm in this with you, right? You know that no matter what dumb things happen with Dad or whoever else, we've got each other."

"You and *Mom* have got each other," Ben said, the comment hitting Taylor right in the gut.

"What?" She tried to laugh it off, waving a hand as they started slowly walking along the shoreline. "Ben, no. Yeah, Mom and I are close, but you know I'm there for you."

"You and Mom are inseparable. And you both couldn't care less about Dad. You guys hate him now."

Well, yes, they did. And Taylor knew that Ben didn't share in her vehement disgust and loathing of their father. She knew he still looked up to Max and was younger and needed him more. Maybe she hadn't been sensitive enough to that. Maybe she and her mother had leaned on each other so much, they'd pushed Ben right out of the equation.

"Ben, I'm so sorry you feel like that." She turned to him. "I know Mom and I can get really buddy-buddy sometimes, and we've definitely supported each other a lot through this. But I'm your sister. And I want to be there for you, too. I want you to feel like you can talk to me about this stuff. About anything."

Ben kicked some water with his bare foot, making it splash around as they kept heading down the beach. "It's fine, Taylor. It just seems like, I don't know, like you're just ready to throw him away and hate his guts and never speak to him again."

And...she was. She most definitely was all of those things.

"But..." Ben continued with a sigh. "Don't get me wrong, I hate what he did to Mom. It was so messed up and awful, and I'm mad at him, too. It's just...he's still my dad. He's still *our* dad. And I feel like, if I wanted to forgive him, or at least give him some sort of chance, you and Mom would hate me the way you hate him. And then we'd all be divided and...yeah."

"Oh, Ben." The words pressed on Taylor's heart, and she shut her eyes tightly. She'd had no idea Ben felt this way, and it definitely explained why he'd become so withdrawn.

He'd felt alone. Taylor and her mom had each other,

and they were attached at the hip. He couldn't turn to Max, who was basically the villain in this whole story, but he also couldn't fully immerse himself into the Hating Dad Club with Taylor and Sam.

She ached at the thought, knowing how badly her brother had been needing her, and how she'd just locked in with Mom and inadvertently shut out the rest of the world.

"We could never hate you," she said softly. "I promise you that. You're free to have whatever relationship with Dad that you want, and I know Mom agrees with that, too. We just miss you! I miss playing *Mario Kart* and beating your butt."

Ben smirked. "You never beat me."

"Remember when we tried to teach Mom to play?"

He laughed, full on this time. "Oh, man, that was a wreck."

"How do I go forward? How do I go straight?" Taylor laughed, too, remembering her mom yelling and shrieking when they handed her a Wii controller and showed her *Rainbow Road*.

Ben shook his head, smiling at the sand as they walked.

"But really. I'm sorry," Taylor said. "I hate that you've pulled away from us so much, but I get it."

"I just don't feel like I have a place in the family anymore."

Taylor cringed at his words, a cocktail of guilt and sympathy rising.

"Benny boy." Taylor wrapped her arm around him,

giving him a side hug and a hair ruffle that he reluctantly accepted. "You will always have a place in this family. Just try to be more present, maybe. Put the phone away now and then. Come down and say hi. And I promise, I will never push you away again. It's not just Mom and me. It's the three of us. And, you know, it wouldn't hurt to talk to Mom about this stuff, too. She'll understand."

"I just know how much Dad hurt her. I feel like it would upset her if I still wanted to see him and stuff."

"No, no." Taylor shook her head. "She's said over and over we have to respect that you don't feel about him the way we do. She doesn't want either of us to hate Dad, although I'm a lost cause. But you should keep your relationship with him. You need that and I promise you, Mom will understand."

"Thanks, Taylor."

She relished the moment for a few extra seconds. The relief of feeling close with her brother again, and allowing him to open up, lifted a weight off of her shoulders, too. She'd been so worried about him, but had no clue how to go about talking to him. He was at such a tender age, and the whole thing was messy.

But Taylor felt like this morning might have been exactly what they both needed, and she knew how important it was to be a good sister for him.

She spotted a faint figure out on the water, and smiled widely at the sight of Kai.

"Oh, look!" Taylor pointed out to the ocean, where the faint figure of a surfer was gliding across the wave in the distance. "There's Kai."

As soon as Kai saw them, he paddled back to the beach, tucking his surfboard underneath his arm as he reached the shore and jogged over to Taylor and Ben.

"Looking good out there." Taylor smiled and gave his arm a friendly pat, trying not to notice the way the wetsuit hugged his biceps.

"Thank you, thank you." Kai shook out his long hair and turned to Ben. "You must be the little bro."

"Hey, I'm Ben." He looked up through his shaggy hair and managed a smile.

"Great to meet you, dude." Kai offered a high-five, which Ben returned. "Your sister's awesome."

Kai and Taylor exchanged a glance that lasted a bit too long, making Ben visibly cringe.

"Yeah, she's all right sometimes," he said with an eye roll.

"So, Ben, you ever surfed before?"

Ben looked at Kai, then out at the ocean. "Uh, no, I haven't. I used to skateboard sometimes with my friends back in Winter Park, but I guess that's not really the same."

"Similar movement," Kai said encouragingly, holding his surfboard out for Ben to get a good look at it. "You wanna try?"

Ben looked back and forth between Kai and Taylor, stuttering a little. "Right...me...right now?"

"Sure, why not?" Kai smiled. "No time like the present, and the waves are absolutely sublime today."

Taylor laughed and clasped her hands together. "Now this I have to see."

"I'll just, uh..." Ben pointed back over his shoulder toward the cottage. "I'll just go throw on a swimsuit."

"Perfect. We'll be here." Kai gave him a thumbs up. "You're gonna love it."

As Ben ran back up the beach toward the cottage, Taylor looked at Kai, not sure what she liked more—the way he looked or how incredibly kind he was to Ben. Both were seriously attractive.

"This is really cool of you," she said. "Thanks."

"Are you kidding?" He laughed and ran a hand through his damp hair. "I always love the opportunity to get someone on a board for the first time. There's nothing like your first time, so it's cool to show new surfers the ropes."

"I'm honestly surprised he agreed so quickly," she said, lifting a shoulder. "He's been kind of isolated since we got here. Not wanting to do much of anything."

Kai gave an understanding nod, leaning closer to Taylor, close enough that she could smell the salty ocean water on him and wonder what a kiss might taste like. "Surfing is good for the soul. It's the best medicine out there. Vitamin *sea*, you could say."

Taylor cringed with laughter. "Well, if you and your terrible puns can get my brother to crack a smile, I will gladly be an enthusiastic cheerleader." Taylor sat down in the sand and clapped her hands. "Woo!"

Kai rolled his eyes and laughed. "I'm gonna get you on a board if it's the last thing I do."

"Well, it would be the last thing I would do. Because

I'd drown. Or get eaten by a shark. Or abducted by jellyfish."

"Ah, yes..." Kai sighed dramatically. "The jellyfish abduction problem has really been getting out of hand in these waters."

Taylor was still laughing with him when Ben came back to the beach, wearing swim trunks and a carefree, boyish smile that she hadn't seen in what felt like years.

"Okay, I'm ready."

"Come on, let's get rolling." Kai jutted his chin out toward the water.

"Just like that?" Ben asked, glancing at Taylor. "We just head right out into the ocean, I don't...like, practice on the sand or something first?"

"Nah." Kai waved a hand. "Can't surf without waves. Let's ride!"

"I'll be right here!" Taylor exclaimed as the two of them rushed into the waves.

She watched as Kai showed Ben how to lay flat on the board and paddle out deeper, which he did with surprising comfort.

She could hear Kai's voice faintly, and she actually heard Ben laugh. Truly laugh, for the first time in God knows how long.

Leaning back, she just drank in the moment, from the sunrise peeking over the horizon to the way her little Benny was starting to inch out of his shell. And Kai, so cool and relaxed and amazing.

She couldn't wipe the smile off of her face as she stared out at the ocean. Ben fell off the surfboard more than a few times, but he kept getting back on, and eventually even rode a tiny wave for a few seconds before splashing down into the water.

Taylor cheered and watched Kai give Ben a big high-five, and she wondered for a second if she'd ever want to go back to Winter Park.

She'd have to, right? Her whole life was there.

But then again...what life? Her dumpy studio apartment and the sticky floors and creepy regulars at O'Leary's? Why would she go back to that?

Well, for Ben. She knew now more than ever that her little brother needed her. He also needed Sam, and they had to be a family.

That was more important than her wistful dreams of living on the beach and running off into the sunset with Kai, who wouldn't even be here anyway.

Whatever. Right now, she didn't want to be in any moment but this one. This morning with a pink and orange sky and streaky white clouds glowing with the sunrise.

Oh, those morning people. They must be on to something.

# Chapter Fifteen

## *Sam*

Sam took one last look at herself in the rearview mirror, fixing an eyeliner smudge and a flyaway hair. She felt a little silly having borrowed a pencil skirt and blouse from Erica, but she wanted to look professional for her first-ever job interview.

Nerves fluttered through her as she went over again and again what she was going to say when they asked her some of the questions that John had told her to prepare for.

*"What do you think your biggest weakness is?"*

When John had read her that one, she'd snorted and said, "You mean besides the fact that I'm forty-three and just moved back to my parents' house?"

Amusing, but not what they want to hear, he told her. His response was something like, "I'm a detail-oriented perfectionist, and sometimes it slows down my work because I spend too much time making sure everything is flawless."

"Right. Perfectionist. That's me," Sam whispered to herself in the mirror. "Because my life is so darn *perfect.*"

She laughed softly and slid her purse over her arm before stepping out of the car and brushing off the skirt.

John's ad agency, Coastal Marketing, was on the third floor of a Cocoa Beach office building, decorated with palm trees around the entrance and an ocean view from the higher floors.

The solid glass panels reflected the sunlight and accentuated the modern finishes and sleek design. Gazing up at it, Sam mentally acknowledged that she'd always been freakishly fascinated by office buildings.

What went on in there, she'd wonder when she passed one. What was it like to dress up, take the elevator to an office—or cubicle—and have some important thing you had to do every day? Meetings to attend or memos to write or, more likely, have a good chat around the water cooler.

It was like Other People's Lives, and now...it could be hers. She had always convinced herself she never wanted to work, she was more than happy with her life as a wife and mom, and that an office job and a corporate career just wasn't for her.

Not that working the front desk of Coastal Marketing was top management, but to Sam, it was new and exciting, and symbolic of her entering a life she never thought she'd have.

Holding her chin up high, she walked through the front doors of the building and into the bright, welcoming lobby. The cool air conditioning blasted her instantly, and her heels clicked on the white marble floor.

Having been to John's office before, she knew exactly where she was going, and headed over to the elevator. As it rose to the third floor, she tried a little encouraging self-talk. Affirmations, she'd heard them called on some podcast she'd listened to.

"I know I don't have any experience, but I am really hard-working. I'm willing to learn as much as I possibly can and do my best to help this team succeed."

The elevator dinged and the doors slid open.

With one more deep breath, Sam walked to the only door on the floor, double glass with Coastal Marketing, Inc. etched onto them, along with a palm tree logo.

Inside, the main reception area blended into the cubes and open tables, where a dozen or so employees were all typing away or quietly having phone conversations. She couldn't see John from here. He, of course, had one of the enclosed offices with views along the back.

She'd never looked that closely when she'd stopped in, but she had to hand it to her brother. He'd singled-handedly built this business with a degree in business and marketing, and a can-do attitude that attracted top local talent. No, this wasn't Madison Avenue, but the agency had many local clients and managed ad campaigns, PR programs, events, and even social media marketing to the tune of several million a year.

What John had built here was seriously impressive.

"Oh, I didn't hear you come in." A cheerful older woman came around the corner and slid into the chair behind the front desk, coffee in hand. "Welcome to Coastal Marketing. Can I help you?"

"Oh, hi there." Sam walked to the desk, which was behind a large, rounded half-wall. "You must be Fran."

"I certainly am." Fran grinned. "What can I do for you?"

"I'm Samantha Sweeney," she said, suddenly quite happy she'd ditched Parker and returned to her maiden name. It sure carried weight around here. "I'm actually, um, here to interview for your job." She gave an awkward laugh and leaned in. "Tell me you love it."

Fran gasped and gave Sam a big smile, her eyes accented by creases. "I do love it, but after fourteen years? I'm ready to go spoil my grandbabies and get in that RV with my husband. But I'm not going to leave until we have the right replacement." She lifted gray brows. "Could that be you?"

"I sure hope so." Sam exhaled with relief, already sensing that this wasn't going to be that intimidating. "Although I know I have big shoes to fill."

"You're too kind. You're John's sister, right?"

"I am, yes." Sam nodded. "He recommended the position to me. I'm sort of..." she lifted a shoulder. "Starting over."

"Well, it's a wonderful office with great people, and we all just adore your brother."

"Who doesn't?" Sam chuckled.

"Speak of the devil, here he comes now!" Fran turned to look at John, who was striding through the office. He gave Sam a playful salute.

"Hey, I'm early." Sam grinned at her brother, who was wearing khakis and a short-sleeved button-down, making it pretty clear that the pencil skirt and heels were probably overkill for a beachside ad agency.

But still. Dress to impress, as Erica said.

"Perfect." John placed a hand on her shoulder and guided her through the office toward one of the back conference rooms. "Thank you, Fran! I'll bring her back to you so you can show her around the front desk."

"Uh-huh, honey. I'll be here." She gave a grin.

"I'm so nervous," Sam said on an exhale quietly to John.

"Don't be." John gave her a classic John Sweeney Everything Is Going To Be Fine Because I Will Make Sure Of It smile. "You're the only candidate right now."

"Really?" Sam winked at him. "Then I'll kill the competition."

He took her to the conference room where only one man sat at a long table, looking at his phone. As soon as they arrived, he put it down and stood, giving her a warm smile.

"Sam, this is Matthew Hart, a one-man HR department, our only attorney, and the guy who signs the checks when I'm not around."

"Ah, the check signer," Sam teased as she shook his hand. "Good guy to know. I'm Sam Sweeney."

"So I've heard." Matt, a solid-looking guy in his mid- to late thirties, looked from one to the other. "I see the resemblance."

"Only I'm prettier," John cracked, easily breaking the ice.

"And way more accomplished," Sam added. "But I'm excited to be here to talk to you, Matt."

"All right, I'll leave you guys to it." John gave a quick

wave and headed out the glass door of the conference room, walking down the short hallway back to his office.

After a few minutes of small talk and an offer of coffee, they settled across the table from each other. Matt opened a file that contained, she assumed, the resume she'd emailed to John.

The lightest of light resumes, with an emphasis on two volunteer projects she'd been involved with for non-profits associated with the hospital, and her stellar success managing the Sally Foster Wrapping Paper Saleathon at Ben's elementary school. Oh, and that year she was team mom for the Winter Park Stars. Go, Stars!

*Ouch.*

"Okay, Sam. This interview is really just a formality, to be perfectly honest with you. Anyone that John recommends is definitely our top choice for the job. Of course, I do have to go through the 'interview process.'" He added air quotes, which really erased some of her stress.

"Helps to know the CEO," she said with a smile. "But whatever you need me to do, I'm here for it. I just really want a chance."

"Well..." Matt arched a brow, scanning the paper in front of him and smiling a little at Sam. "I see you've done some community projects. So you're not unfamiliar with organizing events. What is this...bucket drop you coordinated?"

She bit her lip. "You know when you walk out of Publix and some kids in a uniform hold out a plastic container and beg for support?"

"I can never say no."

"Of course not. That's the idea of a bucket drop. A little pity, a little shame, a little spare cash...and we have new uniforms."

He chuckled. "Ah, I get it. I would imagine that fourth graders are every bit as challenging as a client on a deadline."

"And they come with parents."

Laughing, he put the paper down and eyed her. "Not going to lie, you don't have relevant admin experience, but my guess is you're a quick learner and I know your family is pure quality."

"Oh, thank you." She tipped her head at the compliment. "I do come from a fine group of Sweeneys."

"And I think staying at home with your kids is way underrated these days," he said. "Probably not supposed to say that, but since I'm head of HR, I'll let myself go."

She smiled again. "It's humbling and challenging and fun."

Matt gave a kind smile. "So, let me ask you this." He leaned back in the office chair, studying her. "What unique qualities can you offer us?"

"Well." Sam knew he had said the interview was just a formality, but she still dug hard for a good answer. First impressions were key, and she was definitely a fish out of water in this kind of setting. "As you noted, I spent my adult life as a mom. And while that may not have given me years of relevant experience in the field of marketing or advertising, it gave me a whole lot of knowledge about problem solving—like when an eighth grader walks into your room at six p.m. and announces he forgot the science fair project is due in the morning and *he hasn't started.*"

"The next day? What did you do?"

"We stayed up all night making a solar oven, and as soon as the sun came up, I grilled hot dogs and made cookies on this ridiculous Styrofoam contraption covered in tin foil."

Matt shook his head slowly, his mouth open. "And did he win?"

"Third place." Sam straightened her shoulders proudly.

"That's amazing." He laughed. "And I'd say you're totally ready for the day we get a new business opportunity and the entire staff has to pull an all-nighter to create the pitch."

"I'm ready," she said. "I can even glue things on the presentation board."

"Well, we use PowerPoint on a Mac now."

Of course they did. She felt her eyes shutter. "I'll learn that, too, Matt," she assured him. "I will do whatever it takes to help this team succeed. I know there will be a learning curve and I'm ready for it. But I am really good at solving problems, and, you're right, although I never realized it. Raising two of the world's biggest procrastinators has really honed my skills for working under pressure."

Matt smiled and inhaled sharply, closing the file folder. "Well, I think I've heard all I needed to hear."

She lifted her brows. "Interview's done?"

"And the job is yours." He stood up and held out his

hand to shake hers. "Let's dive into the introductions and orientation and break the happy news to Fran that she will get to the Grand Canyon in that RV this summer after all."

"Thank you!" She shook his hand a little harder. "Thank you so much."

"Oh, and we should discuss pay. I'll get you a letter to confirm everything."

Pay? Yeah. She forgot about that. "That's sounds great."

A minute later, Matt was walking her through the office, gesturing to a cluster of desks and tables against the back half of the ocean-facing window, some music playing from a phone.

"Creative department," he said. "They work all hours, there's always good food back here, and brace for language."

The four employees she saw included one with pink hair, a goateed-man with funky black glasses, and one with dreadlocks hanging around his large, noise-cancelling headset.

"Hello, I'm Sam." She smiled at the group, who nodded or waved as she passed.

"And back there..." Matt guided her to the opposite corner, where a much quieter group of cubicles was set up. "Is our accounting team, who will hound you for time sheets for certain clients who bill by the hour. My office is around the corner, too. The math nerds aren't as much fun as the creatives, but they are every bit as important. I'll take you to account management, where—"

"Sam? Oh my gosh, Sam Sweeney? Is that you?"

Sam turned at the sound of a woman's voice behind her, frowning as someone stood from an accounting cubical and waved.

She looked about Sam's age, with long, dirty blond curls, cheeks dotted with freckles and friendly brown eyes.

Wait a second. She looked so familiar. Sam knew her from somewhere, she had to, but...where?

"It's me, Annie Hawthorne! From Surfside High."

"Holy cow! Annie?"

Standing in front of her was the forty-three-year-old version of one of Sam's closest high school friends. The two of them had bonded in AP Calc, where Annie thrived and Sam, well, *didn't*. She was always more of a right brain, but Annie was a math whiz.

And now, here she was, working as an accountant, which was just so perfectly fitting.

"No way!" Sam rushed over to her old friend and gave her a hug, feeling joyful over this unexpected reunion.

"You're here! And you look fantastic." Annie studied Sam up and down, then turned to Matt. "This lady and I go way, way back. All the way to our high school days."

Matt just laughed and held out his hands. "That's amazing. What a small world. Or a small town, rather."

It sure was.

"I had no idea you worked here, I..." Sam shook her head, taking it in. "Wow. I'm so happy I ran into you."

She had always adored Annie. Smart, witty, and

endlessly fun to be around, the two of them were close pals all through high school, laughing about boys and obsessing over bands and strolling around Cocoa Village on Saturday afternoons.

Sam looked at the woman in front of her, wondering why they'd ever lost touch. She'd always really loved Annie, and they certainly never had any kind of fight or falling out. Annie ended up right back in Cocoa Beach. All these years, they could have been friends. She could have stayed close with her, but...

Sam was short on friends for the same reason she had kept her family at a distance for all these years.

Max. Max made a slow and calculated effort to withdraw Sam from everyone in the world but him, and build a concrete wall around them that no one could get past.

Another person. Another bright, wonderful, positive soul that he kept from her. That he forced her to subconsciously push away.

Well, she was here now. And what could be better for a fresh start than reconnecting with an old friend?

"I just moved back," Sam said. "It's temporary, but it looks like I'm going to work here at the front desk for the time being."

"Oh, that's awesome. It'll be like calc class all over again."

Sam laughed sharply. "Yes, you'll be acing everything and I'll be craning my neck trying to copy your answers."

Annie chuckled and waved a hand. "Hey, when you're done with Matt, let's grab lunch. I'd love to catch up. It's been way too long."

"Absolutely. I'll see you then."

They exchanged another quick hug before Matt guided Sam off to finish the tour and get acquainted with the front desk, her new work home.

"IT's BEEN, what, twenty years or something like that?" Annie stabbed a piece of lettuce with her fork and shook her head, beaming at Sam. "It's criminal that we've lost touch. I've missed you."

Sam felt a weird cocktail of happiness and guilt, mixed in with a hefty portion of regret, but she pushed it away to focus on the positive. "I've missed you, too, Annie. A lot."

The two women sat at a charming outdoor café under an umbrella, just a block or two from the beach. People rode by on bikes and walked past wearing swimsuits and flipflops, making Sam feel extra out of place in her pencil skirt. But it didn't matter. She'd never been anything but comfortable around Annie Hawthorne, and that hadn't changed.

Annie sighed and sipped her iced tea. "Looks like we've got quite a bit of catching up to do. Which is great, because I am definitely in the market for a friend. I spend so much of my time stress baking alone in my little town-house when I'm not at the office, my cat Sterling is starting to worry about me."

Sam laughed easily. "I definitely am in the market for a friend, too. More than words can say."

"Wonderful." Annie clasped her hands together and smiled, reminding Sam so much of her sweet, bubbly friend in high school. "Go on, then. Start from the beginning."

Sam pinched the bridge of her nose. "I'm gonna need more than one lunch to get through this saga."

"We've got time. Give me the CliffsNotes version. I'm dying to know what happened to you! After graduation, you kind of just..."

"Disappeared," Sam finished, the word feeling heavy.

"A little bit," Annie admitted softly.

"Well, I went to UF."

Annie wagged a finger. "I do remember that."

"And my second semester there, I met a guy named Max Parker."

"I figured it was a guy who had you drop off the edge of the Earth." Annie shook her head slowly. "I think that's the last I heard from you, and definitely didn't see you around social media after that became the way to get in touch with old friends."

"I'm pretty sporadic about Facebook and such," Sam admitted. "Anyway, this guy was..." She wanted to say "incredible," but it sure didn't feel like that was a good description of Max. "Short version, I fell for him hard, fast, and could barely form sentences when in his presence. We dated for four months and..." She made a face. "Well, she's twenty-four now and her name is Taylor."

Annie gasped. "You got pregnant? That young?"

"Yes. Nineteen, pregnant, hopelessly in love with

Max. We decided to do the sensible thing and get married."

"After only dating for four months?"

"Hey." Sam tipped her head and laughed heartily. "I never said I made good decisions."

"We all make mistakes."

"So, yes. We got married. And I had my daughter, who is now my best friend in the world."

"Oh." Annie clutched her heart. "Beautiful. I love that. And...Max?"

"He went to medical school and became an orthopedic surgeon. I dropped out, raised Tay, bought a big ole house in Winter Park, had another kid—a boy this time, my son Ben—and I decorated and drove my kids around and grocery shopped and lived the suburban housewife dream. Until it became a nightmare."

Annie stared at her. "Divorce?" she guessed.

"After he cheated on me with his nurse, who he's now living with, and they're expecting a baby."

Her jaw dropped. "Oof."

"Yep."

Annie nodded slowly, leaning back in her seat as she searched Sam's face. "So that's where you've been hiding all these years, Winter Park?"

Hiding was a good way to put it. That's what Max had done to her. He hid her from the world. Selfish and controlling jerk that he was.

"Well, he was a tad controlling." Sam skimmed the droplets of condensation off of her glass while she talked. "But I'm not totally innocent. I chose him over everything, built my whole life around him. It's kind of why we lost touch. It's not personal, I lost touch with everyone. Slowly. He just isolated me, and I never even noticed."

"I don't hold a grudge." Annie shook her head. "Life happens, and you're here now. But I'm so sorry you went through all of that. He sounds awful."

"Perfect description." Sam laughed and shook her head. "That's about the gist of it. So, I'm here on a fresh start. My kids are with me, we're staying at my mom's cottage for the summer."

"Oh," Annie breathed the word. "You're at the cottage. Of course. I always just loved Sweeney House and the cottage so much."

"It's awesome," Sam agreed. "Home was exactly what I needed. But please, enough about my sob story. How are you? Tell me everything." She leaned forward, excited to feel the connection to a close friend she'd been so badly missing for so long and hadn't realized it.

"Well...I don't think I can top your cheating surgeon having a new baby story, but I do have quite a doozy for you."

"I'm all ears."

"As you know, I went all the way up to Cornell for college, froze my Floridian butt off for four long years, got a degree in mathematics, and came back down to the Sunshine State faster than you could blink your eyes."

Sam laughed, waving a finger as the memories of Annie came back to her more and more. "That's right, Cornell. You were always such a brain, Annie."

Annie shrugged humbly and flicked a hand. "I was

just good at math. So, I came down here and moved around to several different accounting jobs and banks, finally landing at Coastal Marketing about eight years ago. I just love your brother, and that Imani is as sweet as can be. I also discovered my secret and unknown passion for baking, and packed on a couple pounds. Oops."

Sam smiled adoringly. "You look wonderful. What do you bake?"

"Cupcakes, mostly. It started out a few years ago, when the big beach church was having a bake sale for charity. I thought, heck, I could whip something up, you know, for the kids. I didn't want any of the premade box stuff, so I sort of concocted my own recipe based on a few others. I decorated them all cute with colors and designs. Had no clue what I was doing, but I was having about the most fun I'd had in years. When I brought them to the sale, everyone was raving and going on about how good they were. And not to toot my horn here, but they were darn good."

Sam smiled. "That's wonderful, you just stumbled upon a passion like that. And you're good at it. And now I want a cupcake."

Annie laughed. "I'll bring a batch to work."

"I would love that. So, what else? Besides accounting and baking, what's gone on in all these years of Annie Hawthorne that I've missed?"

"Well, I guess the main story piece here would be Christian."

"Christian," Sam said softly. "I'm guessing he's the doozy."

"You're guessing right." Annie wrinkled her nose and glanced off to the side, her soft, round cheeks flushed pink at the memory.

Sam placed a hand on her friend's arm, realizing how dear their connection always was, and relishing the fact that years and distance didn't seem to hinder that connection at all.

"You ever heard the phrase *left at the altar*?"

Sam's brows shot straight up as she sucked in a sharp breath. "You're kidding."

Annie shook her head. "I met him shortly after college. We were coworkers. We dated for two years, and were engaged for one. It was my wedding day. Things had been...off, but I figured it was just jitters and maybe a bit of cold feet, but nothing to worry about. Boy, was I wrong." She gave a dry laugh. "I didn't actually *walk* down the aisle, but got pretty darn close before he sent me some cryptic text about how he'd changed his mind and wasn't showing up."

Sam held her hands to her mouth, horrified at the pain her friend must have gone through over this.

"We called the whole thing off, and I haven't had a serious relationship since. That was fifteen years ago."

"I can't even imagine." Sam shut her eyes. "Your *wedding* day."

"I was already wearing my dress," Annie whispered, raising her brows. "But I've done quite a bit of healing since then." She gave a smile, lightening things. "I have a good little life here on the beach. Me, my cat, my spreadsheets and cupcakes. I can't complain."

"And you like working at John's agency?"

"Oh, it's great. My math brain is right at home there." She chuckled. "The people are awesome, nice benefits, good, stable job. In my dreamy fantasy land, I'd open a bakery or a café or something and sell my cupcakes. But that's way too risky in today's economy, and I don't know the first thing about the restaurant business."

"That would be amazing, though. Still, it's good you like this job. I've never had one, you know."

Annie choked. "A job?"

"Nothing real, unless you count being a mom. I rocked the stay-at-home-mom gig pretty hard, though."

For a long time, Annie just looked at her, then lifted her glass and smiled. "To old friends being new again."

"I will drink to that."

They clinked, laughed, and totally lost the rest of the lunch hour savoring the revival of a friendship they both so desperately needed.

# Chapter Sixteen

## Erica

S ome time had passed since Erica got the news about her body's silent shortcomings, and she had given herself a chance to process it and come to terms with the reality of her life.

She would likely never conceive. That she knew for sure.

But the more time that passed, the more she heard Sam's voice in her head saying that she should consider adoption.

As Erica drove the familiar route home from work, the sun was setting behind the palm trees and houses, and she was certain it was time to talk to Will about it.

"Adoption," she whispered to herself, gently turning the steering wheel onto her neighborhood street, trying to picture what it would possibly be like to raise a child that wasn't hers.

She'd had a clear image of her baby ever since the day of her Target Onesie Revelation. The day her life came to a screeching halt, and she suddenly realized she was staring down the barrel of forty and she desperately needed to be a mom.

She'd had an image of a baby with Will's blue eyes

and her small, ski-slope nose that she inherited from Mom and always liked very much. She'd always thought they'd raise the baby and laugh about whether he or she would be visual and creative and right-brained like Will, or extremely analytical and mathematical like Erica. Or maybe somewhere in between.

She'd pictured a boy with Will's voice, playing soccer like he did. Or a girl with Erica's willpower, standing up on her chair at family dinners to declare her political views at the age of eight.

She'd only ever pictured *their* child. A little person who was truly a mixture of her and the man she loved the most, and she'd thought that's what motherhood was supposed to look like for her.

But the more she started to accept the medical facts, the more she realized she didn't have to give up her dream. She just had to picture it differently.

Ever since Sam had mentioned the word "adoption" when she'd visited Erica's office, the thought had been nagging her, worming its way into her brain and her heart.

What if there was a baby out there right now that was meant to be hers? Even if it didn't have Will's eyes or Mom's nose or either of their personalities.

It didn't matter. She could love a baby that wasn't biologically hers. She was certain she could. She wanted one more than anything in the world.

Erica drove down the cul-de-sac in the back of Riverside Palms, where her house sat at the very end of the street, on a round, corner lot. She eased her foot onto the brakes as she cruised through the neighborhood, seeing a couple of children riding bikes in the dead end by her house.

More kids were laughing and running around and playing with a basketball, full of joy and happiness and safety.

As soon as the group of kids saw Erica's car, they ran over to the grass and let her pull in. She could see a couple of the moms from her street sitting in a driveway supervising, with plastic glasses that most likely held wine.

Erica gave them a smile and a wave as she slowly pulled her car into the driveway and then the garage, shaking her head as she turned off the ignition.

This neighborhood screamed for kids. It was already filled with them. Her life screamed for kids. She and Will were beyond happy and in love, they had tons of money, extended family and her mom's cottage right up the road in Cocoa Beach. She needed a baby. And she wasn't going to give up that dream.

Erica got out of the car, feeling a new sense of hope zip through her, something she hadn't felt since right before she took that last dreaded pregnancy test.

Not being able to physically conceive didn't have to mean she'd never be a mother. She could get on a list and get a newborn baby and raise it with all the love and affection and care that she'd give her own child.

Because it *would* be her own child.

And suddenly, as she closed the garage door and

slung her purse over her shoulder, she knew this was an option she wanted to seriously explore.

She also knew it was a long and drawn-out process, and she wanted to be a mom, like, yesterday. So she'd better get started.

That was what Erica did. She made decisions—she chose what she wanted to do, and she made it happen. No waiting, no putting it off, no sitting around and talking about it.

She made moves, and that's exactly what it was time to do.

"Hey, honey." Erica headed through the door and into their beautiful home, hanging her work bag up in the laundry room and walking over to the living room to give Will a kiss.

She wore her usual office attire, a soft pink button-up and black pencil skirt, typically wanting to dress to impress every day as an engineer. Will always teased her that she overdressed, but she was in a highly male-dominated field, and Erica found that the way she looked and carried herself led to her coworkers and team members taking her more seriously.

"You're home early. Ish." He glanced at the clock, which read 7:35.

"Early for me." Erica grinned with a little extra bounce in her step, her head humming with the conversation she knew they were about to have.

After taking one look at the expression on Erica's face, Will drew back and eyed her, a smile pulling at his cheeks. "Oh no."

"What?"

"What are you thinking about?"

Erica faked a confused look as she came around the sofa to sit down next to him. "Me? What do you mean? I'm not thinking about anything in particular."

"Erica." He lowered his green gaze and shot her a *get real* look, wrapping his arm around her shoulders. "We've been together for eight years. I know when something's on your mind. And I'm getting a sense that this might be...a good something?" He smiled at the thought of that, clearly relieved that there might be some positivity on its way, since they'd both spent the better part of two weeks wallowing in sadness.

"Okay, okay. I'm thinking about something. Actually...seriously thinking about it."

He waved a hand, his eyes eager. "Go ahead. I'm listening."

She shut her eyes and took a long, deep breath, letting it out slowly. "I think we should adopt. Or at least definitely look into it."

Will froze for a second, blinking back in shock. "You...you do?"

"If that's something you'd want to do, of course," Erica added quickly. "This would be a joint decision that we make together. I don't want to do anything unilaterally. And I wasn't sure if—"

"Yes!" he blurted out. "Of course I want to! I didn't think you wanted to. I know how you always felt about the precious Sweeney genes and all that, and I didn't want to suggest it when you were feeling upset—"

"I want to." Erica nodded with certainty, inching closer to her husband and feeling a buzz of joy and new hope zing through her. "I really want to."

"Babe!" Will grabbed her face in his strong hands, planting a loving kiss on her lips as they both laughed and smiled and held each other with the excitement of this new revelation. "This is amazing. I never thought you'd consider it."

Erica snuggled close to him on the couch, kicking off her low black pumps and plopping her bare feet up on the ottoman in front of them. "Honestly, I talked to my sister."

"You did?"

"Yeah." She brushed a strand of hair behind her ear and looked at her husband. "I know I was keeping everything so private for so long, but I just...unraveled. I told her everything, and she asked why I wasn't considering adoption. And I..." Erica lifted a shoulder and laughed softly. "I didn't have a good answer."

"There isn't one. It makes so much sense to at least give it a shot."

"I agree! I've been thinking about it for days now, I've gone over every imaginable scenario in my head. Every reason not to. Every reason why it's risky and we should just accept that we can't be parents. But..." She locked eyes with him, emotion gripping her chest. "I don't want to accept that, Will. And we don't have to. There's a baby out there that needs us, I'm sure of it."

"I didn't want to pressure you." He looked down at her, his green eyes twinkling. "I knew how important it was to you that we have *our* baby. You always talked about the little details. How much we'd see ourselves in our child and how beautiful that would be. And that is something we'll miss, for sure. But I'm more than open to adopting. Are you kidding?" He laughed. "I think it's awesome."

Erica squeezed her eyes shut, taking his hands and holding them tightly. "I'm so happy to hear you say that. I want to do this with you."

"Let's do this."

She gave a giddy laugh, drawing closer to him. "You're sure?"

"A thousand percent. I'll start calling agencies and researching tomorrow," he said. "If you wanted to start immediately, of course. I know it hasn't been that long since you found out about...you know." He gestured vaguely.

"I know. But...I'm sure about this," she said under her breath. "I don't want to wait. Our baby could already be out there, waiting for us."

# Chapter Seventeen

## *Dottie*

Dottie walked through the hallway of Sweeney House, looking down at the old tan carpet that she and Jay picked out all those years ago. It was worn and faded and...wow. It was certainly starting to show its age.

The inn was beautiful—charming and cozy and wonderfully unique. But as Dottie walked these halls, she noticed the slight peeling of the wallpaper in the corners and the chips in the paint of the white wooden doors to each room. The outdated, distressed finishings that once seemed so timeless to Dottie now started to look tired and old to her eyes.

She wondered if it was a sign that selling the inn and cottage was the right thing to do. Maybe the best days of Sweeney House lay in the past. And as harsh and sad and heartbreaking as that might be, all things must come to an end. Right?

*Times, they are a-changin'.*

Her heart ached at the thought of the place being bulldozed. The inn had been their livelihood and their life's work together, and the cottage was their home. How could Dottie possibly let some big corporation come in and smash it all to the ground?

Well, because she couldn't handle it anymore. Any of it. The work, the grief, the memories...she had to go. But she didn't. Did she?

"Oh, good heavens," Dottie whispered to herself as she stepped into the little elevator and clicked the button to go down to the first floor. "I'm a mess."

And she was. She felt completely lost without Jay. Dottie had hoped that selling the inn and cottage would bring her clarity and peace and direction, but the very notion of it had her more confused and scared than ever.

How was she supposed to go on without the man who guided her and loved her and supported her through every tough decision she'd ever made? She'd never had to make one alone.

And now, the time had come to be a grown woman and strong and independent—and Dottie was simply crumbling.

The elevator stopped and the doors glided open, letting her out in the lobby.

She slowed her step as she passed the old grandfather clock against the wall by the front desk, a pressing and painful reminder of Jay.

The clock hadn't ticked in decades, and the thing was, well, somewhat of an eyesore. But it was so deeply important to him, having belonged to Jay's father, that Dottie wouldn't dare touch it or mess with it, ever.

She gently put her lips to her fingers and kissed them,

pressing that kiss against the clock as she walked by, as if to tell Jay she loved him.

Karen, her real estate agent, had called early this morning and demanded a meeting with Dottie in person, today, as soon as possible.

Dottie had some rooms to attend to and business to do at Sweeney House, so she told Karen to come by the inn. Which, of course, eager Karen agreed to. She'd find a way to get to Mars if it meant closing this deal.

She was on her way now and would be here any minute, and Dottie had a sinking feeling that this was going to be the end of her stalling period.

She could only hide from this conflict for so long before she had to face it, make a decision, and stick to it.

It was a task so overwhelmingly heavy that Dottie wished she could just walk over to the cottage, curl up in Jay's old recliner and cry.

But that was not an option today.

"Hi, Bella." Dottie smiled sweetly at the capable young woman who had recently started working as a housekeeper at the inn. "Could you doublecheck that 206 is ready for guests? They're checking in today at three."

"Of course!" Bella grinned, her curly blond ponytail swinging back and forth as she whipped around to grab her housekeeping cart and head up to check on the room.

"Thank you, sweetheart."

Another wonderful addition to Dottie's staff. Another poor, sweet person she'd have to break the news to that their place of work, an environment so homey and comfortable that all the staff felt like family, would cease to exist in a matter of months.

Dottie was sick to her stomach just thinking about it.

But before she had the chance to get too far back down the rabbit hole, the front doors of the inn flew open and Karen marched into the lobby, iPad at the ready.

Karen wore black slacks and a white blouse, her hair slicked back in a bun, a look of fierce determination on her face. As always.

Dottie wondered what Karen must think of her, as she looked down at yet another one of the long, flowery dresses that hung loosely on Dottie's bony frame, paired with her pink slip-on shoes.

She smiled to herself as she walked over to the entrance of the lobby. "Good morning, Karen."

"Dottie, hi." She grinned—as close to warm and friendly as Karen could be, Dottie figured. "How have you been? How's your daughter?"

"Oh, she's doing much better, actually." Dottie gestured for Karen to follow her to the small sitting area by the check-in desk, which had a couple of couches and chairs with a coffee table in the middle. "Can I get you some water? I'd offer coffee, but the machine's been broken for a little while now."

"I'm fine, thank you." Karen sat down on the very edge of the couch and crossed her legs. "Already had three cups today."

Dottie chuckled. "Why does that not surprise me?"

"Dottie, I'm going to just get straight down to business with you, if that's all right." She pressed her hands on her iPad and looked Dottie right in the eyes.

"Works for me." Dottie swallowed a ball of nerves and anxiety that rose up in her throat and forced a smile.

"Remember the offer I told you about from the large-scale hotel chain? The top-dollar one?" Karen's brows went sky high.

Dottie cleared her throat, brushing a curl from her face. "Yes, of course. And I'm sorry for postponing, but we agreed I could have more time—"

"The buyer doesn't agree to that," Karen interjected. "They have upped the offer." Her eyes lit up, and Dottie could practically see shiny, glittery dollar signs in them.

"Oh." She drew back, sucking in a breath, not entirely sure how to feel about that.

"By a lot. Almost ten percent over the first offer." Karen leaned forward, meeting Dottie's gaze and lowering her tone. "Dottie, this is a record offer for a property the age and condition of Sweeney House in this area. They're putting life-changing money on the table. For you and your family." She leaned back into the sofa. "You should seriously consider this."

Dottie didn't have the first clue how to respond. She knew how Jay would respond.

*"Tell 'em they can take their offer and stick it where the sun don't shine, because Sweeney House belongs to us."*

But it wasn't theirs anymore. It was *hers*. And she didn't want it. Did she?

"Here." Karen turned the iPad on, the screen lighting

up. "See for yourself." She turned the tablet around and handed it to Dottie, whose hands quivered subtly.

She focused her eyes on the screen, and even without her trusty reading glasses, she could make out the giant number.

Large. Many figures, many zeroes.

"Oh. Oh my." Dottie held a hand to her mouth as she stared at it, knowing Karen was right. This would absolutely set her up and go a long way for her family and grandchildren.

Karen smiled, arching a brow and slowly taking the tablet out of Dottie's frozen grasp. "Bit of a game changer, isn't it?"

"I..." Dottie just stared straight ahead, feeling even more lost and confused than before. "I thought this was exactly what I wanted. I thought I needed a big chunk of money to get away from my past and stop living in my memories and move on."

Karen placed a hand on Dottie's arm, leaning across the white wooden coffee table. "And now you can. With even more security and comfort than before."

Dottie took in a shuddering breath, the dollar figure dancing around in her head. "But I'm still not sure. I want so badly to start over, Karen. To be that independent, strong, tough seventy-two-year-old woman who thrives on her own and takes care of her life and doesn't wallow in loneliness and nostalgia." She wasn't entirely sure why she was dumping her heap of emotions onto Karen, of all people. Probably just because the other woman was in front of her.

But that was Dottie. If she felt something, the people around her were going to know about it. Jay used to say some people wore their heart on their sleeve, but Dottie wore hers smack dab in the middle of her forehead.

"You saw the number, Dottie." Karen's voice was steady and somewhat kind, but she was obviously very eager to close this deal. Of course, she could never understand the history behind Sweeney House and her family's cottage. No one could.

"I did see it."

"That number would make all of that possible." She leaned forward. "You could get a whole new start. A new lease on life. Your golden years as a beautiful, strong, independent woman without being bogged down by"—she gestured around at the inn—"all of this."

Dottie let out a sigh and shook her head. She needed Jay, of course. Maybe she ought to consider talking to the kids about it.

John was sensible. He'd give her an unbiased opinion, wouldn't he?

But...then again, he had three kids who loved nothing more than coming to the cottage for sleepovers and holidays, and even John might put sensibility aside when it came to the sentimental value of the place where he grew up.

He wanted the cottage and Sweeney House to be a big part of his children's lives, and Dottie knew that.

Maybe Erica could be a good person to confide in. She didn't have kids, so no grandbabies to tug at Dottie's heartstrings. She was smart as a whip and would help Dottie make the right choice, wouldn't she?

On second thought, Erica was constantly talking about how she wanted to eventually inherit the cottage, and her husband was a construction manager, and he was always making comments about how he'd love to get his hands on the place for a renovation.

Dottie had always brushed off the idea, knowing Jay would roll over in his grave at the very whisper of changing anything about Sweeney House.

Considering that, was she seriously about to sell it to some company that wanted to level it to the ground?

She had to get away. She had to start fresh. The money...the company...the inn...the outdated décor...the memories...the cottage...

It was all just too much.

"Dottie, are you all right?"

Suddenly, the world went fuzzy and blurry and everything seemed very far away. Dottie heard a loud ringing in her ears and felt as if she might actually faint.

"I'm fine, I'm fine..." She shut her eyes and waved a hand.

Karen jumped over to the sofa where Dottie was sitting, and Bella somehow appeared next to her as well. "Do you need help? You look like you're going to pass out," Karen said.

"I'll get her some water," Bella suggested, hopping up and jogging away.

"I'm okay, really." Dottie took a deep breath and looked around, and things started to feel calm again.

Her vision went back to normal and she could hear clearly. She looked at Karen and saw her very concerned face studying her.

"You're sure you're all right?"

"Here's some water." Bella swooped back in with a cold water bottle and handed it to Dottie. "What happened?"

"I just..." Dottie twisted the top off of the water bottle and took a small sip. "I had some sort of panic attack or something, I-I'm so embarrassed." She laughed uneasily. "I'm not usually so weak and frail, I just..."

"No, don't be!" Bella exclaimed, holding Dottie's arm. "I get my fair share of anxiety, too." Her eyes flashed, but she shook it off quickly.

Dottie turned to her new employee. "You do?"

"Oh, yes. Big time." Bella chuckled. "I try to keep it together around my son, Eli, but I know exactly how you're feeling, and I promise you're going to get through it."

"Eli." Dottie smiled to herself. "How old is he?"

"Two," Bella answered with a wistful smile, something in her gaze giving Dottie the impression that there was more to Bella and Eli and their story than she could have imagined.

She made a mental note to get to know Bella better as soon as she had the chance.

"You're sure you're okay, Dottie?" Karen asked again, tilting her head to scan Dottie's face.

"I'm fine, I promise." Dottie stood up and looked at Karen. "I need some time."

Karen nodded understandingly and packed up her iPad and everything, swinging a black purse over her shoulder. "I know. It's okay."

"I'm sorry, Karen, I really am." Dottie looked at her, feeling her energy come back and the color return to her face. "I don't mean to be so indecisive, and I know you've got a job to do."

"It's completely okay, Dottie. You know the number now, and that is their final offer." She placed a hand on Dottie's arm and gave it a squeeze. "Think it over. You sure you're okay?"

"I'm fine," Dottie insisted.

"I'll keep an eye on her," Bella added with a smile.

Karen nodded and stood up. "Good, okay. You have my cell."

"I sure do." Dottie stood up slowly. "Let me walk you out—"

Karen held up a hand. "No, please. It's fine!"

Bella kept her hand on Dottie's arm. "You should stay resting. I'll have someone call one of your family members to come in and make sure you're okay."

Dottie laughed and flicked her hand. "Please, you're all completely overreacting. I just got overwhelmed, is all."

Karen gave a smile as she turned to head out the front door. She stopped. "Dottie, can I say something? And we'll consider it..." She pressed her lips together. "Off the record, if you will?"

Dottie shrugged. "Sure."

Karen let out a breath and shut her eyes, shaking her

head a little as if she couldn't believe what was about to come out of her mouth. "Look, I know it's my job to sell this property, and believe me, I want to. So, I'm only saying this because I think you're a really good person with a wonderful family and you've been very kind to me, even though I know I can be headstrong about real estate. If you're feeling this much stress and agony and anxiety over something, that's worth listening to. I'm not saying don't sell," she added quickly, with a laugh. "Just...listen to your heart, Dottie. Because I can tell you've got a good one."

As Karen strutted out the door with her heels clicking on every step, Dottie just sat on the old blue sofa and stared at the lobby of the inn.

"Can I get you anything else?" Bella asked sweetly. "You're looking better. Your color is back."

"Oh, honey, I'm fine." Dottie laughed. "It was just a spell."

"If, um..." Bella sat back down, smoothing her hair over to one side and shifting around in the seat. "If you don't mind me asking, am I hearing correctly that you're thinking about selling the inn? I didn't mean to eavesdrop. I just saw you looking seriously ill when I was walking by, and I heard that lady say—"

"Oh." Dottie sighed deeply, shaking her head. "It's very complicated. And, clearly, nothing is set in stone. Bella, would you do me a favor and keep this to yourself for the time being? I've just got to get my wits together and figure out what the heck I'm going to do, and I don't want anyone panicking or spreading rumors."

Bella nodded with reassurance. "My lips are sealed, I promise."

"Thank you. I'm glad we hired you. You're liking it here, huh?"

Bella lit up. "Oh, I love it. Everyone is so kind and welcoming, it really is like a—"

"Family," Dottie finished. "I know."

"Anyway." Bella gave her arm a squeeze. "If you're sure you're okay, I'm going to get back to prepping those upstairs rooms."

"I'm a thousand percent okay. Thank you, dear."

"Your secret is safe with me, I promise." Bella stood up and walked back over to her cart, placing her hands on the handle and rolling it away. "Oh, and Dottie?"

"Yes?"

"I know it's completely not my place to say anything, but...if you ask me, Sweeney House is priceless. It could maybe use a facelift, though." She laughed playfully. "I'll be around if you need anything!"

"Thank you, dear." Dottie waved.

As Bella rolled the cart down the hallway and into the elevator, Dottie sipped her water bottle and messed with the throw pillows on the couch.

That was a big number. A huge number. An astronomical number. It was everything she thought she wanted for the property when Jay died and more.

But things had changed. Her heart had shifted. Sam had returned and they were closer than ever.

Weight pressed on Dottie's heart as Bella's parting

words echoed in her head, unleashing a whole new whirl-wind of ideas in her mind.

"A facelift..." Dottie whispered to herself, rubbing her thumb along the white paint of the coffee table, a few chips of it falling underneath her fingernail and fluttering to the floor.

She could certainly change out the lobby furniture for something more modern and throw a fresh coat of paint on the walls. The hallway carpets could also defi-nitely stand to be torn up and replaced with wood. And some of the rooms could really use some sprucing...

Dottie sat in her lobby, her mind racing and whirling and spinning with ideas and inspiration.

Did she have it in her to renovate the inn? To breathe new life into it and start a new chapter right here in her home?

Was that a possibility? Was that her answer?

She had never wanted to change a single thing about Sweeney House, because all of it reminded her of Jay. Every detail had been chosen and touched and loved by him. But that was the very thing that was making her so sad—the constant reminders.

She couldn't help but wonder, just for a brief second, if the fresh start she was so desperate for was not actually somewhere new, but right where she'd been all along.

# Chapter Eighteen

## Sam

"Thanks for the ride home." Sam smiled at John as he drove down the uneven gravel road that led to the driveway of the cottage. "Boss," she added playfully, nudging her brother in the driver's seat.

John stifled a laugh as he rolled his eyes. "Yeah, yeah. Anytime."

Sam had told Taylor she could borrow her SUV to get around today, since she was on a bit of job hunt herself, and her poor old Honda was in the shop once again.

John, of course, agreed to take Sam to and from the office while Taylor's car was being repaired.

The lane to the cottage was hidden by thick sea grapes and hibiscus bushes that created a lush, green wall along the side of the road. On the other side, of course, was the beach, with small, bungalow-style houses spread out along the sand, each with breathtaking waterfront views and classic Cocoa Beach charm.

Sam pressed her forehead to the warm glass of the window and watched the ocean in the distance.

She was exhausted. Bone-deep tired. Learning an entirely new office, industry, and workplace lifestyle was really quite an undertaking. She'd been enjoying it, though, and everyone had been wonderfully helpful.

Plus, having both John and Annie there was like having two built-in friends, which made things even easier.

Still, she felt totally wiped out, stretching her arms up as she yawned and shook her head.

John laughed and raised a brow at her. "Tough day?" he teased.

Sam laughed, too. "A good day. Just...wow. Work makes you tired!"

"That it does," he agreed, turning the wheel as he pulled the car onto the long driveway that led to Sweeney House and the cottage. "But you've really started to fit in nicely, and it seems like you're picking up the day-to-day quickly. Any trouble so far?"

"Not really. I mean, it's definitely a learning curve. Annie's helping me a ton with Microsoft Excel, which somehow Fran used for literally everything."

"Annie's a whiz with that sort of thing," John said. "And Fran was surprisingly tech-savvy. It's awesome that you and Annie reconnected, though. It completely slipped my mind that you two were friends in high school when I put your name in for the job. Added perk."

"I know. I'm so happy to have a friend." Sam smiled. "I'm really enjoying work a lot. Today was, what, my third day? I already feel like I've learned so much. It's a cool industry, actually. To be perfectly honest, I never actually understood what you did until now."

John laughed, putting the car in Park as he pulled up

in front of the inn, turning to Sam. "Well, we're happy to have you."

"I'm happy to be there. Thanks again for the ride, big brother."

"Anytime."

She slung her bag over her shoulder and gave John one more wave before shutting his car door and heading down the little path that led to the cottage.

She didn't want to let on to her brother how insanely overwhelmed she was by a job that most people would deem pretty simple.

Administrative assistant sounded easy enough, but Sam was working harder than she ever had in her life to figure out how to run an office. It was a lot to take in, and completely different from anything she'd ever experienced before.

As she headed down the little beachside walkway, the humid evening air pressed down on her skin. The sun was still blazing high in the sky, and the sand underneath her feet was radiating warmth and light.

As she approached the cottage, Sam adjusted her sunglasses and felt relieved to be home.

Her SUV was parked out front, so she figured Taylor was back from her job search or errands.

"I'm home," Sam called into the cottage as she swung open the back door, walking through the little entryway and toward the living room. "Anyone here? Tay? Ben? What do you guys want for dinner? I was thinking we could do Chinese. There's that place down the street—"

Sam stopped in her tracks, completely frozen in

shock at the sight in front of her as she stepped closer to the living room.

Taylor and Ben were sitting on the couch, side by side, laughing and playing a video game.

"Hey, Mom." Ben turned to face Sam with a smile—an actual smile—on his face.

Sam's heart suddenly felt light, and she dropped her bag down on the counter and rushed over to join them. "Hi! You guys are..." She gestured at the TV, where it looked like Ben had set up his video games. "You're down here."

"We sure are." Taylor gave her mom a smile, her eyes twinkling. "How was work?"

Sam practically didn't hear the question, because she was too focused on whether or not her eyes were deceiving her or if her angst-ridden and completely withdrawn teenage son had actually come out of his room and was hanging out with his sister. Downstairs.

"Work was good. Ben, you brought your game down?" Sam tried to keep her tone casual, so as not to scare him off.

There was truly nothing more touchy or sensitive than a teenage boy.

"Yeah. Taylor wanted to play some *Mario Kart*," he answered. "And I thought I could use a change of scenery."

Sam almost had to fight tears of joy, but she reminded herself over and over again to play it cool and not freak out over Ben starting to become normal again. "That's awesome. It looks like you two are having a great time."

"Oh, we are." Taylor leaned her head back on the couch, her shiny brown waves falling all around the cushion. "I'm whupping his butt pretty bad."

"Yeah, you wish." Ben smirked. "Mom, do you want to play?"

Okay, now Sam was *actually* fighting tears of joy.

"Yeah, Mom! Play with us. It'll be fun," Taylor urged, scooting over on the big living room sectional to make space for Sam between them.

She was completely fried from a day of work, and just about the last thing on the planet she wanted to do was attempt some insane video game, but Sam knew darn well that this opportunity to spend time with Ben and bond with him had not come in many months, and she was not about to pass it up.

"All right. Set me up a controller thing."

"Yes!" Taylor pumped a fist. "Benny, get her a Joy-Con."

Joy-Con? Sam guessed this wasn't the Wii anymore. Boy, things changed fast.

Ben handed Sam a little red plastic remote with buttons and a moving rubber stick. "You remember how to play?"

Sam practically cackled. "Uh, no."

"Okay, I'll show you." As Ben pointed to the different buttons and explained which one was gas and brake and how to steer your kart and throw bananas at the other players, Sam just watched her son.

For the first time in what felt like an eternity, he showed glimmers of the Ben he used to be. The subtle sweetness in his smile, the gentle nature of his mannerisms.

Since he'd come into this world, Ben had always been calm and quiet and selfless. He hated nothing more than conflict and arguments. He and Taylor never had a fight, even as little kids, because the second conflict would start to arise in any way, Ben would do whatever it took to avoid an argument and raised voices, even if it just meant running away into another room.

Sam thought back on some of the tougher times in her marriage, the late nights when she and Max would have it out over something or other, yelling and screaming and slamming the occasional door or two.

She knew it had destroyed Ben to hear those confrontations. He physically could not stand fights like that.

And then, the cheating happened. And the breakup. And that much conflict had pushed Ben so far away from the family and deep into his own sadness.

But today, Sam watched her boy laugh with Taylor as he gently and patiently explained a video game to her, and she started to see her sweet and wonderful son coming back to life.

It gave her heart more joy than she could ever describe. Sam thought for a second that maybe they could start to feel like a family again, the three of them.

Coming back to Cocoa Beach, the warmth and the sun and the welcoming small town and, of course, the loving family, had been the best thing for their healing, all in different ways.

"Okay, you ready?" Ben asked, clicking some buttons as the screen switched over to the *Mario Kart* race. "We're starting easy."

"This is *Moo Moo Meadows*." Taylor pointed at the TV. "You'll like this one, Mom."

Sam just laughed, nestled between her two babies—who weren't such babies anymore—and held her remote. "Okay, I'm ready. I've got my finger on the gas button."

"And go!" Taylor exclaimed as the race started.

"Oh, no!" Sam shrieked through laughter as she made an embarrassing attempt to race her little kart between the others, getting thrown around and sent way to the back in a matter of seconds.

Ben laughed heartily, the sound making Sam's heart fold. She didn't realize how badly she had missed that sound.

"Mom, throw your shell!" Ben exclaimed.

"Oh! I have a shell?"

"Press the top button," Taylor said, her eyes glued to her own kart flying on the screen.

"Oh, I got it!"

They all laughed as the insanely hectic *Mario Kart* race came to an end, and Sam proudly took dead last.

"You'll get it, Mom." Taylor nudged her mother playfully. "You just have to practice."

"It's been a while." Sam toyed with the remote in her hand. "I've...missed this." She turned to look over at Ben, catching his gaze. "A lot."

His eyes flashed as he glanced down into his lap. "Me, too," he muttered, barely audible, and with enough vulnerability to make Sam feel like being back here in the cottage truly had done wonders for her boy.

"All right, you guys." Taylor stood up and stretched her arms over her head. "That's enough stress for me. My heart can't take any more."

Ben eyed her. "Yeah, can't take any more losing."

She stuck her tongue out and made a face at her brother, giving Sam a heaping dose of déjà vu. "I'm gonna head out for a little. Is it okay if I take your car again, Mom? The Honda is taking longer than expected in the shop."

"Sure, I'm not leaving." Sam shrugged. "You got plans?" She raised her brow and wiggled it teasingly, knowing full well who those plans likely involved.

Taylor made a face and lifted her shoulder, smiling. "Maybe. I'll be back later tonight."

"Bye, Tay." Sam reached out and gave her daughter's arm a squeeze.

She wasn't entirely sure what was happening between Taylor and Kai, but she knew without a doubt that this was the most interest Taylor had shown in a boy in two years. By a long shot.

Sam was well aware of the damage that Max had done to their unsuspecting daughter, permanently embedding in her mind the idea that men were absolutely not to be trusted, because the man she trusted the most betrayed all of them.

Sam knew there could be a good guy out there for Taylor. Was it Kai? She had no idea.

He seemed sweet and he appeared to be very into

her. And obviously, as a female with a beating heart and a set of eyes, Sam could see the appeal.

But he lived far, far away and Sam worried about Taylor getting her heart broken when he left.

Right now, though, she just had to let her daughter be. She was going to figure everything out, and Sam would be there for her, no matter what.

There was a time to be a mother, and a time to be a friend, she'd always thought. And regarding Taylor's dating life, she was old enough that it was a good time for Sam to not "mom" her, and to just love her.

"Have fun, honey," she called as Taylor gave a happy wave and headed out the front door of the cottage.

She shifted around on the sectional to face Ben who, blessedly, did not have a phone in his hand for once.

"Tay's got herself a man, huh?" Sam elbowed Ben playfully, hoping to initiate some level of conversation, but not wanting to push it too hard.

He was so fragile.

"Seems like it," Ben said, pushing some of his hair off his forehead and revealing those beautiful brown eyes that Sam ached to see light up again.

"He's some kind of professional surfer, apparently. Erica and Imani knew who he was."

"I know. He's sort of famous." Ben's face hinted at a smile. "He's really cool, though. I like him."

Sam blinked back with surprise. "You've met him?"

"Yeah, the other morning," Ben explained casually. "I was awake really early and Taylor was going down to the beach, so I went with her. Kai was out there surfing, and he even showed me how to paddle out and stand up. I didn't quite get it, but I feel like I could. You know, if I gave it another shot," his voice trailed off after saying the most words Sam had heard him say in months.

She laughed dryly with disbelief as she pieced together what he was saying. He and Taylor went surfing with Kai? Ben got on a surfboard? He did something that wasn't playing video games or staring at his phone?

Why hadn't Taylor told her about this?

"Wow, Ben." Sam reminded herself to play it cool and not get too excited about anything. She didn't want to scare him off. "That's really awesome!"

"Yeah, it was fun." He nodded. "I would give it another go, maybe. See if I can actually get up on the board."

"I can't believe Taylor didn't tell me you guys did that," Sam said with a smile, shaking her head.

"Mom." Ben raised his brows. "Taylor and I are allowed to have our things, you know. Sibling stuff."

"I do know. And...I think it's wonderful."

And she did. Taylor must have had a serious break-through with Ben, because he was acting far more like his old self than she'd seen in a long time. Whatever they shared, it was between the two of them, and it gave Sam unimaginable happiness to know that her kids were there for each other. She was glad Taylor didn't tell her. Some things should be...sibling stuff.

Sam swallowed, feeling herself practically humming with joy. "Ben, you..." She studied him for a second. "You seem like you're in better spirits. You're enjoying our time here?"

He picked at a loose thread on the seam of the couch. "Actually, yeah." Ben looked up at his mom. "I hated it at first, but I kinda hated everything. I think I'm feeling better. It's nice to be able to see Uncle John, too. I think I might go fishing with him next weekend."

"Fishing? Look at you." Sam couldn't help but draw back and laugh. "You're really embracing the Cocoa Beach lifestyle, aren't you?"

Ben shrugged. "I don't know, I guess. I think Winter Park was starting to get kind of depressing."

"You can say that again."

"Yeah, it's good." He ruffled his long, shiny hair and glanced at Sam. "I'm sorry, by the way. For how I've been."

She could have sworn she felt her heart crack right then and there. Even though his tone was casual and nonchalant, the words meant the world to her.

"Oh, baby." Sam reached over and wrapped her arms around Ben's shoulders, giving him a hug that he didn't actually refuse. "Please don't apologize. I know how much you've been through."

"It's just..." He pushed his hair back again. "I don't know. I was telling Taylor it felt like you and her just wanted me to hate him as much as you guys do. And I get why you hate him, Mom. I get it. But I don't know if I'm... ready to hate him."

She reached out and touched her son's cheek, holding the sweet, handsome face that she still saw as her baby boy. "Ben. I don't want you to hate your father."

"But like, I kind of do," he said, his tone frustrated and conflicted. "But then again, I don't want to lose him. And it's just been really bumming me out. I felt like I didn't fit anywhere. Not with him, and not with you guys."

Sam shut her eyes, her lashes fluttering as she felt emotion squeezing in her throat. Ben was finally opening up to her, and it made her heart soar to see him slowly beginning to move forward through all of the trauma.

Sam carried so much guilt for everything. The weight of her failed marriage pressed on her every time her struggling, angst-filled son pushed her away.

But he wasn't pushing her away anymore, and for the first time, she felt like maybe Ben could start to heal with her and Taylor. In different ways, but together as a family.

"Oh, Ben." She kissed the top of his head and gave him a tight hug. "I'm so sorry you felt pushed out. Taylor and I never meant to do that."

"I know, I know. I was just...feeling some type of way about everything."

"Weren't we all?" She laughed dryly. "Honey, thank you for talking to me. And you know I'm here for you. Whatever kind of relationship you want to have with your father, I will fully support. Taylor and I will always welcome you, no matter what."

Ben let out a noisy sigh, looking visibly relieved to have aired out some of these emotions. "I'm still figuring out what I want to do about Dad. I'm so mad at him. He's having this whole new family. It's like he forgot about us already or something."

Sam so badly wanted to assure her son that that wasn't the case, but she couldn't deny the fact that, in her heart, she felt exactly the same way. Forgotten. Thrown by the wayside. She was still picking up her own pieces.

"He didn't forget, Ben. He's just..." Selfish. Impulsive. Unfaithful. Dishonest. Evil. "He's just made some mistakes," she said instead. "But I know he loves you very much. Let things settle down while we're here in Cocoa Beach, and I'm sure he will miss you and want to see you as much as possible."

Ben arched a brow. "I'm not so sure of that."

Sam just gave his shoulder one more squeeze. "We're gonna be okay, Ben. You, me, and Tay have each other. You're not alone, all right? Don't isolate yourself. You don't have to."

"I'll try not to anymore." A small smile formed at the corners of his mouth, those familiar dimples making Sam laugh as she remembered wiping chocolate frosting off of his face as a baby when she first noticed them. "Just, please, no fighting."

"No fighting. Promise."

"There haven't been any loud fights or yelling or anything since we've been here, and it's made me feel a lot better. When no one is upset, you know?"

"I know, Ben. There won't be any fighting in Cocoa Beach, I promise. Just surfing and family time and lots more *Mario Kart*. I love you, hon."

"Love you, too, Mom."

She blew out a breath and glanced out the window at the beautiful, glistening water crashing in soft waves against the white sand.

Ben was starting to come back to life, showing glimmers of joy and the vibrance that had been dulled for so long. Taylor was maybe potentially opening her heart to love, finding a new hopeful side to herself. And Sam was...healing. Rebuilding old bonds that had been broken by Max's control all those years ago. She was slowly but surely finding her footing, learning who she was without his thumb pressing down on her all the time.

Everything was looking bright, and it seemed the cottage and Cocoa Beach truly was magic.

# Chapter Nineteen

## Taylor

"A secret spot?" Taylor asked Kai, giggling as he guided her through a mess of sea grapes and hanging palm fronds.

He cast a glance at her over his shoulder. "Just trust me."

Trust. Not her strong suit these days.

She kept her grip on his hand as he walked them through this seemingly abandoned alleyway between two condo buildings, leading her to the beach. Taylor was moderately certain they were trespassing, but Kai swore he came here all the time, so she went along with it.

The concrete walls on either side of the narrow path were covered in graffiti and colorful street art. A breath-taking mural of a surfboard gliding through a wave had been painted on one whole wall, as vivid as a photograph.

Taylor ran her finger along the painted wall as they walked by, wondering about the talented artist who painted buildings, likely in the middle of the night.

As they neared the beach, the path grew lush with greenery hanging over the walls, filling the breeze with the scent of sand and salt and beachside air. With Kai's grip strong and tight on Taylor's hand, she couldn't help but savor the feeling of safety as she followed him. Until something brushed her face.

She made a soft squawk, and frantically waved her hand, then wiped her face fifty times. "Okay, I officially felt a spider crawl on me."

Kai laughed and kept walking her to the end of the alley.

"Will you please just—"

Before Taylor could finish her sentence, they reached the end of the walkway, where the concrete walls stopped, the thick green bush opened up, and their feet were on the sand.

The sun had lowered below the horizon, leaving a slight silver and blue glow in the sky around the moon and stars.

"Okay." Taylor took a few steps forward to stand next to Kai, and didn't let go of his hand. "This is beautiful," she whispered, because suddenly the world felt a little...holy.

It was really no different than any other part of Cocoa Beach, but so far from the tourists, surfers, and pier that it was empty and private. Too private.

"Are we trespassing on someone's property?"

He shook his head, the breeze fluttering his long hair. "Nope. There are no private beaches in Florida, technically. How is it that I know more about your home state than you do?" he teased.

Taylor laughed, leaning into him and feeling his warmth and weight against her. "Good question, but you still didn't explain why we're here."

"It's June," he said with a wide and almost giddy smile.

"Yes, it is," Taylor drew the words out. "How is that relevant again?"

"Oh my goodness." He threw his head back and gave a fake groan of frustration. "Taylor Parker, you're a Florida girl, born and raised, and you don't know about the beach at night in June?"

She just laughed at his adorable animation and shrugged her shoulders. "Sorry. I didn't grow up in Cocoa Beach, if this is some local inside thing. I'm a central Florida suburban girl."

"Right. Well, you're beachside now. And that means..." he tightened his grip on her hand as he walked them out a few feet in the sand.

It was cool underneath her toes, and the darkness and silent calm of the ocean made this feel like some sort of hazy, beautiful dream.

"Look."

Taylor looked up to find Kai pointing at a sign stuck right into the sand. She stepped closer, squinting into the waning light to read the words.

"*WILDLIFE WARNING: Do not go past this point between the hours of 6PM and 6AM so as not to harm, disturb, or interfere with sea turtle nesting and hatching. Please avoid using bright flashlights or photography and limit beach activity.*"

"Sea turtles..." Taylor whispered to herself, laughing as she realized why Kai had brought her here.

"We have to stay right here, and it has to be super

dark." He sat right down in the sand and patted the spot next to him. "But it's early hatching season, which means we'll see them."

Taylor gasped a little. "The babies?"

"The babies," he replied. "They have to make a pretty treacherous journey out to the ocean after they hatch, so the wildlife commission does everything they can to make it safe. That's why we can't get any closer, and there's no one out here. The buildings have to limit their light output at night and everything."

Taylor slowly sat down in the sand next to him, tucking her legs underneath her and inching closer to Kai. "Wow. This is incredible. How did you know?"

"I used to look forward to this all year as a kid. Sea turtles migrate their way through all the Hawaiian islands, and the hatching season was the coolest. My uncle and I would come out at night after surfing all day and watch the babies wake up and make their way out to the water. We even saved a turtle one time, who probably wouldn't have made it otherwise. She was stuck in the branches of some driftwood, but we set her free."

"Oh my gosh, my heart." Taylor held a hand to her chest, wondering how on Earth he could possibly be more perfect.

There was no way he was real. Gorgeous, kind, talented, smart, hilarious and wonderful in every way. He saved a baby sea turtle, for crying out loud. Where was the flaw?

Well, aside from the fact that he was a man, and Taylor knew very well what even the most admirable men were capable of. Not to mention his inevitable departure back to Hawaii.

Yeah. Those two facts were not to be ignored.

But still, she was here with him now, and this whole summer in Cocoa Beach had started to feel like some kind of extended fantasy. Like a beautiful, blissful dream where she was far away from everything that hurt and upset and broke her, living on an island of peace and comfort with a dream-worthy man in her arms.

But that's the thing about dreams. Sooner or later, you're going to wake up.

"This was always so special to me." Kai turned to her, the moonlight reflecting on his angular features and strong profile. "I wanted to show you."

Taylor smiled and dragged her gaze from him to the ocean, which was vast and dark and dancing with little glimmers of reflected light.

"Why me?" she asked.

"Because you're...special to me, too."

Taylor swallowed, wondering how the words could make her so happy and yet so incredibly sad at the same time.

He was everything she never knew she wanted, but she wouldn't let herself fall. Not harder than a crush. Not deeper than a fun summer fling.

She almost wished he hadn't said that. She almost wished he'd reject her and just make the whole process easier.

"What's wrong, Tay?"

"I just..." She shook her head, forcing a laugh as a breeze blew her hair back. "Nothing."

"Hey." He placed his hand on her leg, which was certainly not helping her attempt to stop having real feelings for him. "It's all good, yeah? Just relax. Enjoy it."

She knew very well that the "it" he was talking about was the undeniable, inexplicable attraction and connection between them. It was as present as the sound of the waves crashing or the distant flutter of leaves in the breeze.

It was getting bigger and stronger and more intense with every passing second Taylor and Kai spent together, and frankly, it scared her and thrilled her all at the same time.

"Oh, I'm enjoying it, all right."

"Good." Kai reached over, touching her face gently and stroking his thumb along her cheek. "Because I am, too."

In a split second, the world melted away for Taylor as Kai kissed her, making her heart fold and sing and float away.

The Earth stopped turning with that kiss, deepening Taylor's dreaming sensation and silencing all of the voices of hesitation and reason and logic in her head.

They laughed together, smiling as their noses touched and the thrill of falling in love engulfed them both.

"Tay, look!" Kai stood up suddenly, pointing out toward the beach, his voice hushed.

"What?" She got up to join him, still a bit dizzy and

rattled from the kiss, squinting her eyes to see in the moonlight on the dark beach.

She gasped as she saw what he was pointing at—three tiny, adorable, impossibly gorgeous baby sea turtles scurrying through the sand, their little flippers fluttering wildly as they headed toward the water.

"Oh my gosh!" Taylor shrieked.

"Shhh." Kai held his finger up to his lips. "You've got to be quiet."

"Oh," Taylor whispered, giggling. "Sorry."

"They're very sensitive, the babies. They get disturbed so easily." He guided her a few feet to get a better view. "Here, come this way."

In awe, Taylor watched the scene unfold in front of her, completely riveted. It looked like something she'd seen once on *Planet Earth* or another nature documentary. A beautiful phenomenon that didn't even seem real.

Everywhere she looked, another tiny, delicate baby sea turtle scrambled out of its buried nest and hustled toward the shoreline.

She leaned close to Kai's ear. "It's amazing," she said under her breath, her eyes following one particular turtle who hopped and flipped and clumsily, but successfully made its way to the ocean.

Thank goodness.

Kai wrapped his arm around her shoulders as they watched, laughing and smiling, mesmerized by nature's magnificence.

"They're going to start their lives," Kai said softly,

pulling Taylor close enough that she could smell his woodsy cologne. "And you know the craziest part?"

"What?"

"Once these little females are all grown up, when it comes time for them to lay eggs, they will come right back here."

Taylor gasped, looking up at him. "Seriously? To Cocoa Beach?"

"To this exact spot." Kai pointed at the sand beneath their feet. "The mothers will come and make their nest on the same beach where they hatched and entered the ocean for the first time, and then their babies will do the same. And so on and so on."

Chills rose on her arms despite the warm night. "Generation after generation...coming back here. Coming home." She inhaled a deep breath of sea-tinged air, gazing wistfully out at the horizon as it disappeared into the blackness of night. "It's poetic."

"Mmm." Kai held her tightly against him. "My dad used to say that I was like one of the sea turtles. I would swim far, far away, be miles from my family and endlessly distant from my home. But then a certain day would come, and I would know it was time to return. Like the sea turtles. One day, they just know it's time to go home to the beach where they took their first steps. Where they belong."

Taylor could feel her heart sinking as he spoke. "Is that...what you want? To go home to Hawaii?"

"Like I said..." He looked down at her, his dark eyes twinkling with moonlight. "I don't really have a choice.

My dad thinks one day I'll just wake up and feel called to come back to Hawaii and stay forever, like the turtles. But I don't have that feeling yet, that's for sure."

"But you think..." She twisted her toes deeper in the sand. "You think you eventually might have that feeling?"

"No choice, remember?" He gave a dry laugh, then gestured for her to walk back toward the dunes with him.

Taylor just kept her gaze fixed on the sand, her head a swimming mess of confusing and conflicting emotions.

Kai sat down on the sand in front of the dunes and pulled his phone out of his back pocket. "Here, I'll show you."

Taylor crouched down and sat next to him, leaning over to see his phone screen.

"That's the farm," Kai said, swiping through a couple of photos.

"Oh, wow."

The photos showed vast fields of tall, green stalks of sugar cane, with breathtaking mountain views as a backdrop. The colors were rich and vibrant, the rolling landscape foreign and exotic to someone born and raised in flat, flat Florida. The farm looked way bigger than Taylor had pictured, giving her a chance to understand the depth of the family history and tradition that must be embedded in a place like that.

"Here are my parents." Kai swiped the screen to show another picture, of an older Hawaiian couple standing in front of a three-story wooden farmhouse with a decorative railing around the porch.

"Aww, they are beautiful." Taylor inched closer,

looking at the slender woman with long, braided hair next to the tall, stern-looking man who Kai greatly resembled. "And that house is stunning."

"Our family home. And my parents? They're great." He clicked the phone off and put it away in his pocket. "They're wonderful people. They just don't quite understand me, I guess."

Taylor nodded, hugging her knees to her chest as she looked out over the ocean, wondering how far the little baby sea turtles had made it on their journey so far.

"It doesn't look like a bad life," she mused. "Nice house, good farm, great family."

"Oh, it's not bad at all," Kai said quickly. "And I don't mean to sound ungrateful. I've just...always wanted something different than the cane farmer's life. They see surfing as a hobby. A phase, even."

"A hobby?" Taylor laughed. "You're literally a professional."

"My parents don't really look at it that way," he said, looking straight ahead. "They're proud, but someone has to take on the family business, run it, and grow it, and hand it over to the next generation of Leilanis. And that someone is me."

The certainty of that reminder made Taylor's heart ache a little. He was leaving. In a matter of a couple of months, Kai would be thousands of miles away. And even if he continued surfing for a few more years, that's where his life would be...six thousand miles away in Hawaii.

Despite how wonderful he was, she knew better than to get attached.

# Chapter Twenty

## *Erica*

"If you'll just sign here..." Abigail Banks, a soft-spoken adoption coordinator at Space Coast Family Connections, pointed at the bottom of a form with a highlighted line.

"Of course." Erica squeezed Will's hand under the desk before scribbling her signature on the line and taking a deep breath.

The agency had been booked out a few months, but somehow Will's refusal to take no for an answer, which he wrapped in persuasive charm, had gotten them squeezed in with an agent this week.

Once her signature was on the paper, Erica leaned back and took a moment to look at her surroundings, a bright, busy office humming with purpose. Will had chosen a top-notch agency that was clearly a well-oiled machine, giving her real confidence that these people could make her dreams come true.

She looked over at her husband, who gave her a barely noticeable wink, making her heart feel even lighter.

This wasn't the path she had imagined, but it was her path now. The right path. The path that was meant to be.

She had complete peace with the idea now, certain that being an adoptive parent was her destiny, as right and real as engineering.

She could already picture a tiny little nose, sweet, fluttering eyelashes, rosy pink cheeks...her heart kicked up just thinking about it.

"Now..." Abigail smiled from across the desk, looking back and forth between Erica and Will. "Because you are adopting, you do get to put in some preferences about the child that you'll eventually end up with."

"Preferences?" Will asked with a dry chuckle. "We're not buying a Mercedes, we're adopting a child. We'll take whatever baby is in need of a loving home, and give them just that."

Abigail held a hand to her chest and gave Will an adoring grin. "You have no idea how much joy it brings me to hear potential adoptive parents with that attitude."

"We're very open," Erica added, inching forward on the edge of her seat. "We really want a baby, Abigail."

"And we really want to find you one." She skimmed her big computer screen, narrowing her gaze as her eyes slid over the words. "Okay, so absolutely no preferences on gender, background, ethnicity, birthplace, biological parents..." Her voice trailed off. "None of that?"

Erica shrugged and looked to Will for backup. Was any of that important? The gender, the race, the background? No, she would love her child however that baby was made and delivered.

"Should we consider any of that stuff?" she asked Will. "I suppose we could think about—"

"Of course not," Will replied quickly, turning back to face Abigail. "We want to be parents, Abigail. We are completely open."

Erica sucked in a breath, trusting fate to bring her the right baby. Her baby. The baby meant to call her Mommy.

"We are open," Erica agreed with a nod, tightening her grip on Will's hand. "To anything."

"Wonderful."

"Does that increase our chances of getting a child sooner rather than later?" Erica asked eagerly.

"It can." Abigail tapped a few more computer keys, then turned back to face Erica. "I can't make any promises right now, but you are certainly setting your-selves up for a faster adoption. But fast is a relative term in this world."

"I know it's a long journey," Erica said on a sigh.

"It can be. However..." Abigail scrolled through something on her computer screen, pushing a pair of thin-rimmed glasses up onto the bridge of her nose. "Are you open to an immediate adoption, in the case that a child would become in need of a home due to sudden unforeseen circumstances?"

"Immediate?" Erica asked. "Like...this week?"

"It could happen any time," Abigail said. "And you'd need to be able to take that child into your home."

"Yes," Will blurted out, looking at her for agreement. "Of course we are. Right?"

"Yes, we are," Erica added with a nod, clearing her throat.

She knew she couldn't wait for "the perfect moment." They'd just adapt and adjust, and work would have to accept that she'd need a maternity leave. She couldn't fit an adoption into her launch schedule, for crying out loud.

Nerves and anticipation swirled through her, but she held Will's hand tightly, which brought comfort and stability to every situation, and took some deep breaths.

Abigail reached behind her chair to grab something off the top of the printer. "Okay, I'll need you both to sign this form stating that you will be willing to take in, care for, provide for, and love this child as your own in the case of an immediate adoption."

"Okay." Will clicked his pen and signed the bottom, then slid the page over to Erica.

She took the pen and signed it as well, her hand shaking a little.

"And in the situation where an adoption is sudden and immediate—we call them foster-care adoptions—you would have six months before you finalize it. But you would have to take the baby immediately."

"We wouldn't change our minds," Will said with certainty, squeezing Erica's hand. "Once a baby is ours, it's ours forever."

"Absolutely," Erica said. She certainly wasn't going to *return* it for one that fit better.

"Well..." Abigail stacked some papers and slid them into a blue folder with the agency logo on the front. "I fully believe that, and appreciate it. All I'm saying is...you wouldn't be the first."

Will and Erica shared a sideways glance, wondering

what kind of people would give a baby back after they adopted it. She supposed anything was possible, and it wasn't her place to judge.

The words didn't scare her, though, because Erica was so sure that whatever sweet little baby they were given was going to be the absolute light of her life, no matter where it came from.

"Okay." Abigail handed Erica the folder full of paperwork. "You have my card. Call me if anything changes. We'll be setting up a home visit in the next couple of weeks to assess your fitness as adoptive parents, but you've passed the preliminary interviews and background checks. This is just standard protocol."

"We know," Will said on a soft laugh. "That's okay. Our door is always open."

Erica nodded in agreement. "Whatever needs to be done. We just want our baby."

Abigail smiled at both of them before standing up and holding out her hand. "Wonderful meeting you both, seriously. Keep your phones on you, and we will be in touch."

Erica shook her hand. "Thank you for everything."

"We really appreciate it." Will reached out to shake her hand as well. "We'll be holding our breath."

Abigail gave him a look. "I wouldn't. It could be years."

Erica shut her eyes, disappointment and worry curling through her chest at that possibility. "Please don't say that."

"I'm optimistic for you guys," Abigail added, walking

them over to the entrance of her office and holding open the door for them. "I just can't make any promises, and I do want you to keep your expectations on timeline relatively realistic."

"We understand." Will gave a friendly wave and flashed a smile.

"Thank you again, Abigail," Erica said over her shoulder as they headed out.

"We'll be in touch," Abigail called after them.

"God, I hope so," Erica whispered to Will as they headed out through the lobby of the adoption office.

The afternoon sun beamed down on the parking lot, and they walked to their separate cars because, of course, Erica had to go back to work. Not that she could focus on anything right now, but the Eagle project was definitely a good distraction.

She hoped that the math and science and physics would keep her mind occupied for most of the day and stop it from wandering off to Babyland, although that seemed like an impossible expectation.

"Come here." Will wrapped his arms around her and kissed the top of her head. "How are you feeling?"

"I just want our baby now," she said, her words muffled against his chest. "I just want to fast forward. I hate the waiting. I hate not knowing."

Will sighed. "You and me both, babe. But it's going to be worth all of the waiting and trouble and pain in the world. And one day, when our kid is old enough to understand, we're going to get to tell them the story of how badly we wanted to be their parents. And what we went through to have them. And that kid is going to know truly how wanted and loved they are."

Erica's heart squeezed with love, and she held on to her husband for one more extra second before pulling away. "You're so right."

"Don't worry." He took her chin in his hand and tilted her head up to meet his gaze. "Our baby is coming."

"Our baby is coming," Erica repeated, her voice barely above a whisper.

"And you..." He kissed her lightly. "Need to get back to building rockets. And I need to get back to remodeling bathrooms."

"Wanna trade?" she teased, digging her keys out of her purse.

"Not for a billion dollars." He smiled at her, shielding his eyes from the sun as they walked to their cars. "Love you, honey."

"Love you more," Erica called back with a wave before sliding into the driver's seat of her Range Rover and letting out a long, shaky breath.

A wave of excitement and anticipation rolled over her as she held the soft leather-covered steering wheel in her hands.

Erica had found herself in a position she truly thought she'd never be in, and that in and of itself was strange and foreign to her. From the time she was eleven, she wanted to build rockets. She'd watched the launches from the beach outside the cottage growing up, and was completely obsessed.

She'd turned to Dottie once and said, "Mom. I'm going to make one of those."

And she was right. She'd pictured herself as an engineering student at MIT. She'd pictured herself getting a job with NASA right out of college. She'd pictured herself in a wonderful and happy marriage with an amazing guy like Will Armstrong.

She'd even pictured the exact white Range Rover she was sitting in, which had been her teenage dream car.

She'd envisioned every detail of her life, and everything had always gone according to plan.

Until now. This was Erica's first dive into a vast unknown.

She tried so hard to envision this.

Who would her baby be? Would she have a boy or a girl? Would he grow up and play sports? Would she like to dance? Would Erica and Will be at the hospital for the baby's birth? Would Erica hug the birth mother and thank her?

As Erica wondered about all the unanswered questions surrounding her future child, she only knew one thing for sure.

She couldn't wait to hold her baby.

# Chapter Twenty-one

## *Dottie*

It was just after five o'clock in the morning, and Dottie was wide awake. Ever since she'd had the idea of possibly renovating and keeping Sweeney House instead of selling, she could hardly think about anything else.

Yes, it would be a massive expense, but couldn't she get a loan against the value of the property? Was it the right thing to do, or a crazy idea that would put her in debt and bury her in stress and problems?

She just didn't know.

Jay would know. When they faced a big decision like this, she'd wake up in the middle of the night and could tell that he wasn't asleep from his breathing.

He'd roll over and say, "I've been thinking, Dot."

And he would have made the right decision, and she would trust him.

But he wasn't here to roll over and whisper his thoughts, so she had to make that decision without him. The more she thought about it, the more she wanted to take the leap. If it didn't work out, she could sell anyway, right?

"Oh, Jay! What should I do?"

The only answer in her heart was...more ideas. How

to make this suite gorgeous, for one. Refinishing the hardwood floors, maybe repurposing the antiques. Did they have room for an actual kitchen on the first floor? Maybe it was time for that, since all the competition had one.

Oh, and paint. Beautiful coastal colors everywhere, and some new windows to replace the beat-up ones that had been through so many storms over the years.

But...what would Jay say? Her heart thudded as she wondered if he'd respond with a resounding, "Are you out of your mind? What would you change?"

And she'd understand that. Every single detail in all ten rooms had been hand-selected by him, and the thought of getting rid of so many of his personal touches and sentimental pieces still felt sort of wrong to her.

And then, of course, there was the offer. Maybe he'd say she was out of her mind to say no to that kind of money, which would give Dottie an entirely new future and life.

Not that she wanted a new life, not like Sam did. She wanted her old life, with her old husband, and her old chair, and old paint.

Fact was, she didn't know what she wanted, except for Jay to help her figure it out. Just one more conversation, she thought wistfully as she started to rise for the day. One more day, one more decision together.

The longing was strong enough to make her fall back against the pillows and ache.

What would Jay want for her? Well, he'd want her to be happy, more than anything. He certainly wouldn't want her to be so racked with grief and guilt and confusion.

And while the thought of a potential inn renovation certainly made Dottie a little giddy with the excitement and the possibilities, she felt like getting rid of the original designs and decoration of Sweeney House was like erasing Jay. And turning down that money might be irresponsible, if not downright dumb.

With a moan of frustration, she slid out of bed and pulled on her soft blue robe, tightening the ties with a powerful yank. She folded her arms over her chest and stepped into her slippers, walking over to the sliding door of her suite that led out to a large second-floor balcony.

There, she drew the curtains, staring out at the pitch-black water and the reflection of the moon dancing on its surface.

Dottie opened the slider and walked out onto the balcony, leaning against the railing to watch the first whisper of morning hit the horizon.

The way Dottie saw it, she had three options.

She could sell Sweeney House and the cottage to Bartram Properties, make a small fortune, and start over somewhere new. Financially wise, emotionally...challenging.

Or she could do nothing. Turn down the money, keep the inn the way Jay made it to be, make her kids happy by not selling their childhood home, and plod through life without her partner.

Finally, she could bring this property up to date and it would be worth even more. A ton of work, a big investment, and the risk of changing Sweeney House into something that wasn't...Jay's vision. Would renovation dishonor his memory by turning Sweeney House into something he wasn't a part of? It was a silly consideration, she supposed, but very real in her heart.

"Jay..." She whispered, pressing her palms onto the metal railing, her whole body aching for his presence, his voice, his company.

How could the hole in her heart still be this big? Would she ever stop missing him? Constantly, deeply, endlessly...mourning.

A strong breeze blew in, swirling warm ocean air around Dottie's face, lifting her hair up and blowing it around.

She leaned forward against the rail of the balcony, sucking in the salty air.

"Send me a sign, Jay. Please?" she whispered, emotion tightening her throat. "Just tell me what I should do. If I sell it, I can start a new life. But that means the end of Sweeney House."

She waited, quiet, as if he'd actually answer. The only thing she heard was the soft splash of the waves in the distance.

"If I update it and redesign it," she continued, "I can turn over a new leaf right here at the inn, but it means erasing so much of your touch and influence. Would that erase you?"

No answer, but she closed her eyes and inhaled again.

"Yes, I could keep it as it is, and continue my days

missing you, needing you, but honoring you by preserving your memory in every corner of this place. But that means choking on my grief every day and getting swallowed up by the past. Honestly, that's the least favorite of my options, although it is by far the easiest way out."

She squeezed her eyes tight, still wishing he'd say something.

"I need your blessing, Jay, because...I think I want to renovate."

Dottie could still see his face, those big dimples on either side of his wide, magnetic smile. His eyes would crinkle when he laughed, and sparkle when he said he loved her, which he did every single day many, many times.

"Give me a sign," she begged on a whisper. "Tell me if that's the right thing to do."

Ten seconds ticked by. Then thirty. Then a full minute.

She stared at the sky, hoping for a shooting star. She'd know for sure that was Jay giving her his blessing and his approval. Or maybe the haunting coo of a mourning dove, a sound Jay loved to imitate. A light on the horizon? A few drops of rain? *Anything, Jay. Anything.*

But the only change was the sky that slowly grew pink and orange with the glow of a glorious East Coast sunrise.

Jay was silent.

Dottie shut her eyes, feeling a tear slide down her cheek. This new idea had taken full form in her head and in her heart, but she wasn't ready to do it if she felt like it didn't honor him.

Not to mention she didn't exactly have the funds for a major, ten-bedroom inn renovation just laying around. But that wasn't really her main concern. If it was meant to be, Jay would make sure everything lined up.

She knew that. If it was right, the money would come. The answers would be clear. But without Jay, how could she know it was right? How could she know anything?

With no signs from heaven, Dottie headed back into her suite and shut the sliding glass door, deciding it was time for coffee. She toyed with the idea of talking to Sam about all of this, since their relationship had recently started to become closer than ever.

But Sam had all of her own struggles going on. Plus, she wasn't ready to admit that she'd been keeping such a whopping secret from her daughter this entire time. John was up to his eyeballs with work and three active kids, and Erica was putting a rover on Mars.

And Julie? Well, Dottie didn't even know what part of the country she was in right now, and that thought broke her heart in an entirely different way.

She'd have to make this decision on her own, that much was clear. Jay wasn't going to whisper his blessing like some kind of ghost in the morning light.

"Because he's gone," she said to herself, repeating the truth she'd spent the last year trying so hard to accept. "Gone. And I'm alone."

Dottie pulled on a comfy cotton dress and fixed her

hair a bit before heading down the elevator to go over to the cottage and get some coffee, since her coffee maker was still broken, like so many other things in Sweeney House.

*Facelift* might have been an understatement. The place needed an overhaul.

Dottie walked into the lobby of the inn, past the old clock, and through the front doorway, stepping out into the morning sunshine that bathed the shell-covered parking lot.

It was quiet and still at this hour, hardly a car on the road, the sunrise painting the sky in pastels and the birds just starting to sing their morning tunes.

Dottie walked through the parking lot slowly, over the path cloaked in sea grapes, palm trees, and hibiscus bushes.

In the break in the shrubbery, she could see A1A, the main beachside road that ran all up and down the east coast of Florida, and was the quickest way to just about anything in Cocoa Beach.

She stood there for a moment, watching a few cars rumble by, early birds headed to work. Shaking her head, she let out a sigh, taking one last look through the trees out at the main road. For some reason, she didn't move. She just stared like she was...waiting.

Still waiting for the answer that wasn't—

She blinked as a vehicle approached and seemed to slow. No, not a vehicle. That was a yellow pickup truck. Vintage. Classic. In fact, it looked exactly like Jay's 1965 Chevy short-bed.

How was that possible? Jay's beloved and precious Chevy that he hung on to for years and years after they stopped making parts for it.

And then it was gone, whizzing down A1A like...its mission had been accomplished.

Dottie held her hand to her chest and blinked back the tears.

"Jay!" Dottie exclaimed, rushing to the end of the parking lot to crane her neck through the sea grapes and get one last look at the classic truck as it stopped at the light. The grill was the same. The back lights. And that color, canary yellow designed to turn heads and get attention.

As the light changed, she blew it a kiss, tears rolling down her cheeks.

"Thank you, my dear, dear husband," she whispered.

Finally, Dottie knew what she wanted to do. She wasn't sure how, but refused to worry about that.

For the first time since he died, she felt the glorious glow of peace in her heart. She had Jay's blessing, and she was ready to move on to the next chapter of her life.

# Chapter Twenty-two

## *Sam*

"So, the cost per click is different from the advertising cost of sale?" Sam shook her head as she sat in the passenger seat of John's car, enjoying yet another ride home from her brother-boss.

She decided to make good use of the short commute to pick his brain for answers to her mountains of questions regarding the advertising and marketing world, knowing her own brother couldn't judge her no matter how rudimentary those questions may have been.

Well, he *could* judge her. She just didn't care, because it was John.

"Sort of," he answered. "The cost per click—CPC, it's usually called—is the actual amount of money that it costs for one click, on average, of a particular ad. The ACOS—advertising cost of sale—is a percentage that's used to represent the success of an entire ad campaign as a whole. Based on how much it costs for customer acquisition per purchase."

Sam rubbed her temples, knowing how helpful it would be at the office to at least have a basic understanding of what people were talking about when they used this kind of terminology. But, dang, it was foreign to her.

"Okay, right. Gotcha. I'm just trying to get a grasp on some of this."

"Sam." John turned to her as the car rolled to a stop at a red light, giving her his signature older brother look. "Stop stressing. You're doing fine. It's only your second week working at the agency."

"It's my second week working. Period. Ever." She snorted.

"Exactly. So cut yourself some slack." He turned the car onto the uneven gravel road that led to Sweeney House and the cottage.

Sam leaned against the passenger door, thinking about the concept of giving herself some slack. She felt like she'd been giving herself quite a bit of slack lately and wondered if it was maybe time to toughen up a bit.

The world had been seeming brighter these days, and her heartbreak was less of a bleeding wound and starting to become a scar. A very slow-healing, tender, sort of ugly scar. But scars, however ugly they may be, showed strength.

And for once in her life, Sam felt like maybe she could have some of that.

She'd been strong, as a mother and as a wife. She's always showed up for her kids every second of every day, and would never stop fighting for them. She was strong in that regard, and she was proud of the people she'd raised. But her strength was built around her love for her children and her selflessness as a mother.

Now, she was starting to find her own inner strength, the kind that didn't come from anyone or anything but herself.

"Thanks for the ride. Again." She nudged John's arm.

"You know I got you." He unbuckled his seatbelt after parking the car in front of Sweeney House. "I'm gonna run inside for a second, actually. Mom said there were some boxes of Dad's stuff in the storage room at the inn she wanted me to have."

"Oh, Dad's stuff. I'm intrigued. There's got to be some old gems in there, no matter what it is," Sam said, pushing open the passenger-side door and stepping out of the car. "I'll join you. I hope Mom's pawning that horrific old grandfather clock onto you, because I really don't want to deal with it."

John laughed. "I don't think she's ever going to part with that thing, thankfully."

Sam walked into Sweeney House side by side with her brother, the warm afternoon sun baking down into her skin.

"Hey, Jeanine," John said to the woman who'd been working at the front desk of the inn for many years.

"John, Sam." Jeanine smiled. "How are you guys?"

"We're good. Hanging in there." Sam walked over to the counter where Jeanine sat.

John nodded at the woman. "I'm supposed to pick up some things of my father's. Do you know where I might find that? I know my mom had to run out to a doctor's appointment, but she said she'd leave them for me."

"Oh, yes." Jeanine stood up. "I believe she marked them in the back storage room. Hang on. Let me go check on that and I'll come back and let you know."

John gave her a thumbs up. "Sounds good."

"Thanks, Jeanine." Sam waved.

Suddenly, the big glass front door of the lobby flew open, and a determined, sharp-looking woman in a pantsuit who Sam didn't recognize came marching in.

"Is Dottie here?" she demanded without bothering to introduce herself to Sam or John.

"Uh, not at the moment," Sam said, glancing at John to see if he showed any signs of recognizing the woman. Sam had certainly never seen her before. She'd remember the sharp business suit and expensive chunky jewelry.

Maybe an event coordinator looking at the place? Or a mother of the bride planning a wedding and looking for a room block?

"She's out right now," Sam said. "But I'm going to see her in a minute. Can I give her a message?"

The woman inhaled so deeply her nostrils flared. "Yes, I think you better, because time is of the essence. My name is Karen, please tell her that I stopped by, and I have to talk to her about the Bartram offer. They need an answer or they are simply going to withdraw the offer to buy this property."

Sam blinked, and next to her, she heard John hiss a breath.

"The...did you say buy this property?" Sam repeated, certain she hadn't understood.

"Yes." Karen lifted a brow. "That's generally what we real estate agents do."

"Bartram?" John frowned. "Bartram *Properties*?"

Impatience straightened the woman's back as she shot him a look. "That's correct."

John actually chuckled. "I think you might be in the wrong place. This is a family-run inn. There's a Marriott down the road that might be what you want. Sweeney House isn't for sale."

Her eyes narrowed as she looked from one to the other. "I better deal with my client, Dorothy, and not her employees. She's the seller."

"*Seller?*" Sam choked.

Karen grimaced and swore softly under her breath. "I think I've..." She closed her eyes. "You must be the kids she talks about so much."

Sam looked up at John, who was as pale as she imagined she was right then. "She's...*selling?*" she breathed the question.

"Not in a million years," he said.

Karen gave a dry laugh. "Well, it does feel like it's taking that long for her to make a decision on this offer that I've had on the table for weeks."

*Weeks?* And Mom didn't tell her? Sam almost whimpered. None of this could be true. Could it? It had to be a mistake or a misunderstanding. Maybe there was an offer, but her mother couldn't seriously entertain it.

Could she?

John inched closer to Karen, who was visibly

annoyed. "Are you sure that this is all correct?" he asked, an edge in his demand.

"Yes, I'm sure and perhaps if you see the offer, you can talk some common sense into your mother. Who is very sweet, but good heavens, the woman can't make a decision to save her life."

Irritation tweaked at Sam, who watched in silence while Karen whipped an iPad out of her shoulder bag, flicking at the screen with long acrylic nails. She turned it around for them with a smug look.

"Listing is here. With the price. And the offer is well above that."

Sam and John stood frozen in complete astonishment as they stared at a full market commercial listing for the Sweeney House Inn and Cottage.

How could their mother do this? Without telling a soul? There was no way. It was not like her. Dottie was honest and open and... Sam had trusted her.

"Did..." She looked at John, whose eyes were glued to the screen of the tablet as if he, too, was working hard to comprehend the reality of what they were looking at.

"She's not selling it," Sam said to John, then turned back to the uptight woman who had come in here with the sole purpose of ruining everyone's day. "She's not selling it," Sam repeated, this time to Karen.

As if the more she said it, the more it became fact.

"Um..." Karen lifted beautifully drawn-in brows, then scrolled to the very bottom of the iPad screen and tapped one coffin-shaped red nail at the signature on the dotted line at the bottom of the listing contract.

*Dorothy Sweeney.*

"Yes, she is," Karen added. "Now, can you please tell her I stopped by, and that the offer from Bartram is going to disappear if she doesn't act now. And I mean *now*."

Sam felt like the ground below her was suddenly shifting and tilting, and she grabbed onto the counter in front of the desk for stability.

It was so unlike Mom to do something like this. Sweeney House was everything to them, it was their livelihood and the cottage was their home. They worshipped this place.

Mom lived to preserve and honor Dad's memory. It was all she'd talked about since he died. How on Earth could she even be considering *selling* the inn?

And to a major corporate hotel chain? Bartram? It just simply couldn't be. It made no sense.

Karen, the wicked witch of luxury real estate, whipped around and headed out the door, like some sort of fleeting spirit that brought horribly confusing and terrifying news.

Sam and John stood side by side in silence for a few seconds, both completely frozen with shock.

"Was that real?" Sam looked up at her older brother, whose expression was puzzled and concerned. "Is Mom seriously selling the inn and the cottage? It's not possible. I mean, she would never..."

"I don't know." John ran a hand over his face and let out a noisy, distressed sigh. "She didn't tell a soul. I'm sure if Erica knew about this, she'd have told us."

"Erica's got her own stuff going on," Sam said softly.

John furrowed his brow. "Huh? What stuff?"

Erica hadn't confided in any other family member about her infertility news or struggle to become a mom, and that wasn't Sam's secret to share.

"Nothing, never mind." Sam waved a hand. "We've got to talk to Mom and see what the heck is happening."

"It's pretty clear what's going on," John said with an edge in his voice. "She's selling the place to Bartram Properties."

Sam paced a little back and forth around the front desk, running a hand through her hair as she tried to make some sort of sense of this. "I'm calling her."

"Sam, wait." John held up a hand. "We should talk to her about it when she gets home from her appointment. I'll stay here with you, and we can have this chat with Mom together."

She puffed out a sigh and nodded. "You're right, you're right. I mean, maybe it is just a misunderstanding or...something."

"That listing was no misunderstanding."

Sam made a face, unable to argue that. "Bartram is huge. Would they tear it down?" Even as she said the words, they hurt. The very thought was just too awful for words.

John clenched his jaw, clearly trying to keep his composure. "Yeah. Probably. I don't know. I just..."

Sam walked over to him and placed her hand on his back.

"I am so mad at Mom," he admitted, accentuating the

exclamation with a dry laugh, as if he could hardly believe the words he just said.

Sam imagined it had been a long, long time since there was so much as a whisper of conflict between Mom and Perfect John. But he was truly upset, and so was Sam.

"I just hate that she didn't tell us." Sam threw her hands in the air as the two of them walked over to the little sitting area in the corner of the lobby. "If she had just been honest...the hiding it is what's so weird and awful."

"Exactly. I know." John sat down, anxiously running his palms along his thighs, shaking his head with frustration. "I would sort of understand if Mom had some kind of revelation or whatever and wanted to downsize and go somewhere else. I would get that. But to keep it a secret? To basically lie to us about it?"

Sam flopped down on the sofa, emotion rolling over her in waves. "It's so not like her to hide something like that. To keep anything from the family."

"You know, she hasn't been the same since Dad died," John said, his voice barely above a whisper. "She can hardly function without him. She used to be so strong and self-assured."

"That's not fair," Sam insisted, surprising herself as she quickly came to her mother's defense. "She can function."

"Lying to us? Selling Sweeney House out from under the whole family?" John ran a hand through his hair. "I mean, what if one of us wanted to take over the business?

I mean, hell, you and your kids are literally *living* at the cottage."

Sam groaned. "Why wouldn't she tell me when I got here?"

"She should have..." He shook his head. "She should have told you. She should have told all of us. In fact..." He pulled out his phone. "I'm going to call Erica and see if she can come over here after work. We need to all be together and figure this out as a family. I wish Julie were here. Not that she cares too much about the inn, but still."

Sam pressed her lips together, her mind flashing back to the conversation she'd had with Dottie on the porch of the cottage the other day.

They'd connected. They'd been so raw and candid and open with each other. They'd almost reconciled over all the problems of the past, or at least that's what it felt like to Sam.

How could Mom not have mentioned this? How could she have looked Sam in the eyes and held her hand and been so real and loving and open with her and kept such a massive and life-altering secret?

The listing of Sweeney House on that iPad was burned into Sam's brain, and she didn't understand how her mom could be so secretive about something so monumental.

As Sam sat there, a familiar hurt threaded up her chest and left a metallic taste in her mouth.

Betrayal.

Was there anything worse? First, her husband; now, her mother?

Biting back tears, she pushed up and walked out to the deck, facing the ocean, waiting for the breeze to wipe away the pain. But all it blew away was that fragile new relationship she'd forged with her mother and Sam felt completely alone again.

# Chapter Twenty-three

## *Taylor*

Taylor had spent most of the afternoon driving around, sipping iced coffee, and thinking about the endless vortex of possibilities for where her life could lead her.

She and her family had been in Cocoa Beach for just about a month. and she had started to look at her life with a new sense of optimism.

Only several short weeks ago, she'd been pouring beer and mixing rum and Cokes for whatever obnoxious group of men stumbled into O'Leary's and made sideways comments to her. She'd been apologizing to her manager for not being insanely friendly to every guest at the bar, even the creepy ones. She was getting home at 3 a.m., showering the stickiness of beer off of her, snuggling with Mr. Minx, and feeling, well, kind of hopeless.

She'd always coped with humor and sarcasm, laughing at herself for ditching med school to serve drinks. Making jokes out of her seemingly pathetic existence. But she had absolutely no regrets about dropping out of school. She knew medicine wasn't her path. Problem was, she had no clue what her path actually would be.

But on this island, in the sunshine, next to the ocean, surrounded by loving family and laughter and hope, Taylor had started to feel like she could find something.

She didn't know what, but she knew that she could find it.

And even though she hadn't found a career path or a purpose or a passion just yet...she'd found Kai.

She'd found someone who made her feel like she *wanted* to trust him. She wanted to give in, and let herself feel something. Something real. Something close.

She hadn't had that desire really, well, ever. And everything that Kai made her feel was new and exciting and liberating.

Terrifying, of course, at the same time. But for the first time in Taylor's twenty-four years, she was starting to think maybe the risk was worth the reward.

She walked down the tropical backstreet that led straight to Sharky's Sea Shack, where Kai had asked her in a text to meet him tonight for dinner.

The invitation delighted her, because he usually spent all afternoon and evening working with his trainer out on the water or preparing for the contest. A dinner date was a rare and exciting thing, worthy of the white and pink sundress she'd picked out, paired with little white sneakers.

Praying her hair wasn't a complete ball of frizz from the sticky Florida humidity, she took a deep breath as she walked up to the restaurant.

There was a time not so long ago that she didn't think she'd ever be vulnerable and trust a man. But Kai...was different. He was honest, thoughtful, and deserved her trust, which she was starting to give him more of with each passing day.

She had no idea what the future held with this man, but that shouldn't stop her from telling him how she felt. He should know how much he meant to her, and maybe —just maybe—that would affect the future.

Who knew? The only way to find out was to confess her feelings. Taylor decided, right then and there as she walked up the old wooden stairs to the entrance of Sharky's, that she was going to tell Kai tonight...she was falling for him.

"Just tell him," she whispered to herself as she smoothed down her hair one more time and took a deep inhale of the ocean air.

Cocoa Beach had her feeling very far away from her baggage and her past and her pain. Everything was new, and whatever sort of magic was floating around in the air, she'd certainly caught a whiff of it.

As soon as she stepped onto the outdoor deck of the restaurant, she spotted Kai sitting alone at a high-top right at the edge of the wooden platform, looking out at the ocean.

Her stomach instantly filled with butterflies, and her head hummed with excitement as she walked over to him, wondering if the bounce in her step was noticeable.

*Just tell him. Just say it. Just put it all out there.*

"Hey, you." Kai hopped off the stool and instantly gave Taylor a tight hug, holding her close for a couple of long, extra, wonderfully reassuring seconds.

"Hi." Taylor smiled, holding his gaze as she sat down at the table, her jittery nerves instantly calmer in his presence.

"You look absolutely stunning." Kai gestured at her. "I love the dress."

"Thank you." Taylor laughed softly, holding out one of her feet to show her white Keds. "Even the shoes? My mom says wearing a sundress with sneakers makes me look like I'm in the third grade."

Kai laughed heartily as he sat down across from her. "I don't agree. I'm a fan of the shoes, personally."

"Glad we're on the same page about that." Taylor rested her chin in her palms, hoping they'd also be on the same page about the other, much more significant topic she was absolutely determined to bring up. "So, you had a free evening, huh?"

"I did." Kai took a slow breath, glancing out at the ocean. "And, of course, I wanted to spend it looking at the ocean and...you."

The words squeezed Taylor's heart as she continued to lean into this unfamiliar and uncharted territory of emotions. She felt safe with Kai. "Well, I was so happy when I saw your text. I know training has been insanely busy, so it's nice to see you sometime when it isn't, you know, before the crack of dawn."

He tipped his head, his long hair falling around his face. "It is, isn't it? I know how much you love mornings." He winked.

"They're kind of growing on me, actually." She took a sip of an iced water that she didn't even notice a waiter put down on the table. "Or maybe you're just growing on me," she admitted softly.

His eyes flashed, and he glanced down for a second, then back at Taylor.

"So, the Ron Jon Invitational is, what, in August? Almost two months away?" She leaned closer and lowered her voice. "But you'll be here training that whole time." And that was enough time to fall in love. *More* in love.

Kai sucked in a breath like he wanted to say something, but then quickly changed his mind. "There's something I need to tell you, Taylor."

He locked his gaze with hers, and she felt a little chill zip down her spine.

Was he about to beat her to the punch? Was he going to be the first one to say he was falling in love and these feelings were real and this was way more than just a summer fling?

Excitement and nerves and a foreign kind of giddiness rippled through her.

"I think I know what you're going to say." She smiled, reaching across the table to take his hand and giving it a squeeze. "I wanted to tell you the same thing."

"You *what*?" He blinked back with confusion, his dark brows furrowing.

"Look, Kai." She shut her eyes, feeling them flutter as she took a deep breath and gathered herself, gearing up to be as real and vulnerable as she could ever remember being. "I really, really like you. And I know that all of the logistics make no sense, and I know your family is in

Hawaii and you travel constantly and none of this makes sense, but...I think I'm falling for you." She let out a breath, the weight of the words soaring off her shoulders. "There. I said it."

"Taylor." Kai looked at her intensely, his gaze suddenly seeming worried and sad.

Taylor's heart dropped hard and fast. Did he not feel the same way? Was that not what he wanted to say to her?

"What is it?" she asked.

"I really like you, too." He ran a hand through his hair, his expression conflicted. "A lot. A ton. I feel everything you just said."

"Okay," she said slowly, giving a dry and nervous laugh. "Why do I have the feeling you're not happy about that?"

"Because I'm leaving."

"I know," Taylor said quickly. "After the invitational. I know that. But we have two months before that, and we could figure things out and just enjoy being together. We could—"

"No, Taylor. I'm not leaving in two months. I'm leaving..." He swallowed. "Tomorrow."

Taylor felt her breath leave her body as she drew back, her heart pounding and her mind whirring.

"Tomorrow?" she whispered, the word coming out as almost a croak.

Heat rose in her cheeks as she pulled her hands into her lap, tucking them under the table and wishing, for a second, that she could melt away and disappear into the floorboards of the wooden deck.

Kai shook his head, his eyes dark with sadness. "I'm so sorry, Taylor. You see, my dad just found out he needs a knee replacement, pretty quickly, and my mom can't run the farm without him. He's down for the count for at least a couple of months and I...I have to be there. I've got to help them out while he recovers from the surgery."

"Oh." It was the only word she could say.

Taylor lifted a slightly quivering hand and pushed some hair behind her ears, swallowing hard and trying desperately to keep her composure. She cleared her throat and shifted in the tall barstool, which was suddenly wildly uncomfortable.

"He's okay, though, right?" she asked quietly. "Your dad?"

"Oh, yes, he's fine. Just arthritis and wear and tear from decades of physical labor. Like I said, they just need some assistance. I have to go back."

"What about the invitational?"

"I'm still going to compete," he explained gently. "My trainer said I can work and practice in Hawaii in my free time, and my spot in the competition is secure. So I'll fly back for a week in September, but..." He let out a long exhale, apologetic sympathy written all over his face. "But that's it."

*That's it.*

The words sliced right through her. She could feel her eyes start to sting, and she was suddenly warm with embarrassment.

He brought her here to say goodbye, and she thought he was going to say, "I want to be with you."

Her heart sank into her gut and her body felt heavy with sadness and heartache.

"I'm so sorry, Taylor, I—" Kai reached his hand across the table and touched hers.

Taylor instantly jerked her hand away, knowing that every second, every touch, every moment of connection would make this even more painful than it already was.

"It's okay." She looked at him, hoping he didn't notice the tears welling behind her eyes. "It's your family. You have to be there for them. I understand, I just..." She folded her arms over her chest and slouched. "Feel kind of stupid."

"You shouldn't feel stupid." His gaze was intense and passionate, and so familiar it hurt to look at. "Everything you said is mutual. I feel the same way, and in some other universe in some other lifetime, there would be something absolutely incredible here." He took a breath. "But I can't deny my own reality, Taylor. It's a situation I can't change. I hope you don't hate me."

"I could never hate you, Kai." Her voice caught a little, and she was truly surprised by just how deeply this news was cutting her.

She knew she had strong feelings for him, but, wow. This hurt *bad*.

"They're your family." She finally, reluctantly looked at him. "Thanks for telling me and not just disappearing."

"I wouldn't do that in a million years." He shook his head. "And, hey, I'll be here in September."

"For a few days," she whispered, the weight of that reality crushing her.

"I know, but...I know. I'm sorry, Tay. I never expected this. I never expected to meet someone like you and feel this way. It wasn't in the plan, you know?"

She snorted. "Oh, believe me, neither did I."

"I'll write to you," he said, his tone fervent.

"It's not the 1940s, you can just text me or give me a call." She smiled a little, still adoring him even through the pain of losing him.

"But letters are more romantic, so I'll do all of the above. Okay?"

Taylor shut her eyes and felt a tear fall down her cheek and drop onto the table. "Okay," she whispered.

She couldn't even be mad at Kai. He hadn't broken her trust—he'd told her from day one he lived in Hawaii and would someday go back. She couldn't get angry and spiteful and scream out the lyrics to Taylor Swift breakup songs in her car, because he hadn't done anything wrong. He just had to go. She always knew he'd have to go, eventually.

She just had no idea how badly it would hurt when he did.

Taylor looked out at the ocean and watched the sky turn dark and the moon come out from the clouds. She took a deep breath and looked at the waves crashing onto the sand, one after another.

She realized, in that moment, she'd had no clue how badly she wanted love until she had to kiss her first real chance at it goodbye.

# Chapter Twenty-four

## *Dottie*

As Dottie pulled into the parking lot of Sweeney House, the whole place looked different to her. Not in reality, but in her imagination, and she couldn't see anything but her renovated, updated property.

Even with the heavy cloud cover and gray skies that threatened a typical late-afternoon summer storm, she could imagine her finished, renovated inn.

Maybe a soft coastal blue paint with white siding and dark shutters. That would be magnificent. She would definitely replace all the old carpets with wood and redecorate each bedroom in something bright and clean and fresh. A room with white beadboard, or maybe another with a coastal mural.

And then she'd put flower boxes on every balcony at the inn, like the ones in the windows of the cottage.

Oh, and the cottage! She wanted to keep it yellow, just like Jay's truck, but a fresh, new, brighter yellow. And the floors could be light, beachy wood. And all new furniture, of course, or she could reupholster some of what she had.

Yes, the more she thought about it, the more Dottie was confident that she could preserve and honor Jay's memory and his character while also reviving and revital-izing Sweeney House. It was the perfect balance, she was sure of it.

And ever since the other morning, when Dottie saw that yellow Chevy drive by and felt Jay's heavenly hand on her shoulder, she had peace in her heart. She knew, without a shadow of a doubt, that he was behind her with this plan.

And truly, she hadn't been this excited about some-thing in a very, very long time.

Dottie continued to ponder all the renovation possi-bilities as she climbed out of her car, thinking about that annual checkup with Dr. Farnsworth, another thing that put her in a good mood.

She was declared to be in relatively perfect health, and for a seventy-two-year-old woman, Dottie was proud to not be on a single medication. Her bloodwork, testing, and vitals were all normal and healthy, and Dottie decided that was yet another sign from Jay that the reno-vation was a good idea.

She was feeling young, strong, hopeful, and even, dare she say, happy.

The next thing to do was break the news to Karen, and figure out how to get a loan of some sort. Oh, and telling the kids. She'd have to tell them, of course, but Dottie had a feeling they'd be a whole lot more excited about renovating the inn than selling it. They'd certainly all have opinions and ideas.

Everything about the decision felt right in her heart and soul, and as she walked through the lobby of the inn and looked around with all of her new ideas floating through her mind, she almost laughed at the fact that she had been so unbelievably stressed about the decision of what to do. The answer had been so obvious all along.

"Hi, Jeanine." She waved at the woman who'd been sitting at that front desk for years now, and it brought Dottie joy to realize she wouldn't have to break any bad news to Jeanine or anybody else on the Sweeney House staff.

"Dottie, you're looking spritely today." Jeanine grinned.

She laughed and jokingly fluffed her hair. "I'm feeling spritely, actually. I just got a clean bill of health and I think I'm finally ready for a new chapter."

"Oh, Dottie." Jeanine, who was all-too-familiar with Dottie's long and painful journey of grief and healing, held her hands to her heart. "That's wonderful."

"It truly is, isn't it?" She held up a finger. "Oh! Did John stop by? I had some boxes of things I needed him to sort through and take from the back storage room."

"Yes, he did. Actually, all of your kids are here. Well, besides Julie, of course. I think...I think you'd better get over there."

Dottie laughed and frowned with confusion. "They're here? Erica, too?"

"Yes." Jeanine nodded. "John and Sam went back to the cottage, and Erica showed up shortly after. You should go and talk to them, Dottie."

"Really?" Dottie angled her head, uncertain of the

tone in Jeanine's voice. Was something wrong? "Well, I'd better head over there, then."

With a quick wave, she hustled out the side door and headed down the path between the inn and the cottage. With every step, she started to feel a small thread of concern worming its way through her heart, hitting her just as the first raindrops started to fall.

Why were Erica, John, and Sam all together right now, with no occasion? Had something happened? Jeanine had sounded weird. Surely, Dottie would have gotten a phone call if there were any serious matter, right?

The back door to the cottage was unlocked, and she stepped inside before the rain got too heavy.

"I heard talk that three of my children are here," she called out brightly. "Is there a birthday I forgot?"

As Dottie walked down the hallway and into the living room of the cottage, a sudden heaviness loomed in the air around her.

Erica, John, and Sam all sat together on the sectional, and it was very obvious that they were upset about something.

Dottie's heart rate spiked, and she rushed over and sat down across from her kids. "What happened? Is everyone okay?" She searched their faces. "What's going on?"

"Everyone is fine, Mom." Erica nodded.

"Then why all these frowns?" Dottie glanced at each of them, relaxing a little, but still feeling a strong sense of uneasiness in her gut.

"Mom." John leaned forward, his deep and strong

voice reminding her so much of Jay. "Are you selling Sweeney House?"

Oh. That was why they were here. They'd found out.

Dottie shut her eyes, holding up a hand. "Let me explain."

"Oh my gosh, you *are* selling it!" Erica exclaimed. "John and Sam called me and I told them they were completely nuts. But they're right, you're selling it. Mom, why didn't you tell us?"

"I'm not selling it," Dottie said.

"Please don't lie anymore, Mom," Sam said softly, the hurt in her voice making Dottie's heart crack in half. "Why did you keep this from us? Why didn't you say something? I just moved in here, and—"

"I know, Sam. I know." Dottie placed a hand on Sam's arm, but she pulled it away, reminding Dottie all too much of those million fights they'd had when Sam was younger.

Dottie would reach for her, and she would run away, straight into the arms of Max Parker.

"I'm *not* selling it." Dottie looked at her grown kids, all so beautifully different and uniquely wonderful. And, clearly, opinionated. "I've changed my mind."

"So you *were* going to sell it?" Erica pressed. "You really were? Without telling us?"

"Mom, why would you keep this hidden from us?" John's voice rose in frustration. "This is our home, too."

"You all have your own homes now."

"I don't, not really," Sam interjected, making Dottie instantly regret her words. "But this was Dad's pride and joy. You were just going to pawn it off to some massive company and not tell any of us?"

Dottie felt her eyes shutter as she dug for composure. "For the record, *you* are all Dad's pride and joy. And I was going to tell you guys when the deal was done."

As they reacted to that, she slipped into her favorite chair. "But it's not for sale anymore. I changed my mind, so none of this is even relevant."

John puffed out a sigh and Erica shook her head.

But Sam just stared at her, eyes welling with obvious hurt.

"Mom..." Her voice was subdued and breaking. "How could you keep this from me? I came here when I had nowhere else to go. You knew that. And you let me trust you and open up to you, and you kept such an enormous secret. What would have happened if you sold it? You would have just told me to pack up and get out?"

"No." Dottie stood up, emotion flooding through her. "You are my daughter. You know I would never do that to you."

"You would have, though. You were about to." Sam stood up, too. "I saw the listing, Mom. You looked pretty damn close to doing just that."

"I changed my mind!" Dottie heard her volume rising as she desperately clung to her truth and prayed this would not end in the way all her previous conflicts with Sam had ended—with her defiant and strong-willed daughter leaving the house, slamming the door, and shutting her out.

Dottie could feel peace and control slipping away as the emotions swirled through the air around them.

"Sam, listen to me." Dottie reached for her again, but Sam snapped her hand away.

"You lied!" Sam exclaimed. "You sat out on the porch with me and we...we almost, I don't know, made up or something. I felt like we had a breakthrough!"

"We did have a breakthrough!" They were yelling now. Good thing Dr. Farnsworth wasn't checking her blood pressure now, because she knew it was climbing sky high.

*Don't go, Sam. Don't run away again.*

Sam threw her hands up in the air with frustration. "You looked me in the eyes and you kept that from me, Mom. You let me open up to you, and be vulnerable. You told me I could heal here, and the entire time you were secretly about to sell the whole place? How could you do that?" Sam's tone rose even louder with anger.

John, the peacemaker, held up a hand. "It's okay, Mom. Let it go, Sam. Let's just cool off and we can talk about it when we're all a little less emotional."

Dottie was grateful for her son's steady and unwavering composure, and his attempt to defuse a situation that the whole family had seen many times before.

But she was laser focused on Sam right now, every fiber of Dottie's being anxiously wanting her daughter to understand, to pause, to listen to her and not run away and build up another twenty-year wall.

Suddenly, as if the weather outside wanted to mirror the mood in the living room, a booming thunderclap echoed loudly through the sky overhead, accompanied by a bright flash of lightning.

They all gasped, startled by the sudden and extremely close storm.

"Sam..." Dottie calmed her tone and held her daughter's fiery gaze. "You have to listen to me—"

"It's Dad's place!" Sam cried, inching forward. "You were going to sell Dad's place."

"It's *our* place!" Dottie shouted back, composure flying out the window. "Mine and your father's. And I can do what I want with it. He and I built it together."

"So you *are* selling it?" Erica chimed in now, studying Dottie with worry in her eyes.

"No, I am *not* selling it. Can you kids just listen to me, please?" Dottie threw her hands up as if to surrender.

Rain poured down in loud, roaring sheets onto the roof of the cottage, and thunder rumbled around them, making the floor shake with the booming claps.

"You lied to me," Sam insisted. "I trusted you and you lied to all of us. We saw your signature on the listing and I have to say, it hurt, Mom."

Another flash of lightning punctuated the statement, followed by a loud clap that meant the storm was close.

"Seriously, Mom." Erica folded her arms across her chest. "Why didn't you talk to any of us?"

"We had no idea you were even thinking about this," John added.

"How could you, Mom?" Sam yelled over the next rumble of thunder.

The words cut Dottie like a knife, and suddenly, all

of her anger and irritation and swelling frustration melted away, and she was overcome with a tidal wave of sadness.

Dottie's body went weak, giving in to the overwhelming ache of sorrow as tears fell from her cheeks one after the other. She slumped down onto Jay's old recliner, took a deep inhale and smelled the old worn leather, and started to sob.

Her tears fell as fast as the pouring rain outside the window, and Dottie felt like her heart was breaking all over again.

"Mom." John rushed over, placing a strong hand on her shaking shoulder.

"Are you okay?" Erica joined her brother, leaning against the side of the recliner.

Dottie looked up, her gaze falling on Sam.

"I'm sorry." Sam stepped over to the recliner, crouching down next to it and putting her hand on Dottie's arm. "I'm so sorry. I got so emotional and I was wrong. Mom, please, I'm so sorry for yelling at you."

For the first time in decades, Sam was reaching out to *her*.

The realization startled Dottie, and gave her a shot of relief.

"I didn't mean it, Mom." Sam's eyes were wide and deep and loving. "I shouldn't have said all that."

"It's all right, Sam." She squeezed her daughter's hand, savoring the moment that Sam wasn't running away. She wasn't leaving or slamming a door or driving off.

She was here. To stay.

"Oh, you guys." Dottie gave a tearful laugh. "I was lost. I was just so darn lost."

"We know you were, Mom," John said.

"We understand, really." Erica smiled. "We all just felt hurt that you'd sell Sweeney House and the cottage and not tell any of us about it. It seemed out of character for you, Mom."

"Of course you did. You had every right to be hurt." Dottie pushed some of her curls out of her face and took a deep breath. "It's your home, too. And I'm sorry you all felt betrayed and lied to. I'm really sorry, Sam."

Sam met Dottie's gaze, a new kind of warmth in her eyes as she gave a soft smile. "It's okay."

Dottie breathed out a sigh of relief, clinging to Sam.

"I was lost and confused, and looking for any imaginable way to stop missing your dad. Every second of every day, the inn reminds me of him. Constantly. I was desperate to stop grieving, and I went to an extreme."

Sam nodded, her own tears falling.

"But I was serious when I said I changed my mind." Dottie looked back and forth between the three of them. "Sweeney House is no longer for sale."

"Mom." Sam shut her eyes. "If selling the inn is what you feel like you need to do to heal, then we support you. I just felt like...you should have said something."

"I know," Dottie said quickly. "But ~~I am serious when I say that I changed my mind~~. Selling Sweeney House is not what I want to do."

"Either way..." Sam exhaled. "I'm sorry for how I

acted. That was not...that was not the new me. That was the old me."

"The screaming match did feel a bit familiar, huh?" Dottie teased lightly, her heart soaring as she realized Sam wasn't going anywhere.

Her girl really had changed. And this was proof that they could find a new relationship going forward. And nothing made Dottie happier.

"Too familiar." Sam shook her head.

"I thought you were going to leave and slam the door."

Sam pressed her lips together, putting an arm around Erica and the other around John. She looked at each of her siblings, and then back at her mom. "Not this time. I'm not going anywhere. I'm not walking out on this family ever again."

They all hugged for a long moment, and Dottie let herself melt into the love of her children that she so desperately needed.

"~~But really, I'm not selling it.~~" She pulled away and grinned at them. "I've decided there's another way that I can get a fresh start."

"Really?" Erica asked.

Sam angled her head. "What is it?"

"Before I do, I have to ask you a question, Sam. I need you to be honest with me."

"Of course."

Dottie opened her mouth to speak, but before she could get a word out, the sliding glass door that led out to the back deck flew open, and they all turned in surprise.

A rain-soaked, shivering, miserable-looking Taylor stepped into the house.

"Tay." Sam stood up, rushing over to her daughter with instant concern. "What happened?"

As Taylor got closer, Dottie could see that rain wasn't the only thing that drenched her face. Taylor had been crying.

"Kai left. I..." She waved a hand, her long hair dripping all over her soaking wet sundress. "I don't want to talk about it right now. Aunt Erica, Uncle John, what are you guys doing here? Did I miss a dinner party?"

Sam chuckled softly. "Not exactly. Here, let's get you dried off and we'll fill you in on all the drama."

Taylor looked up through mascara-stained eyes. "Is everything okay?"

Sam glanced back at Dottie, sharing a mutual, subliminal mother-daughter glance that brought Dottie's heart a wave of peace. "Everything is fine," Sam murmured.

Taylor grabbed a towel from the linen closet in the hallway and wrapped it around her, squeezing her hair. "So what's going on? Please make me think about something other than my own sad life."

"I'm so sorry about Kai." Sam reached for her daughter's arm.

Taylor waved a hand. "We can talk about it later."

"Well, Taylor." Dottie leaned forward in the recliner as Erica and John sat back down on the sectional. "Before you walked in, I was just about to ask your mom a very important question."

"Why does everyone look upset?" Taylor glanced around, frowning. "Was there a fight or something?"

"It's over now," Sam assured her, glancing back at Dottie. "What did you want to ask me?"

Dottie could feel butterflies in her chest, and she shut her eyes for a second, hoping and praying this would go well. "Well, you know how I said I thought of a way I can get a new start and heal from my grief without selling Sweeney House?"

"You're selling Sweeney House?" Taylor blurted out with astonishment.

"No!" Erica, Sam, John, and Dottie all answered in unison, their synchronicity making everyone laugh.

"I'm so confused." Taylor shook her head.

"Yes, Mom." Sam smiled at Dottie. "What did you want to ask me?"

"I wanted to know..." Dottie swallowed, keeping her gaze fixed on Sam. "If you would help me renovate the inn and cottage. You have such an eye for decorating and design and all of that, and I truly think this place could use a hefty facelift. What do you say?"

Erica laughed and held her hands together. "What a wonderful idea! I'm sure Will would love to help with any construction needs, too."

"I was already planning on that," Dottie admitted with a cheesy smile.

"That's awesome." John nodded in agreement. "It's a great plan, Mom. Really."

"Mom." Taylor turned to Sam, smiling enthusiastically for her. "You should do it with Grandma. You should help renovate, you'd love that."

Sam's eyes were wide with disbelief, but the smile on her face told Dottie everything she needed to know. "I—"

Before she had a chance to finish, Sam's phone started buzzing loudly. "Hang on." She pulled it out of her pocket and frowned in confusion as soon as she looked at the screen. "I'm sorry, I'm going to take this. I don't recognize the number, but it could be some legal crap with Max that I can't miss. They call at all hours. Two seconds."

Sam stepped off to the side into the kitchen, pressing her phone to her ear.

"So." Erica grinned brightly at Dottie. "You're going to remodel Sweeney House? Top to bottom?"

"That's the plan! And I think it could be wonderful for Sam to be involved."

"Are you kidding?" John chuckled. "She'd love that. And I've thought for a long time this place could use an upgrade."

"I have a great feeling about it, I truly do." Dottie smiled, feeling like in that moment, everything was good.

It was the first time she'd ever fought with Sam where it didn't end badly. In fact, it ended beautifully.

They really did have a breakthrough. This was progress. She'd spent so many years walking on eggshells with Sam, just wanting her to stay close. She'd spent so long feeling like Sam was keeping her at a distance, but not anymore. She was here to stay, and Dottie felt like, right now, there was nothing in the world that could mess this up.

"You guys." Sam raced back into the living room, her face ghost white and stricken, her hands shaking as she clutched her phone. "Ben's been in a car accident. It's serious."

# Chapter Twenty-five

## *Sam*

S am had never been a religious person. She'd spent most of her life worrying more about school projects and soccer practice than her relationship with God. She hadn't prayed or been to church in probably a solid decade.

But right now, as Taylor drove them to Orlando Regional Medical Center, Sam prayed hard. And she texted Max, but then remembered what day it was, and knew he could be in surgery.

So she left a voicemail and went back to trying to pray.

"He's going to be okay." Taylor placed her hand on Sam's leg as she sped down the highway in her little red Honda. "I know he is."

Sam just swallowed and nodded, her body racked with nausea and panic, quivering as she squeezed her daughter's hand.

There were a thousand unanswered questions that echoed through Sam's mind, but she tried desperately to keep them quiet until they got to the hospital and she could get some answers.

Where had he been driving? In the thunderstorm? In

Sam's car? Why was he in Orlando? Why did he leave and not tell anyone?

Sam shifted in the old, worn-out leather seat and took in a shuddery breath as Taylor stayed focused on the road.

All they knew so far was that Ben was in a wreck on the Bee Line headed toward Orlando. It was in the peak of that raging thunderstorm, and he was driving Sam's SUV.

He took it without telling anyone. Without asking. He just left in the middle of the storm.

Sam's heart ached and her mind spun as Taylor switched lanes and passed a couple of trucks, counting the exits until they got to the hospital.

Erica, John, and Dottie followed in two separate cars, and were only a couple of miles behind them, all racing to get to Ben.

Sam wiped her hand over her face and leaned her head against the window, trying to will herself to stop shaking.

She shut her eyes and thought about Benjamin John Parker. Her sweet and gentle boy. He was soft-spoken from the day he could talk. Bright, insightful, observant Ben.

Ben was never the center of attention. He loved to let others have the spotlight. Especially his big sister. He would always sit back and watch, think, and understand. Ben was methodical and quiet and wonderfully sensitive.

Sam thought about Ben's first soccer practice when he was only four years old, and how he would run as fast as he could to get to the ball, but then he'd shy away from actually kicking it. Sam would give him a big thumbs up from the sidelines, but he'd just shake his head. He'd wanted no part of that ball.

She thought about the way he and Taylor would jump into the back of her car when she picked them up from school and instantly ask if they could go to 7-Eleven and get Slurpees.

*Please, Mom! Pleeeeease!*

She thought about his first day of high school, when his hair was so long it was practically covering his beautiful brown eyes, and Sam had to trim it with scissors that morning. Oh, he'd hated that. But it was a crime to cover those eyes.

She thought about the way he laughed so hard he cried the first time he ever watched the movie *Spaceballs*, and how his favorite ice cream was mint chocolate chip. *"It's so underrated, Mom. Everyone sleeps on mint chocolate chip."*

"Oh, Ben," Sam whispered though a shivering sob. "Please be okay."

Taylor just held her Mom's hand tightly as she finally, blessedly, took an exit and drove them down the road to the emergency entrance of Orlando Regional Medical Center. "We're here, Mommy."

The childish name made Sam fold in half with aching emotion. She whipped the door open the second Taylor parked the car, reaching for her daughter's hand as they rushed into the hospital together.

Her heart pounded in her chest, so loud she could hear it in her brain.

"I'm here for Benjamin Parker, I'm his mother," she called the words before she could even reach the check-in desk.

Taylor jogged next to her. "I'm his sister, we need to see him."

The woman at the front desk smiled at them. How anyone could smile at a time like this was completely beyond Sam, but she couldn't really think about that right now. She couldn't think about anything besides getting to her baby. Nothing else mattered. Nothing.

"Parker..." The woman repeated the name, tapping some keys as she scanned her computer screen on the desk in front of her. "Okay, I have a Benjamin Parker—"

"Where is he?" Sam asked desperately. "What room?"

"Unfortunately, ma'am, I cannot disclose that right now because he's in the intensive care unit and being closely monitored at this time."

Intensive care unit? Sam nearly collapsed.

"Please, he's..." Sam's voice broke as frustration and fear bubbled up in her chest, threatening to choke her completely. "He's my son. I need to see him."

"I understand that, ma'am, and I promise you that as soon as you are able to see him, we will allow you to do so."

Taylor leaned against the desk, inhaling sharply. "Can you just tell us what's going on? Is he all right?"

The woman pressed her lips together. "His condition

is stable, that's all I can tell you at this time. Please have a seat in our waiting area, and the attending physician, Dr. Clark, will come out and get you as soon as there are any updates."

Sam kept her palms pressed onto the cool white surface of the counter, feeling as if it was the only thing keeping her upright.

"Come on, Mom." Taylor wrapped an arm around her waist. "Let's go sit."

Sam nodded and followed her to an empty corner of the waiting room, wondering why it had to be about five degrees in here. Shivering was not helping right now.

A few seconds later, Dottie, John and Erica burst into the waiting room, looking around frantically.

"Where is he?" Dottie ran over to Sam, her flowery dress billowing around her. "Is he okay?"

John walked up to the front desk and Erica came over to the chairs, sitting down right next to Sam and giving her a big hug.

"We don't know anything yet." Sam shook her head and squeezed her eyes shut. "He's stable, that's all they'll tell me right now."

"The doctor will come out as soon as there are updates," Taylor explained, tucking her knees into her chest and curling up against the armrest of the chair.

Dottie sat down by Taylor and took each of their hands in hers. "We're here for you. We're here for Ben, and we're in this together."

"He's the toughest kid I know," Erica said softly, holding Sam's gaze. "He's going to be okay."

Sam desperately wanted to believe that. But no matter how many times she heard it from others and said it over and over to herself, she wouldn't be convinced until she saw that smile on his face again. Until she saw those dark eyes for herself and heard his laugh and kissed his silly, overgrown Justin Bieber hair.

"Thank you guys for coming." Sam felt a tear fall and a sob threaten. "It means a lot to have family around."

John walked over, placing his hand on Dottie's shoulder. "That's what we're here for."

The sliding doors to the waiting room opened again, and this time Imani came in, with Damien, Liam, and little Ellen all in tow. She held a cardboard carrier with a bunch of Starbucks cups in it.

"Hi, everyone." She set the coffees down on the table. "Thought we could maybe use these."

Sam reached out to her sister-in-law and took her hand. "Thank you, Imani."

"Of course." She went to John, who put his arm around her as the three insanely well-behaved kids assumed spots in chairs and sat quietly. "Any news on Ben?" Imani glanced around.

John and Erica filled Imani in, and shortly after that, Will showed up with a box of donuts.

Sam just tried to keep her head above water.

"Great minds think alike," Will joked with Imani after greeting everyone and giving Sam a big hug.

The little Sweeney corner of the waiting room just seemed to keep growing, and Sam felt like, for the first time in as long as she could remember, she was surrounded by an ocean of love and support.

She could fall apart, because they would pick up the pieces. It was okay to trust them. It was okay to need them. In fact, it was more than okay. It was beautiful.

Worry and fear and anxiety rocked her, like one tsunami after another. But she wasn't alone. Far from it, actually.

She couldn't stop thinking about her boy. What had happened. Had the car flipped? Was he scared? Why did he leave?

He must have been upset. It must have been...the fight.

Oh, God. The realization in Sam's mind was like getting that dreaded phone call all over again. Ben left because of the argument. Ben couldn't handle conflict, and she and Dottie were having a pretty loud one at the time of the storm.

It was her fault. If he wasn't okay, it was her fault.

She suddenly felt nauseous and dizzy and wanted to sob and scream and run away.

"You sure you don't want something to eat?" Imani asked Sam, stroking her arm.

Sam forced herself to keep her composure. He was stable, apparently. That meant alive, right?

"I can't really." Sam waved a hand and shook her head. "I just need some sort of update. I just need to know."

Imani nodded with kind sympathy and under-standing.

She needed to know if she was the reason her boy would be permanently damaged. Or worse. She couldn't bear the guilt.

Why had she yelled at her mom? Why did they have to fight? Why didn't she think about the fact that Ben was upstairs; she knew how much he couldn't handle those things. Why didn't she remember the way he'd cower under his bed when she and Max would have it out?

Sam just forced herself to focus on breathing and squeezed her hands together. She looked over at Taylor.

Taylor pressed her forehead into her knees. Poor girl had gotten dumped right before this, but all focus was on Ben now.

Damien walked up to Sam, his dark, curly hair dancing around his pretty eyes. "My brother and sister and I made a card for you and Taylor and Ben."

Liam chimed in. "We drew it on the way here."

"Oh." Sam pressed her hands to her chest and shared a sweet look with John and Imani. "Thank you. That is so thoughtful."

"Here, Aunt Sam." Tiny, adorable little Ellen handed Sam a pink piece of cardstock that was folded in half.

The front of it said, "Get well soon, Ben!" with a hand-drawn picture of all the cousins as stick figures hanging out together at the beach, complete with palm trees, surfboards, and waves.

"This is beautiful," Sam said as she opened it up and read the inside, her heart still ripping.

It had little messages from all three of the kids and was signed by each of them, telling Ben how much they couldn't wait to hang out for the rest of the summer, and they hoped he'd feel better fast. Damien added that he heard Ben was learning to surf, and he wanted to learn, too, and they'd have to go together sometime.

"You guys." Sam took a deep breath and pressed the card against her chest, holding it tight. "I love it. And Ben is going to love it, too. Thank you."

"When can we see him?" Damien asked.

"Not yet," Imani answered her son quickly. "Aunt Sam is going to see him first when he's ready, and we're going to wait patiently and quietly, okay?"

"Okay." He nodded and went back over to play a small handheld video game with Liam, while Ellen pressed crayons onto a coloring book.

"You holding up okay?" Will asked Sam, sharing a look of sadness and sympathy with Erica.

"As best I can, I guess." She shivered a little.

"We're all here for you, my girl." Her mother squeezed her hand, the gesture making Sam ready to start crying again.

"Family of Benjamin Parker?" The man's voice suddenly cut through the room, making Sam jolt and stand up as fast as possible.

"Right here." She rushed over to the doctor, heart racing, palms sweating. "I'm his mother."

"I'm Dr. Clark." He held out a hand and shook hers, his dark eyes kind and freakishly youthful for a doctor, so likely a resident. "I've been treating your son. Is this your family?"

Sam stepped aside and looked back at the group of

people big enough to fill half the waiting room. "Yes, this is my family. They're all here with me."

"Hello," he nodded, his focus on Sam. "Benjamin is out of the woods and going to be okay."

"Oh, thank God." Sam let out a breath she felt like she'd been holding for two hours, and practically sank into the floor. "Oh, he's okay. He's okay."

"Now, that doesn't mean he's in great shape," he continued. "Ben sustained some serious injuries in the accident."

As Sam finished hugging her family and breathing true relief, she looked back at the doctor.

"He's lucky, too." Dr. Clark folded his hands together and held Sam's gaze. "From what he told us, he hydroplaned in the thunderstorm and sped into a tree."

Sam winced, the image so unbearable she thought for a split second she was actually going to throw up. "What kind of injuries?" she managed to ask.

"A minor concussion, a fractured rib, and a broken wrist. Also some substantial bruising and open wounds that have all been stitched up. However, no internal bleeding, which is what we were initially most concerned about, so that's a big relief. He'll be able to be transferred out of the ICU shortly."

A lump rose in Sam's throat, the thought of her baby in such bad shape causing her physical pain. But he was okay. He was okay. He could handle a broken wrist and some bruises. "Is he awake?" Sam asked.

"Yes, but he's pretty groggy and a little out of it from

the medication, so only immediate family is recommended to visit at this point in time."

"Tay?" Sam looked at Taylor, who was already getting out of her chair and rushing over to join her mom and Dr. Clark.

"I'm his sister," she explained.

"You two can follow me." The doctor tipped his head to the double doors in the back of the waiting room that led to the corridor.

Sam looked over her shoulder and saw her family. Mom, with misty eyes and her soft gray curls, clasping her hands together and smiling. John, with his arm around Imani, both visibly relieved. Their sweet and adorable kids, giving cheesy grins and joyful waves and celebrating the good news.

Erica and Will sat side by side, holding hands and giving Sam reassuring nods.

"I love you guys," Sam mouthed to them as she walked into the hallway with Taylor and Dr. Clark, every step one step closer to reaching Ben.

At Room 403, the doctor stepped aside and gestured for them to enter a hospital room. "Right in here."

Sam couldn't physically get into the room fast enough, practically lunging toward the door.

"Oh." Her hands flew to her mouth and a sob choked out of her throat as she laid eyes on her son.

"Hi," he croaked, barely awake.

It looked like twenty different cords and wires connected his body to machines and monitors. One of his eyes was completely bruised all around, and he had a line of stiches in the corner of his forehead. His arm was elevated in front of him, wrapped in a hard cast, and there were still some dry bloodstains around his hairline and neck.

The sight broke Sam and shook her to her core, but she rushed over to him and grabbed his uninjured hand.

Taylor came around to the other side of the bed. "Benny boy."

"Oh, honey. You're okay." Sam cried through the words as she clutched his non-casted hand, tears falling onto the sheets of the hospital bed. "You're okay."

Taylor let out a shaky sigh, leaning close to her brother. "Ben, you scared the crap out of us."

"I'm sorry." His voice was broken as he looked at Sam. The eye that was bruised was swollen and couldn't quite open all the way, but his other eye was bright and wide and familiar and filling with tears. "I'm so sorry, Mom. Ouch...my ribs." Just talking made him wince in pain.

"Don't cry, Ben. Don't cry. You've got a fractured rib."

Ben swallowed and gave a strained nod, then looked over at Taylor. "You're here, too."

She laughed sarcastically and tearfully. "Of course I'm here. The whole family is here, Ben. In the waiting room."

He lit up. Well, as much as someone who'd just survived a serious car wreck could possibly light up. "Everyone? All of them?"

"All of them," Sam said.

"Why..." he rasped. "Why are they all here?"

"Because they love you, idiot," Taylor quipped. "And so do we."

"I can't believe the whole family is here for...for me." He stirred a little, and Sam held her hand on his not-broken arm.

On a sigh that came from deep inside her, Sam collapsed onto the side of the bed, reaching to stroke Ben's soft brown hair.

"Honey, what happened? Why did you leave like that? You could have been killed." Sam held back the sob that threatened in her throat.

Ben's eyes shuttered closed. "I was...I was upstairs, and I heard you and Grandma fighting really loud. You guys were, like, screaming at each other." He worked to speak without pain. "And it made me freak out a little, like I was having a panic attack or something. It reminded me of when you and Dad would fight."

Sam inhaled sharply, the words pressing on her chest. She closed her eyes and clenched her jaw as waves of guilt and pain rocked her. "I'm so sorry, Ben."

Sam hadn't been thinking. She'd been totally engulfed by the emotions of her fight with her mother, and she forgot Ben couldn't handle it. She didn't think about how it would make him feel to hear that kind of yelling and conflict. She couldn't believe it slipped her mind.

"I just...I just took your car and I left. I had to go. Because I felt like everything, all the good stuff that's happened since we moved there, it was going to all just disappear. You and Grandma had one of your crazy screaming fights and I thought it was all going to go away. Everything has been so much better and it sounded like we were about to lose it all." Ben wet his lips and looked at Taylor, then back at his mom. "I had to get out of there, and I wanted..." He hesitated. "I wanted to see Dad."

That cut Sam's gut like a dagger, but she swallowed the pain and nodded, understanding how upset Ben had been in the moment.

"Ben, you cannot be reckless like that," she pleaded. "I'm so sorry there was an argument, but I promise I'm done running away. Grandma and I are fine. More than fine! We're going to renovate the inn together this summer."

"You are?" Taylor and Ben asked in unison.

Sam hadn't realized her mind was made up until those words had just tumbled out of her mouth. "Yes." She nodded slowly, smiling at the thought of it. "We are. And we did have an argument, but it's okay now. It's better."

"I thought you were going to want to leave like usual," Ben said. "I thought we'd have to go. Whenever you and Grandma fight, we leave."

"Not anymore." Sam shook her head. "No more leaving."

"Mom?" Ben asked, looking up at her.

"Yes, honey?"

He thought for a long second, pressed his lips together, and then inhaled. "You can take longer than the summer if you want. For the renovation."

"Well, we will have to see what happens. I'll be commuting for work and it's only an hour, so—"

"I don't..." Ben started, coughing a little and sitting up, meeting Sam's eyes. "I don't think I want to go back to Winter Park."

Shocked, Sam and Taylor looked at each other from across the hospital bed.

"You don't?" Taylor asked eagerly.

"It was bad there. I wasn't happy. And I feel like I could be happy in Cocoa Beach. The whole family is out there in the waiting room, you know? I never thought I'd have family like that. They all...care. I want to stay. Can I finish high school there?"

Sam's heart soared, and she tried to stifle the joyous laughter that bubbled up in her chest.

"Ben are you..." She looked back at Taylor, who was grinning and nodding enthusiastically. "Are you sure?"

"I'm positive," he said, his voice husky as he readjusted his broken arm in front of him. "Please?"

"Yes, of course!" Sam exclaimed, giving Ben the world's most gentle hug.

Taylor squealed with excitement. "Now I'm seriously going to get on the job search. Especially because I won't be distracted by you-know-who."

"Kai?" Ben asked, looking at her.

"He's leaving. Tomorrow."

"Tay, I'm sorry. That's awful."

Taylor waved a dismissive hand. "I'm just glad you're okay. That's all that matters. Plus..." She pointed to his forehead and laughed. "It looks like you're going to have a cool Harry Potter scar."

Ben chuckled. "That is pretty cool."

"I guess I know who you'll be for Halloween," Sam teased, laughing with her kids, all sharing the hospital bed as relief and happiness and hope settled in the air around her.

"Hey, family." The sudden, familiar, and startling voice echoed through the room, making Sam jump up and turn to the doorway.

"Max," she breathed his name as he walked in, still in scrubs, obviously having rushed from his last surgery the minute he saw her texts.

"Dad?" Ben sat up and furrowed his brow. "You're here?"

"Of course I'm here, son." Max walked over to the hospital bed, his gaze catching Taylor. "Hi, Tay," he said awkwardly. "Holy cow, Ben. I'd hate to see the other guy."

Taylor stepped away to make room for him. "I'll be in the waiting room." Without another word, she hurried through the door and down the hallway.

Max winced at how obviously Taylor just blew him off, but he turned to keep his attention on Ben. "Ben, how you holding up?"

"I'm all right." Ben tried to lift a shoulder. "Mom's whole family is here. Isn't that cool?"

"I know they are." Max slid Sam a look. "They gave me quite a warm welcome when I walked past them in the waiting room."

Sam almost snorted. "I'll give you two a minute." She walked out of the hospital room and into the hallway, where a couple of nurses strolled by with a cart and a doctor answered a phone call.

Sam leaned her back against the cool, hard wall of the hallway, tipping her head back and letting out one massive sigh as the adrenaline dump rushed through her body. What a day.

"Hey, Sammi. Can I talk to you for a second?" Max leaned out of the room and angled his head, looking at her.

"Um, sure." She waved him over to the side of the hallway and folded her arms across her chest, trying not to roll her eyes at the hated nickname. "What is it?"

Max puffed out a sigh and ran a hand through his thick, salt-and-pepper hair, looking maybe a little more sallow than the last time she'd seen him. But he might have done five knee surgeries today, and he always looked rough after a long day in the OR.

"Listen, I'm...I'm having a new baby."

She choked on a soft laugh. "Yeah. I know. You told me already, and believe me, that's not something I would forget."

"I know, I know I told you. I just...I'm starting this new chapter with Kayla."

She closed her eyes, not wanting to talk about this. "I know," she repeated. "I have other things on my mind right now, like our son, who was darn near killed."

He exhaled. "Okay, okay. Then I'll just cut to the chase."

"What chase?"

"I want to stop paying you alimony," he said, matter-of-fact.

Her jaw dropped. "Now? You want to discuss this—"

"I have a better idea," he interjected, holding up a hand to stop her arguments. "I want a clean break. I want to be able to leave my past and my mistakes and all of this behind so I can move forward and let go of some of the guilt."

Guilt? About time he felt some of that. "What are you saying?" She narrowed her gaze, because guilt or not, he *had* to pay her alimony. She was his financial dependent for twenty-five years and it was set in stone in the divorce papers.

"I want to pay you a lump sum. In cash. All of what I owe you at once. I want to write a check, break the ties, and let go of the past. What do you say?"

Sam leaned harder against the wall for support, not sure she could physically handle yet another insane curveball today. "Cash? All at once?"

"We can work it out with the lawyer, plus what I would have gotten for the house. It's a fat amount, Sammi, close to seven figures if you agree. But after this? Clean break financially."

"Why would you do that?" It didn't make that much sense, at least not for him.

He shifted from one foot to the other. "It bugs Kayla when I send you money. This way, we'll be over and done with it. And of course I'll continue payments for Ben until he's eighteen, and in college." He sighed. "I owe you all at least that much."

*At least*, she thought, but she didn't say anything, because the last thing she wanted to do was be bitter or snarky.

Her life had changed, even more than she ever dreamed it could. "All that money...at once?"

He nodded, watching her and waiting for her response, which was almost to throw her arms around him and squeeze. Almost.

She could be financially independent, and live comfortably off smart investments. And the first one: the renovation of Sweeney House. She could help! She could cover most of it for her mother! And the money the inn would make in future business would more than cover the investment.

"Max." She looked into a set of eyes that had once mesmerized her, and other times broke her. Now they made her feel...nothing at all. "I never thought there would be a day where you would make me happy again. But you just did."

He gave a tight smile. "Everyone deserves a second chance, Samantha. I hope you take it."

"I intend to."

# Chapter Twenty-six

## *Erica*

It had been a week since Ben's accident, and Dottie called a mandatory family dinner to celebrate both Ben's health and the new, exciting undertaking of the Great Sweeney House and Cottage Renovation.

Erica had welcomed the recent distractions and craziness, because it gave her an opportunity to focus on things and people and events that didn't involve staring at her phone, willing Abigail from Space Coast Family Connections to call and say they had a baby for her.

No surprise, that hadn't happened yet. In fact, they hadn't heard a peep from the agency since they finalized their adoption application weeks ago. The waiting wasn't doing anything for her productivity at work, and she'd been so focused on getting this baby that she'd missed a huge error in some of the engine plans for the Eagle.

Erica was jumbled, and felt a bit out of control, sick of reminding herself to be patient. That wasn't one of her virtues, and in this case? She had less than none.

"So happy you guys made it." Sam put her arms around Erica and Will as they stepped into the cottage, which was already humming and buzzing with conversation and family.

Ellen and Liam sat on the couch with Taylor, playing with a bouncy Mr. Minx and trading off turns with the *Mario Kart* controllers.

Mom was talking to John and Imani in the kitchen, pouring drinks with a big smile on her face as she laughed at something Imani said.

The sliding glass doors in the living room were wide open, letting in the salty evening breeze and the warm sunshine of the beach.

"How's Ben?" Erica asked after the first hug.

"Doing really well, actually." Sam led them to the kitchen and their mom's signature charcuterie board. "He's up and about, and already talking about learning to surf when his rib and wrist heal up."

"That's awesome," Will said. "Kid's tough. I'll grab us some wine. White for you, babe?"

"Yes, please." Erica smiled at him, then turned back to her sister. "You must be so relieved."

Sam blew out a sigh and placed her hand on her chest. "You have no idea. Also, there's some other exciting news, actually, that I'm going to share with everyone tonight."

"Ooh. News. Tell me first, because I'm your sister." Erica grinned. "Plus, I have no patience, as my husband and I just discussed in the car on the way over."

"Well, find some, because I'm only making my announcement once."

"Fine." She studied Sam, whose eyes were already significantly brighter and clearer than when she'd first arrived in Cocoa Beach. Even her hair seemed shinier from the salt air and her smile easy and optimistic. What-ever her news, it was good. "But I'm so intrigued."

"Stay that way. First, I'm going to go check on Ben and make sure he's not showing Damien something that's very against Imani's video game rules." She laughed and shook her head, turning to jog up the stairs.

A pang hit Erica's heart as she took a cracker and a piece of brie from the board, greeting her mother and John and Imani with hugs and kisses. A pang of envy, because she wanted to be the one with exciting news. She wanted to tap her wine glass and tell everyone that she and Will were adopting a baby. She ached for that moment, that joy.

"Here you go." Will handed her a glass of white wine and kissed her forehead.

"Thank you." She sipped the Pinot Grigio and took a deep breath. "Apparently, Sam has some exciting news."

"About the renovation?" Will asked.

Erica shrugged. "Not sure, but I would imagine it has something to do with it."

"Dottie is already throwing all kinds of ideas at me." He shook his head and chuckled. "Family contracting is always fun and challenging and...not terribly profitable."

Erica laughed. "But it's family. Are her ideas crazy?"

"Doable, not crazy. Also, I have some ideas of things I've been wanting to try out on a willing client, so it's all good."

"Hey, everyone," Sam called. "Gather 'round. Big announcement!"

Erica glanced at Will and knew he was thinking the

same thing—one day, their big announcement would come. Holding his gaze, they headed into the living area with the others, all looking at Sam on the stairs with Ben.

She walked down with her arm lightly around Ben's shoulders, guiding him slowly down each step. He leaned against her, his smile visible from the kitchen. His bruising had started to fade, and he was becoming a newer, brighter version of himself.

Damien followed after them on the stairs, and the three of them stepped into the living room.

Sam's eyes danced with an inner joy Erica hadn't seen for a long, long time. Her husband may have only been caught cheating on her seven months ago, but that light had been absent for a lot longer than that. No doubt she subconsciously knew something was very wrong in her marriage and life.

But now, it looked like everything was very right.

"We have an announcement." Sam raised a glass as she walked over to Taylor, John, and Imani in the kitchen.

Mom looped her arm through Sam's, and looked at her, beaming.

The room fell silent as Sam and their mother commanded all of the attention. Even the little kids paused their video game, and Mr. Minx stared in complete fascination, perched on the edge of the sofa.

"As you all know," Dottie said slowly, looking around the room at her kids and grandkids, all happily eating and drinking and truly enjoying each other. "We have decided to undergo a remodel and renovation of this cottage and the Sweeney House inn."

"Woo!" Taylor chimed in, lifting up a glass.

"So..." Sam took over, glancing at her mom before looking back around at the rest of the room. "We have a lot of big plans, and we have tons of ideas for how to preserve the character of the inn and honor Dad, while also making it modern and updated. And what I wanted to share with you all is...everyone knows Max, my almost-ex?"

Erica snorted. "Unfortunately."

John laughed and shook his head and Imani's eyes widened with curiosity.

"Well," Sam continued. "Seeing as he totally broke my heart and wrecked my family, as we all know, he seems to be wallowing in a bit of well-deserved guilt, and decided to rewrite the financial terms of our divorce. Meaning..." Sam paused for a long time for dramatic effect, and everyone stared at her in riveted silence. "He's giving me a crap ton of money, and it's going to easily pay for the entire renovation!"

"Oh my gosh!" Erica blurted out and rushed over to hug her mom and sister. "That's incredible."

Cheers and the sound of celebration echoed through the room as John hugged Will and the kids jumped around, not sure what they were excited about but bouncing off the walls nonetheless.

"I'm so happy you guys are doing this," Imani said, giving Dottie a quick hug.

"Me, too." Erica grinned. "Sam, you're glowing."

"I am?" She laughed. "I have to say, I feel a bit glowy."

"I have an announcement, too." Suddenly, Ben's newly deep voice rose up through the loud, humming room, and caught everyone's attention.

Young, troubled Ben looked happy and calm, and despite the cast on his arm, appeared to be in great spirits.

"What is it?" John asked.

"I decided to transfer to Surfside High School," Ben said quickly, not loving the sudden influx of attention. "We're staying here."

"Oh!" Erica's heart soared, and she gave Sam yet another hug. "For sure?"

Sam nodded. "For sure."

"I am so happy." She squeezed her sister's shoulders, knowing how wonderful it was going to be to have her around all the time. "So, so happy."

"It was his decision," Sam said proudly, her gaze shifting to Ben, who was laughing about something with John and Will. "He told me that's what he wanted to do. So it looks like you're stuck with me."

"Stuck with all of us." Taylor swooped in on the conversation, her long brown hair bouncing around her pretty face. "We're here to stay, Aunt Erica."

"I am so happy about that. But...I'm so sorry about Kai leaving. That's a bummer." Erica tilted her head and gave her niece a sympathetic look.

Taylor just flicked a hand. "I'll live."

"And you..." Erica turned back to Sam. "You're really

doing this with Mom, huh? This is gonna be a lot." She made a face. "A lot of fighting?"

"Nope. Those days are gone, and we're headed into Sam and Dottie 2.0."

"Awesome. I'm so—" Erica stopped talking when her phone vibrated in her pocket. "Hang on." She slipped to the side and pulled it out to read the screen, praying it wasn't a crisis on the project at work.

The name on her phone screen made her heart do a somersault.

*Abigail Banks.*

Gasping to herself, Erica swiped the Accept button as quickly as she could and pressed the phone up to her ear.

"Hello? This is Erica."

"Erica, hi. It's Abigail, with Space Coast Family Connections. I hope I'm not catching you at a bad time."

"No, no. Not at all." Erica cupped the phone against her ear and stepped outside, over the deck and to the beach where it was quiet and private. On a calming breath, she asked, "What's going on?"

"It's a time-sensitive situation and I need your immediate response, okay?"

A chill flew down her spine. "Okay."

"We do have a child here who is in need of a foster-care adoption, and you and Will were next on the list. She has no father in the picture—he cannot be traced—and this child was just removed from her home with her mother by Child Protective Services."

"Oh my gosh!" Erica gasped.

"If she doesn't get an adoptive home, she'll go straight into the foster system. But if you would agree to take her as a trial—"

"Yes!" Erica blurted out the word, her head dizzy with unexpected joy. She paced around on the sand, feeling like she could float away at any second. "Yes, yes. We'll take her."

She knew without a doubt that Will would agree.

"I'm very glad to hear that," Abigail said. "Can you send me your current location? We need to get the child placed tonight, if possible."

"Right *now*?" Erica's heart was beating out of her chest, and she felt a wave of relief when she looked up and saw Will jogging out of the house and down to the beach to join her.

"Everything okay?" he asked softly, but could definitely quickly tell from Erica's wild smile and bright eyes that this was a good phone call.

She pulled the phone away from her ear and covered the microphone with the palm of her hand. "There's a baby! There's a baby, Will. And we're getting her tonight, literally right now."

"What?!" He laughed with shock and joy. "That's amazing."

Erica picked the phone back up. "Abigail? I'll send you my location. I'm at my mom's house in Cocoa Beach. Is that okay?"

"That's perfect. We're coming in a car now. Thank you, Erica."

"Thank you." Erica breathed out the words as they disconnected the phone call.

She slowly looked up at her husband, meeting his gaze as they shared in this crazy moment of joy and uncertainty and disbelief all at once. "We're having a baby," she said softly, the words not even sounding real.

"We'd better go tell the family."

"And borrow a crib from the inn," she added. "Oh, and diapers! And clothes! And a bottle! And, oh, I need so much, Will."

Laughing, he ushered her back to the house. "What we need is our baby. After that, we'll take it one day at a time."

When they stepped back through the sliding glass doors and into the living room, everyone turned as if they sensed something was going on.

"Since we all seem to be giving announcements, I think it's our turn," Erica said, nerves audible in her shaky voice. "Some of you knew that Will and I have been trying to have a baby, and we've been running into some problems. But all of that is over now, because we are adopting a baby girl, and she's on her way now!"

"What? Whoa!"

"On her way here now?"

"No way! Seriously?"

The cascade of questions and congratulations were drowned out by the pounding pulse in Erica's head. She laughed and tried to answer and kissed Will and realized that however different this was from the way she'd planned to have a baby, this was the perfect way to do it.

She wiped a few tears and hugged and hugged and hugged them all. Her head felt floaty and the world was buzzing. She truly couldn't believe this was real. In a matter of minutes, she'd be holding a baby.

A girl! The very thought brought tears of joy to her eyes, and time floated away on a cloud of laughter and planning and giddiness, until her phone buzzed with a text from Abigail.

*Pulling in now.*

"Oh my gosh," Erica breathed shakily, grabbing Will. "They're here."

"You two go alone." Dottie placed her hands on Erica's shoulders, giving that classic warm and comforting smile. "You two should meet your baby for the first time together, and then we will be next."

Erica nodded frantically. "Okay." She sniffed. "Okay. You ready?" She looked at her husband, who was beaming with joy.

"Absolutely."

Hand in hand, the two of them stepped out of the cottage and into the driveway, where they could see a big, black SUV pulling in, the tires crunching on the shells and gravel.

Erica's heart was racing, and she squeezed Will's hand as hard as she could.

Breathing slowly and methodically, she kept her gaze fixed on the car as it came to a stop and Abigail climbed out of the passenger seat.

"Abigail, hi." Erica rushed over, anxiously craning her neck to try and see the baby.

"How are you?" Will, slightly more composed than his wife, gave Abigail a handshake and a smile.

"Hello, Armstrong family." Abigail's gaze lingered on Erica for a long time. She looked a bit worried and stressed and...not like someone who was about to give a couple the happiest day of their life.

Erica tried to shake off the nerves. "Is she here?"

Abigail nodded. "I'll get her now, if you're ready."

She and Will looked at each other, holding their gazes together for an extra beat.

"We're ready," they agreed in unison.

Abigail opened the back door, but didn't reach in for a car seat or a baby carrier, but leaned in and spoke to someone.

Wait. Was this baby...not a baby? A toddler, perhaps?

After a couple of seconds, Abigail moved aside and out of the car stepped a lanky, thin, preteen-looking girl with long, dark hair that hung in front of her face. Her shirt was dirty and worn out, her jeans were ripped, and all she had was one pink backpack slung over her shoulder.

She stood frozen in the driveway, her gaze glued to the ground, and didn't say a word.

"Erica, Will..." Abigail put a hand on the girl's shoulder. "This is Jada Perez."

Erica frowned, her gaze dropping to the girl's stomach. Was she pregnant? Was she going to have a baby that...

No. No...she *was* the baby.

This grown up, angry-looking teenage girl with a

name and a past and a personality...this was the baby she was adopting.

Speechless, Erica turned to Will, who was slack-jawed and wide-eyed as the realization hit him, too.

For a long moment, no one said a word. For five, six, seven painful heartbeats, they just stood there. Then Will inhaled softly and walked over to the young girl.

"Jada," he said in a whisper. "I'm Will. It's wonderful to meet you."

Erica swallowed, swamped with emotion and pride in her husband. She joined him, reaching out her hand. "And I'm Erica," she said. "Welcome...to our family."

She couldn't be more than twelve or thirteen, with a perpetual frown and downturned lips, at least from what Erica could see behind messy, uncombed black curls.

She hunched with slender arms crossed in front of her, looking at the ground. "Hi."

Abigail cleared her throat and stepped forward. "Jada, Erica and Will are going to be taking you in. Please be good."

Jada didn't say a word, and neither did Erica.

She still felt completely stuck in shock. This was certainly not what she or Will or anyone had envisioned, and right now, she had no clue *how* to feel. Sorry for the poor thing, and, yeah, disappointed.

But there would be time for that later. Now, they had to do something for her.

"We don't live here on the beach," Erica said, sounding ridiculously chatty. "But this is my mother's place and we'll come here all the time."

Jada finally lifted her face, looking up at Erica for just a second, giving her a tiny glimmer of brown eyes, then back down again.

"I know you're probably really freaked out right now," Will added gently. "That's okay."

"I've got to get going. We'll be in touch." As Abigail said the quick goodbye, Erica had the impression that a speedy getaway was part of this process. Maybe so the child didn't wail and beg to go back to...wherever she'd come from.

Taken from her mother by child services with no father to be found, Erica remembered, and her heart fell to her feet. She had to forget her disappointment and shock. This kid had to be reeling.

Erica looked over her shoulder and saw her mother standing in the doorway, watching the stunning scene unfold.

"Jada, this is my mom, Dottie." Erica stepped aside and gestured at her to join them.

Her mother got the message, hustling over with a bounce in her step like she was happily greeting a new guest at the inn.

"Jada, what a beautiful name," Mom cooed.

Jada managed a tiny wave, but kept her eyes down.

"Well, I hope you're hungry, because if there's one thing Sweeneys can do, it's eat." Will gave her the tiniest nudge to the house. "Want to meet everyone, Jada? Talk about baptism by fire. But hey, once you've met the Sweeneys..."

His voice trailed off as he led Jada to the cottage and Erica stood frozen in place next to her mother.

"Not expecting that, were we?" Dottie whispered.

"What do I do? I don't know thing one about a teenager and I thought... What do I do with her?" she asked in a ragged voice. Erica watched Will and Jada disappear into the house, the sound of introductions floating out.

In all of her plans, her blueprints, her schedules, and her visions, she never could have pictured...this. Not in a million years.

But this was what life had given Erica Armstrong. And in the most unexpected, terrifying, and unorthodox way imaginable, this girl walked in and made all of her dreams come true. Sort of.

Now, all Erica had to do was learn how to be a mother to a broken, scared, shy, and troubled girl.

Dottie just laughed and shook her head. "You do what you do with any kid."

"And what's that?"

"Jay always said, 'You get what you get. And you love 'em no matter what.' So, she's what you got. You wanted a child, and there's one that needs you. Badly." Dottie put her hand on Erica's shoulder and met her gaze. "Now, go be a mom."

*Want to know what happens next for the Sweeney Family? Don't miss book two:* **Cocoa Beach Boardwalk***! Or sign up for my newsletter to get the latest on new releases and more!*

# The Sweeney House Series

The Sweeney House is a landmark inn on the shores of Cocoa Beach, built and owned by the same family for decades. After the unexpected passing of their beloved patriarch, Jay, this family must come together like never before. They may have lost their leader, but the Sweeneys are made of strong stuff. Together on the island paradise where they grew up, this family meets every challenge with hope, humor, and heart, bathed in sunshine and the unconditional love they learned from their father.

# About the Author

Cecelia Scott is an author of light, bright women's fiction that explores family dynamics, heartfelt romance, and the emotional challenges that women face at all ages and stages of life. Her debut series, Sweeney House, is set on the shores of Cocoa Beach, where she lived for more than twenty years. Her books capture the salt, sand, and spectacular skies of the area and reflect her firm belief that life deserves a happy ending, with enough drama and surprises to keep it interesting. Cece currently resides in north Florida with her husband and beloved kitty. When she's not writing, you'll find her at the beach, usually with a good book.

45260207R00189